Praise for *Empire's End*

"As a former newspaperman and one of America's most respected biographers, Jenkins has the know-how to assimilate massive amounts of data about the life of the apostle Paul. However, as a best-selling novelist, he also knows how to unpack this information and turn it into a fast-paced, highly entertaining story. We readers get to enjoy this double bonus."

Dr. Dennis E. Hensley, Chairman, Department of
Professional Writing, Taylor University

"Once again Jerry Jenkins's amazing imagination and literary skills captured my interest, and I found *Empire's End* pure intrigue! The relational surprises were fascinating, but more importantly I was blessed spiritually with Jerry's unusual ability to weave relevant passages from Paul's subsequent letters into what may have been God's personal messages to him during his three years in the Arabian desert!"

Dr. Gene A. Getz, Pastor, Professor, Author

"The best writers don't explain history or spin tales, they show us our own hearts. This is what Jerry Jenkins has done in *Empire's End*."

Chris Fabry, Award-Winning Novelist & Host,
Chris Fabry Live, Moody Radio Network

"Jerry Jenkins takes biblical records and historical data to weave a fascinating story about the apostle Paul. The intrigue, danger, and mysterious romance in *Empire's End* will keep you turning the pages and leave a 'wow' in your heart. Be entertained and inspired."

Sammy Tippit, Author and International Evangelist, San Antonio

"When Jerry Jenkins crafts a novel, he makes every word count. Our senses are engaged and our hearts beat faster as the story moves at breakneck pace. In *Empire's End,* we find all that and more. The apostle Paul lives and breathes on each page, and the God who calls him on the road to Damascus clearly speaks to us as well. Biblical truth and storytelling excellence make this a wonderful read."

Liz Curtis Higgs, *New York Times* Best-Selling Author of *Mine Is the Night*

"Built upon good knowledge of both what the New Testament says and what it does not say, Jenkins enhances Luke's history with his own masterful storytelling skills while still restraining imagination by theological respect."

Wallace Alcorn, Ph.D., Biblical Scholar and Author

"The divine revelation poured into the apostle Paul would help launch a movement that would change the world. *Empire's End* brilliantly tells the powerful, supernatural yet very human story as Jerry Jenkins imagines a journey through Paul's extraordinary calling and early ministry life. I couldn't put it down, and highly recommend it!"

Ray Bentley, Senior Pastor,
Maranatha Chapel, San Diego

EMPIRE'S END

EMPIRE'S END

A NOVEL OF THE APOSTLE PAUL

JERRY B. JENKINS

WITH JAMES S. MACDONALD

WORTHY®

PUBLISHING

Published by Worthy Books, an imprint of Worthy Publishing Group, a division of Worthy Media, Inc., One Franklin Park, 6100 Tower Circle, Suite 210, Franklin, TN 37067.

WORTHY is a registered trademark of Worthy Media, Inc.

HELPING PEOPLE EXPERIENCE THE HEART OF GOD

eBook available wherever digital books are sold.

Library of Congress Control Number: 2015937636

Scripture quotations marked NKJV are taken from the New King James Version®. Copyright © 1982 by Thomas Nelson. Used by permission. All rights reserved.

For foreign and subsidiary rights, contact rights@worthypublishing.com

ISBN: 978-1-61795-007-0 (trade paper)

Cover Design: Brand Navigation
Cover photography: Parthenon Image—Getty Images, Street and Trees Image—iStock, Sky Image—iStock, Parchment Overlay Texture—Dreamstime
Digital Illustration: Mike Chiaravalle

Printed in the United States of America

15 16 17 18 19 RRD 8 7 6 5 4 3 2 1

To Trisha White Priebe

with thanks

CONTENTS

PREAMBLE

After having distanced himself from the execution of Jesus, Roman Prefect of Judea Pontius Pilate further alienated Jerusalem's Jewish leaders by failing to maintain the protocols of his predecessors.

Those before him had deferred to the sensitivities of the Sanhedrin by not allowing Roman troops to enter the capitol city bearing the ensigns and effigies of Caesar. Pilate allowed them in under the cover of darkness, which only infuriated the citizenry the next day. Then he assigned mounted troops to surround the protesters and threaten them, backing down only when they expressed willingness to die before accepting such a desecration of Mosaic Law.

Later Pilate installed gold-plated shields outside Jerusalem's Herod's Palace, so antagonizing the Jews that when he refused to remove them—claiming they were meant only to honor Emperor Tiberius—the people appealed directly to the emperor himself. Tiberius, apparently sensing the shields were meant to annoy rather than to honor, forced Pilate to move them to the great Mediterranean port city of Caesarea, where the prefect's administrative offices were housed.

The next time Pilate addressed the Jews on an unpopular topic, he infiltrated the crowd with soldiers incognito. When the protest arose, he signaled his troops to randomly attack and kill several to keep them from appealing to Tiberius.

Eventually Prefect Pilate learned of a contingent of Samaritans planning to visit Mount Gerizim to view holy artifacts they believed had been buried by Moses himself. To draw attention away from himself, Pilate left Jerusalem for Caesarea and summoned the most ruthless military leader under his charge, General Decimus Calidius Balbus, to his administrative headquarters.

The prefect had never seen General Balbus dressed other than for battle, armed, and ready to strike. When Pilate pointed to a chair, Balbus told him he preferred to stand.

"Do you ever smile, General?"

"When something amuses me."

"And when was the last time?"

The general squinted, a hint of crow's-feet appearing around eyes matching the color of his short gray hair. "During our last campaign one of my men delivered to me the severed head of a woman who reminded me of my wife. That made me smile. At least the wench has borne me no children."

Pilate roared. "I wish I could say the same of mine! Yet you keep her. Why?"

"Maybe I *will* sit, Prefect."

"Please."

"I keep mine for the same reason you keep yours."

Pilate studied him. "Ambition. You seek higher office. There's that smile. You seek *my* office!"

"I don't deny it."

"And why should you? You're right that a divorce would hinder you.

But I won't hinder you. It's no secret I seek Vitellius' chair myself, so my own may soon be vacant."

General Balbus nodded. "I can see you as governor of Syria. But you didn't call me here to tell me that."

"True enough." Pilate told him of the planned Samaritan foray to Mount Gerizim.

The general shook his head. "Why can't they just exercise their superstitions where we allow them—in the temple where they belong?"

"Precisely."

He tilted his scabbard and crossed his legs. "Well, they'll have to go through Tirathana, that village at the base of the mount. Just tell me where you got your information and the result you desire. I'll have some scouts infiltrate, determine how many are going and when, decide how many troops to take with me, and it will be done."

"Do what you have to do to keep them from the mountain, and bring me the leaders. I will reward you with a private home right here in Caesarea, and you will be my handpicked successor when the time of my ascension comes."

~

General Decimus Calidius Balbus led a heavily armed infantry and cavalry that easily overwhelmed the large contingent of Samaritans. He and his men killed several in the village before they got near the mountain, captured the leaders, and chased off the rest. Pontius Pilate made good on his promise of a private house in Caesarea for the general, then had the Samaritan leaders executed without trials.

In short order, Roman Syrian Governor Lucius Vitellius deposed

Pilate and ordered him to Rome to answer to the emperor for his actions, but by the time he arrived, Tiberius had died and Caligula had succeeded him.

To General Balbus' abject disappointment, Vitellius appointed his friend Marcellus as prefect to replace Pilate. But then Marcellus stayed largely in Caesarea and looked the other way when the Jerusalem Sanhedrin stoned to death a zealous follower of The Way named Stephen. Carrying out a punishment to the point of execution was something the Sanhedrin was not to do without the permission of Rome—even if the guilty party had been a devotee of the crucified Galilean the Jews considered a blaspheming false messiah. So suddenly Marcellus was out, and Balbus believed his time had come.

When the governor invited the general to his Caesarean office, Balbus was so convinced of his good fortune that he dressed not for battle but for pageantry and even deigned to have his despised wife accompany him as a masquerade of domestic harmony.

By the time he and his driver and aide-de-camp set out from his new home for the meeting, Caesarea was alive with rumors that the emperor himself was in the city. When the streets leading to the administrative offices proved impossible to navigate, General Balbus knew it was true. Had the emperor sailed all this way just to see him installed as prefect of Judea?

Balbus directed his driver through an alleyway that led to a rear entrance, but as they rattled near he was alarmed to see Lucius Vitellius in the back of a plain wood wagon—a conveyance far beneath the dignity of his station—shoulders slumped, his head in his hands.

"Governor Vitellius!" he called out. "I've arrived! Where do you want me?"

Vitellius turned slowly with a forlorn look. "I'm no longer your governor. Publius Petronius is your man now."

"I barely know him! What—?"

But Vitellius waved him off as his wagon pulled away, and the general climbed down, not knowing what to do. Petronius appeared with a younger man hurrying along beside him. "General Balbus, isn't it?"

"Yes, sir, I—"

"Why are you not in uniform?"

"Well, I was given to understand—"

"And who is this?"

"Sir, this is my wife, she—"

"No women are allowed at this entrance," Petronius said, grabbing the general by the arm and turning his back on the rest of Balbus' party. "This is Marullus. You know each other?"

"We've met."

"He's the new prefect and he has an assignment for you. Now I must get back to the emperor. I wish you'd have come in uniform. You could have appeared with us. No matter. Marullus, you may meet with him in the library, but find me in ten minutes. Balbus, as you're out of uniform you'll have to join your party around front."

The general set his jaw. He would do no such thing. As soon as he was finished with this young man who had the job he believed should have been his, he would find his wife and his men and head back to his home—he didn't care how it looked. New emperor, new governor, new prefect, same old general to do their dirty work.

When he and Marullus were alone in the cavernous library, he told his new superior he preferred to stand.

"It wasn't a suggestion, General," Marullus said. "It was an order."

"Very well, sir," Balbus said with an edge, sitting.

"Have no fear. Your role is secure."

Actually, that is what I was afraid of.

The new prefect sat with his back straight and his hands clasped before him. "Everyone from me on up knows that all you did was what you were ordered to do."

"That's all I've ever done, sir."

"And you've done it with excellence and honor."

"Thank you."

"And General, there is more for you to do. The emperor believes the time has come for Rome to support the Jewish leadership in Jerusalem. What better way than to have our best military leader aid them in their quest to maintain order among their own?"

"I don't understand."

"They have an insurrectionist. One who for years had led the opposition to The Way, those the Jews believed were threats not only to them but also to Rome, has become a traitor."

Marullus sat back as if to let that sink in.

"What? Who?"

"The name is Saul bar Y'honatan of Tarsus. He was assistant to the vice chief justice of the Sanhedrin."

"Nathanael?"

"That's the one."

"His assistant has what, become a follower of The Way?"

"So it appears. And this was the man instrumental in the stoning of the man these people now call their 'first martyr.'"

"How did this happen?" the general said.

"No one knows. But he is abetting these people who are a threat to Jerusalem, to all of Judea."

"To us."

"To Rome, General. We could show no greater support to the people under our jurisdiction—and the emperor wishes to make up for many recent missteps—than for us, for you, to find this man."

"I can find anyone."

"We believe you can."

"May I stand?"

"You may."

"Tell me the result you desire."

"My desire is the desire of the governor, which is the desire of the emperor, which in this case is the desire of the Sanhedrin: the end of The Way."

"Which means the death of this Saul."

"Prefect!"

Marullus looked up with a start at the voice of Governor Petronius. "Coming, sir."

General Balbus leaned close as he walked Marullus out. "I will deliver the heads of Saul and as many members of The Way as I can find, but I want the truth. What's in this for the emperor? He's no more interested in pleasing the Sanhedrin than you are or I am."

"The Temple."

"The Temple?"

"He sees himself as Saturn. A statue of him as Saturn is being built, and he wants it moved to the Temple in Jerusalem as soon as it's finished."

"The Sanhedrin will never—"

"He believes they will, if you deliver Saul."

Part One

CALLED

1

TERROR

I NEVER REFERRED TO the stoning of Stephen as murder, because even standing close enough to hear the blows that tore his flesh did not weaken my belief that we had carried out the judgment of God Himself.

A student of the Scriptures, I knew the sin of putting another god before the one true God. The Jesus-followers had the audacity to elevate that common carpenter to the position of a Christ, the Messiah. And even though this Stephen had been able to conjure some of the same miracles, he had also proved merely mortal in the end.

Now would they worship their new leader, the uneducated fisherman Peter, who may not have had the silver tongue of Stephen but was convincing enough to persuade thousands to become followers of The Way?

Or would they revere Peter's brother James, or the other James among them—one of the brothers of Jesus? Perhaps the new favorite would be young John, who apparently everyone agreed had been Jesus' favorite.

It didn't matter to me. I had undertaken a new assignment with complete confidence that I served as an agent of God. It also raised my stature with the chief priests and most of the rest of the Sanhedrin. Most, because some agreed with my old mentor, Rabbi Gamaliel, who felt the council had overreacted in the matter of Stephen. Gamaliel tried to reason with me, but his advice fell on deaf ears. He had lost my respect. I felt no need of his approval, as I had for so many years.

I admit, however, that the death of Stephen did not have the effect on the people of The Way that I expected. Continuing to insist that Jesus had resurrected from the dead, they referred to Stephen as their first martyr. Rather than cowering in fear of the same fate for themselves, some expressed envy that Stephen had been privileged to be persecuted for Jesus' sake!

His violent death seemed to have discouraged no one from stepping up to replace him—neither the young men of the sect nor even their mothers. Within days of his burial, dozens of devout believers seemed determined to take his place. Their new leaders were bolder, their proclamations louder, their resolve more intense. Even worse, they now began traveling to distant lands to expand the influence of their lies and subversion.

The daily tasks I had handled for Nathanael for years, challenging as they had been, held little interest for me anymore. I took personally the failure of the Sanhedrin to hinder the burgeoning growth of The Way. I had gotten a taste of blood, and I liked it. But this was not violence for violence's sake; rather it was the purest form of justice. Arresting, imprisoning, and killing these people were the only ways to stop the spread of apostasy.

Caiaphas, the high priest, made me his special assistant, with all the power and authority of his office, telling me, "I want The Way driven from Jerusalem. You have proven yourself able and committed."

I was eager to get started. "I will proudly bear your authority, but I need men, weapons, horses."

Caiaphas said, "Consider it done."

Imagine how pleased I was the next morning when a complement of brawny horsemen arrived, every one about twice my size, yet fully understanding who was in charge. For several weeks, I led my men on daily raids before sunrise, surrounding houses owned by Jesus' wealthy followers. We stormed every entrance, denouncing them in the name of God, whipping any who tried to flee, binding them and tethering them to our horses to be dragged off to prison.

I was infused with righteous anger, a godly hatred of these opponents of the Scriptures. My team and I were merciless, swift, and brutal. Fear in the eyes of my prisoners or pleading on the parts of mothers not to separate them from their children had no effect on me. I had been born for this, schooled and trained for this, uniquely equipped for the task.

The fact was I enjoyed it. I was not a tyrant to gain power for its own sake. I was enforcing the will of God. What could be a higher calling? I even told Gamaliel, "I feel alive, fulfilled, as if I am living life to the fullest, defending and glorifying the name of the Lord." My goal was to do anything contrary to the name of Jesus of Nazareth. I cast my votes for many death sentences in Israel and other cities.

Learning that many of The Way had scattered into Judea and Samaria and as far as Damascus, I went again to Caiaphas, breathing threats and murder against them. I asked for a letter of introduction to the synagogues of Damascus. "Any disciples of Jesus I find there, men or women, I will bring to Jerusalem in chains."

This seemed to please the high priest. "Damascus is outside Roman law," he said, "so you will encounter no restrictions."

He supplied me with the letters, and my band of enforcers and I lit out for the great walled city about 135 miles north of Jerusalem. On horseback for the better part of four days, we traveled the way of the Sea of Galilee, crossing the Jordan River by bridge a few miles north of the Dead Sea. My excitement built as we neared Kaukab, about twelve miles south of Damascus.

I pointed into the distance where the road rose to a slight ridge. "The wall will appear on the horizon as we clear that incline, but don't be misled. The city is still almost half a day's journey from there."

I had slowed my great black mount as the sun reached its apex and we neared the crest, when suddenly we were struck by a light so bright it made my horse rear and emit a piercing whinny. I held fast to the reins as I slid from his back, my full weight hanging from the leather straps several feet off the ground. I had just enough presence of mind to let go so I wouldn't pull him over backward and kill him.

The other horses and men cried out as they, too, crashed to the ground. I hit hard and the breath rushed from my lungs. I lay there, eyes shut tight, face pressed into the dirt, but even that did no good against the sudden brilliance that radiated not just from above but also from all around me.

I heard men struggling to their feet and trying to calm their steeds. I fought to move but lay rigid with fear. Suddenly a loud voice implored in Hebrew, "Saul, Saul, why are you persecuting Me?"

Astounded I could find utterance, I moaned, "Who are you, Lord?"

"I am Jesus of Nazareth, whom you are persecuting."

In that instant my world changed. I had believed with my entire being that Jesus had been an impostor and now was dead. There was no time to wonder, to question, to make sense of what was happening. Jesus Himself had clearly spoken to me. The light was the light of God, and it permeated my soul.

I said, "What shall I do, Lord?"

"Rise and stand, for I have appeared to you to make you a minister and a witness both of the things you have seen and of the things I will yet reveal to you. I will deliver you from the Jewish people, as well as from the Gentiles, to whom I now send you, to open their eyes, in order to turn them from darkness to light, and from the power of Satan to God, that they may receive forgiveness of sins. Now go into Damascus, and there you will be told all things that are appointed for you to do."

I struggled to my feet as the men came to my aid. "Did you see that?" I said, unable to control my shuddering.

"Yes! We were scared to death. The horses are still spooked."

"Did you hear the voice?"

"Yes, but we saw no one!"

"It spoke to me, the voice of God. I must get to Damascus with all haste, but I cannot see!"

Two led me by the hand and helped me remount my horse, but the big animal skittered and stutter-stepped and I could feel in the reins his shaking his head. "Hold on tight," one said. "We will lead him slowly."

Several hours later the sounds of the city told me we had arrived.

"Where should we take you, Saul?"

"To the home of Judas on the street called Straight."

2

NARROW ESCAPE

DAMASCUS

I HAD NEVER BEFORE prayed as I did at Judas' house on the street called Straight. I sat blindly on the floor of the bedchamber, murmuring deep penance and rocking in the heat of the sunlight streaming through the window.

Earlier that day on the road into the great walled city I had come face-to-face with Christ Jesus, whom I had persecuted with all that was in me. I moaned, my spirit wracked with sobs, tears forcing their way past the oozing sores. My quivering fingers traced great crusty coverings over both eyes. "Oh, God, forgive me! Cleanse me! Create in me a clean heart like David of old. Make me a man after Your own heart."

Judas laid a hand gently on my shoulder and whispered urgently that I should eat, balancing in my lap a plate of steaming meat and vegetables.

I continued, "Be merciful to me, a sinner . . ."

"At least sip some wine, Saul. You must. I'll leave it here."

I left the pungent food and drink untouched.

Late that day, my supplications turned to every praise I could remember from the Psalms.

Outside the wide wooden door, I heard Judas plead with someone to leave me alone. One of the men from my detail, obviously speaking to his superior, said, "You will not have to answer for returning without him, sir. As it is, we'll likely have to put down his steed."

My horse? Why?

It had not been lost on me that my superior, the vice chief justice of the Sanhedrin, had issued me a colossal black stallion that allowed me to tower over my troops. Each man was at least a head taller than I and weighed much more, but they all reported to me. I'd had to leap just to reach the four-horned saddle, but I loved being astride that enormous horse.

"Why?" Judas whispered. "What's wrong with the animal?"

"You can see for yourself. But if the stable man's not paid by tonight . . ."

"I'll pay him and let Saul decide when he's up and about."

"How long before we're able to get him back to Jerusalem?"

"The man is blind, sir!"

"But can he travel?"

"That is not for me to say."

As footsteps approached, I fell to my face on the floor and cried out, "Jesus, I praise You, Son of the living God, slain to take away the sins of the world, now risen!"

"There's our answer," my man said. "He's mad."

"I told you," another said. "It was a spell, a seizure."

"That's for those at the Temple to decide."

All I knew was that I would never return to Jerusalem in the same role

I had left it. Whether I would regain my sight, I neither knew nor cared. God had found me. Christ had changed me. Jesus had made Himself known to me. Able to see nothing else, I saw myself for who I was.

Three days hence, Ananias and I were brought together by God, my sight and strength were restored, and I immediately began preaching Christ and Him crucified to both the believers and the Jews in Damascus. All who heard were amazed and said, "Is this not he who destroyed those who called on this name in Jerusalem and has come here for that purpose, so that he might bring them bound to the chief priests?"

Though I had been a scholar from my youth and knew the Scriptures almost wholly from memory, I felt clumsy holding forth on an entirely new topic in the synagogues and in private homes with gatherings of followers of The Way. Besides having to convince them that I was not a fraud, merely trying to ingratiate myself in order to turn the tables on them and arrest them en masse, I was suddenly preaching sermons diametrically opposed to what I had espoused for two decades.

Passionate and earnest as I was, I found myself stumbling over my words as I gushed with all my evidence and proofs, rolling the sacred scrolls this way and that, feverishly pointing out every prophecy I could remember that pointed to the promised Messiah. "He was to come from the lineage of David, be born of a virgin in Bethlehem, called Immanuel . . ." I went on and on, thrilling the believers with the fact that Jesus met all these criteria, and clearly alarming the Jews.

I glanced up at my listeners as I paced about, referring to the scrolls and then interspersing my personal story, recounting my credentials, my training, my devotion to God, my commitment—just weeks before—to persecuting the very people I now strove to encourage or win over to my side of the argument.

In the eyes of the followers of The Way I saw both the hope that I was genuine and suspicion that I might not be. *Could it be true?* their expressions seemed to say. *Dare we embrace this man whose dark reputation preceded him?* In the Jews I saw anger and sometimes more—resentment? Worse?

Gradually, as I knew more and more of the brothers and sisters—as the believers were wont to refer to each other—they seemed to embrace me as one of their own. Yet, every day I wondered when I might hear of a band sent from the Sanhedrin to transport me back to the Temple.

Mostly I devoted myself to prayer and whatever God wanted to teach me. I felt like a newborn calf in a pasture of cows. All I had were passion and enthusiasm. I knew what I knew and was eager to persuade, yet I also wanted to grow and mature.

What would my family make of this? I could hardly conceive of it. My sister, Shoshanna, and her husband, Ravid, had a son and three daughters, but they had moved back to Tarsus soon after I had begun making a name for myself persecuting followers of The Way. My parents had both fallen ill and, proud as they were of me, said they wanted to spend their final years back at home too. To my shame, I had not kept up with them as I should have.

I had once heard from my sister that they had taken a turn for the worse, and she included a personal letter from the local rabbi. If my work brought me close to my childhood home, Rabbi Daniel informed me, the congregation would welcome me as the hero I was. He wrote,

> *Reports of your great work on behalf of the Temple only confirm what your family and I and your many friends here in the congregation at Tarsus have known of you since your childhood. Continue*

*making us proud and do come and see us, should the opportunity
ever present itself.*

In my pride I had responded with a generous donation to the Tarsus
temple and a formal expression of gratitude I had grandly dictated to
an amanuensis with beautiful handwriting on expensive parchment,
which I had him roll and seal with the mark of Nathanael, the vice chief
justice.

Shoshanna wrote me back.

*While Rabbi Daniel is impressed, as you clearly knew he would
be (along with most of the people of the congregation), you must
know that your dear father and mother would have appreciated
even more some personal message. While your garish parchment
is now on conspicuous display at the synagogue, your parents remain chiefly unable to attend except on their best days and yearn
only for the unlikely possibility of seeing you once more before they
pass.*

*I don't mind that their care has fallen to me, Saul, I truly do
not. It is a privilege to honor parents who were as good to me as
they were to you. But if you must know the truth, as successful as
Father's business was, rabbinical school, not to mention moving a
family from Tarsus to Jerusalem and back, depleted any excess. If
you have drachmas to spare, perhaps consider sharing the wealth
within the family.*

Imagine my pique. Admired, respected, even bowed to on the street
by most in Jerusalem, I was gushed over by my childhood rabbi and those
who had attended synagogue with me. But what did I hear from my own

parents? Nothing. They were sick, fine, and that troubled me. But if I could dictate a letter, why couldn't they?

And my own sister scolding me? Wouldn't most siblings be proud of a brother who had risen to such heights?

My response had been to not respond at all. At times I wavered and hoped nothing would happen to either of my parents. But I assumed someone, the rabbi if no one else, would give me fair warning if either truly began to fail.

In my anger I could have sent Shoshanna a gift that would have made her feel small for having asked. I had the means, and because I had not married, my needs and expenses were few. All I desired was respect, and if it was not forthcoming from my family, I got plenty from my colleagues and the citizens of Jerusalem.

Naturally the memory of that ugly self-righteousness sickened me now that I had become a believer, and I craved the opportunity to make things right. I prayed it wasn't too late, but I didn't dare risk revealing my whereabouts to the authorities by sending written messages. Sadly, the news of my conversion to Christ would be a far greater offense to my family than appearing to have become an ingrate in adulthood.

No, if word had already reached them of what I was suspected of now, the parchment would have long disappeared from the wall of the local synagogue. My parents would have been disgraced and surely disowned me. A missive in my own hand would be rejected, even if they knew it to contain a generous contribution to the family coffer. They would not see me as one who had discovered the long-awaited Messiah. I would not be considered even a Jew anymore, let alone a Pharisee. I would be seen as a traitor, a heretic, apostate, anathema, an abomination.

Not welcome in the home of my youth, I'd feel as if I had never been born.

One afternoon while I was praying about what I would impart to a group of believers in a Damascus home that evening, a young boy from the stables arrived to tell me the owner wanted me to come and see about my horse. I followed him to find the stable man demanding, "Either take the beast, pay more, or I'll be forced to put him out of his misery."

He led me to the back, where I would not have recognized the animal except for his saddle draped over the rail. The once-magnificent mount, which had stood head high, ebony coat shining, now shifted warily, eyes wide, hide faded. His ribs protruded, and a wood bucket full of feed proved his lack of appetite.

As I approached, the horse stamped and banged a shoulder against the wall. I reached to pet his neck and he jerked away.

"Cruel to that horse, were you?" the stable man said.

"We suffered a trauma together."

"Aah, that's plain. Well, he won't be ridden again, at least not by you."

I took that as a challenge and believed I could win the steed's confidence again if I took the time. For now I had no actual need of him. I lived day to day at the mercies of Judas and Ananias and on the few coins dropped in a box each time I spoke to a small gathering of believers. Though such wouldn't have paid half a day's worth of the luxuries I had grown fond of as an agent of the Sanhedrin, it took care of my needs now. I wanted no more. If I spent the rest of my life making amends for my sins against Jesus and His people, that would amount to a treasure for me.

I pressed a few coins into the stable man's hand and persuaded him to give me a week before he took any action with the horse. Every morning thereafter I slipped through the narrow alleyways to the livery. At first the horse allowed me close enough only to speak quietly. Eventually I was able to caress his muzzle and tousle his forelock. Finally he let me saddle him, but that made him stand stock-still and I wondered whether he would ever trust me again. How could I blame him? He associated me with a terrible day and a blinding light that had made him rear and throw me before he crashed to the rocky ground.

I found myself living for the evenings, longing for the camaraderie afforded me when Ananias took me to various homes of followers of The Way. Some had been fortunate enough to see and hear Jesus. He had referred to Himself as "the way, the truth, and the life." My former self scoffed at that, called Him a heretic, a charlatan, and worse. I imprisoned people who identified themselves with The Way, and yes, put some of them to death.

Now I knew that He *was* the Way.

Many of these believers told me they could see it in my eyes, hear it in my voice, sense from my very countenance that I was genuine. At first they had been suspicious—and why not? Why trust me any more than my horse did? But now we prayed and sang together, and they chuckled with me at how poorly I warbled. "It proves your earnestness," one said.

Not surprisingly, I was learning that I was not so well received in the synagogues. Since I had come to Damascus as a celebrated dignitary from the Temple in Jerusalem, charged with ridding the local congregations of followers of The Way, the leaders knew my men and that I bore the authority of the high priest.

The story quickly spread that I had been escorted into the city blind by men who had since abandoned me. And when I did appear in the synagogues, I did not roust out interlopers of an opposing sect but rather proclaimed Jesus of Nazareth as the long-awaited Messiah.

Despite being a novice, I debated, preached, cajoled, persuaded. And just about the time a congregation seemed ready to rise up and cast me out, I moved on to another synagogue. But finally the day came when the Jewish leaders had had enough of me. If the Sanhedrin was not going to do anything about me, they would.

Rumors flew everywhere. Would they capture me, bring me before a tribunal, bind me, and spirit me back to the Temple in Jerusalem?

At sunset one day I was holding forth in a synagogue, my finger on a passage that foretold of the Messiah, when Ananias rushed forward and whispered in my ear, "They mean to kill you, Saul! We must go now! Follow me!"

Amidst a great murmur that rose to shouts, I followed him out the back and into an alley, surprised at how the older man could run. He led me down one street after another toward the eastern wall. "I have sent for your horse!" he called over his shoulder. "When did you last eat?"

"It's been hours."

"I had no time to get you anything," he said, as he emptied into one of my pockets coins from a small purse. "You'll have to find something on the road."

"I don't need all these," I said.

"Of course you do. Who knows how many days you must make them last?"

"Where am I to go?"

"I had no time to think about that either. Jerusalem?"

By now I was panting. "I would be no safer there! It's likely death here or prison there!"

Ananias led me to one of the homes built into the wall, and we dashed inside and up long narrow stairs. There was no way out except through the city gates, for the outside walls were smooth. I had met the couple residing there at one of the meetings of believers. After a hurried embrace, the man said, "We're two hundred paces from the eastern gate."

"No good," Ananias said. "The Jews are watching all the gates. We must lower him out the window."

"Thirty feet down?" the woman said.

I followed her and peered out. In the disappearing twilight I could barely make out the ground. "Ananias . . ."

"You're not a large man," she said.

"Still, I would split open like a piece of fruit."

"You will fit in my basket."

"Surely not."

But when she fetched it, I could see she was right. By removing my sandals and tucking them beneath me, I was able to wedge my feet inside and tuck my head between my legs, my hands clasped firmly behind it, elbows pressed to my sides. I leapt out and helped Ananias and the couple fashion ropes from linens, anchor them in the room, and then bind them to the handles of the basket.

"The stable boy should have your horse a hundred yards east of the gate," Ananias said. "Pay him two coins, and give the watchmen wide berth."

I folded myself inside the basket, barely able to breathe, and the woman began pressing fruit and loaves of bread around me. When they lifted me to the edge of the window, the sun had vanished, and I felt cast into outer darkness.

The basket bumped and scraped the wall, and more than once it almost tipped me out backward and then forward as they fought to control it. First the fruit and then the bread sailed out and thumped to the ground in the gloom. Worse, the coins from my pocket rattled out and pinged against each other in the night air as they flew from me. Was it possible I'd lost them all? How far could I go penniless?

My ragged descent seemed to take forever and I had no idea how far

I'd gone or even whether we had allowed enough makeshift rope until finally, mercifully, I slammed to the ground.

I grabbed one sandal from the basket and was feeling around in it for the other when the three began quickly raising it again. I backed up to where I could see the window but didn't dare holler at them, and suddenly the opening went dark. Why had they doused their lamps? Were the authorities checking every house?

I waited, hoping at least they would notice my sandal in the basket, and sure enough, a moment later it flopped behind me. I followed the sound and presently stumbled upon it—all the while digging deep into my pocket for any remaining coins. I found two.

I hopped on one foot while sandaling the other, then raced into the night for my horse. I had so hoped to coax him gently to run beneath me again, but in the light of day when he could read my calm demeanor. What would all this rushing about in the darkness mean to him, especially if my pursuers appeared close and I had to force him to bolt?

As I neared the gate, a cacophony of voices assaulted me. Clearly everyone attempting to get in or out of the city was being questioned and searched. I slowed, covered my head, and kept to the shadows, blocking the flickering torches from illuminating my face. Ananias had pulled me away just in time. There would have been no other way out of Damascus and certainly there was no way back in now.

I found the boy just east of the gate, not as far as I had expected. He held the tall stallion by its mane and seemed to struggle to keep it from startling, both his and the horse's eyes wide and wary.

"No bridle or bit?" I said. "And no saddle? How am I to ride him?"

"There was no time," the boy whined. "I was told to get him here fast."

"Did you ride him?"

"Bareback? No! He wouldn't even let me get a rope around his neck. I just got here. They asked me at the gate where I was going with him. I said out to exercise him. I don't think they believed me, but he stamped and nickered and I think they were afraid of him."

I thanked him and gave him my last two coins. As he ran toward the gate, I called after him, "You should return through another gate!" But it was too late. Someone demanded to know what he had done with the horse, and guards were dispatched to find it.

There was no time for sweet-talking the steed now. Knowing my knees and elbows would be worn to bone within a mile, I leapt to reach his mane. Because of my stature I had to pull all my weight the rest of the way up by that coarse hair. I feared that would cause him to throw me or crush me against the wall, but he merely straightened his forelegs and steadied himself till I rearranged my grip and planted a knee on either side of his back.

Men approached, armor clanging, and the great creature stood as if waiting for me to tell him what to do.

"I will call you Theo," I whispered. "Gift of God. Go!"

3

THE FIRST MIRACLE

DAMASCUS TO ARABIA

"THAT'S HIM!"

"Halt!"

"That horse belongs to the Sanhedrin!"

"Stop him!"

But on my simple command, the stallion instantly returned to the magnificent form I'd remembered. He thundered away from the wall and onto the well-worn path, causing sojourners into the city to scatter. He deftly pivoted around those who heard his pounding hooves too late and would have otherwise been trampled.

The shouting, clanging guards faded quickly. I peeked back to see they had resorted to their own mounts, but by the time they reached top speed, Theo had hopelessly outdistanced them. I would love to think I was steering my charger to this prodigious feat, but no doubt he barely felt my death grip on his mane or my bony, bowed knees in his sides.

I was hardly steering. I was hanging on for my life.

And he wasn't mine anyway, was he? I had indeed stolen a horse that belonged to the Sanhedrin. I would have to make that right. But how? I didn't even know where I would find my next meal. Strangely, in the excitement, my hunger had subsided. And unless I was mistaken, the horse felt full size and full strength beneath me. Had someone been exercising him? I would have guessed he'd lost up to two dozen pounds when first I'd seen him. What had put him back on his feed?

Theo had reached a speed as fast as I had ever ridden him in a saddle, and without one I would not have expected even to stay astride. But he had also settled into such a strong rhythm that I felt one with him, rocking with his pace and feeling none of the discomfort I expected from his bristly coat.

Clear of pursuers and encountering no one else coming toward Damascus, I eased my grip on Theo's mane and expected his gait to slow. But no. He rushed on. We had been at full gallop for little more than twenty minutes when we neared Kaukab, about twelve miles south. This was the stretch where my Lord Christ had confronted me and my horse had thrown me and landed on his side.

Surely this memory would slow him. But either Theo didn't recognize the spot or didn't care, for he surged on. It was as if he had a mind of his own, a destination only he knew, and I would find out when we got there. We flew past Kaukab and soon left the road and angled southeast, hurtling over rougher, rockier terrain without slowing.

This could not be good. Was Theo spooked? Would he sprint until he collapsed? Then where would I be—in the middle of nowhere with no resources and a spent horse? I gently tugged him to the right, trying to urge him back toward the road of the trade route, where I knew we would eventually come to a place I could rest and water him.

But he ignored my prods and stayed his own course. What was I to do when I needed to eat or relieve myself? He could hold out much longer than I, so it made no sense to wait until he flagged. Without money I would have to find berries or a way to trap small game or locate a body of water where I could devise a way to catch fish.

Half an hour later, as Theo dashed on through the night, I wondered if I would have to leap off. He showed no signs of slowing, and when I reached to feel for foamy sweat on his flanks, I detected none. How was this possible? I soon realized that I felt none of the effects of the exertion either. I should have been pouring sweat as well. My muscles should have ached, my heart should have been pounding, my breath short, my fingers cramped, my knees and elbows worn raw.

Yet I felt fresh, strong, rested, as if I had enjoyed a long night's sleep. My only ordeal had been vexation, worry over what to do next. I had agonized over how I would stop, where I would stop, where I would eat, what I would eat, where I would rest, how I would water and feed the horse, how I would keep him on course, but on what course? I had no idea where I was going.

And yet Theo seemed to know. He didn't slow, showed no hesitation.

Suddenly I felt as if God Himself were telling me I should relax and trust my horse. Tearing over rough terrain at top speed bareback, I had not come close to being thrown. I had been vigilant, eyes alert, squinting into the night. Now I leaned forward and rested my cheek on the back of my hand in his mane and let his fast, steady rhythm soothe me.

An hour later I realized I had been actually dozing as we flew past a way station on the trade route and men called out.

"Slow down!"

"You'll kill that horse!"

"You all right, man?"

I waved and settled back in. Theo sprinted on without effort, so seemingly unaware I was even astride him that I was able to stop worrying about my safety or where he was taking me. Clearly this was of God. He had a plan. Escape had been my aim. Hours into this miraculous flight I was devoid of concern and only looked forward to whatever destination He had in mind.

It struck me that I had actually slept, unaware of how long, and had not suffered from the chill of the black night. Theo's gait never waned, even when I felt the softening of the earth, breathed in moist air, and realized he was kicking sand in high plumes behind us. He had set his nose on a direct route about twenty feet from the edge of the Red Sea, heading due south.

When the western horizon to my right began to lighten to the faintest pastels, I comprehended that the magnificent animal had been at this for more than ten hours. How long would he go? How far might he take me in the light and heat of the day? Still I felt no discomfort, no hunger, no call of nature, no fatigue. Whatever God was doing, He had imbued us both with ceaseless power.

A dozen Roman cavalrymen, swords drawn and standard flapping, surged from a thicket of trees about forty yards to my left. They galloped directly into my path and stopped in a line, anchored at the middle by a taut, wiry, gray-haired man, the reins of a white stallion in one fist and the other raised over his head.

"Halt in the name of the emperor!" he thundered. "Saul of Tarsus?"

Hopelessly outnumbered, I yanked Theo's mane to stop him and trusted God to protect me. But my horse was having none of this! He slowed not a whit but flew between the man and his number two as I yelled, "Whoa! Whoa!"

"I am General Decimus Calidius Bal—after him!"

Now I was torn. A Roman citizen, I fully intended to obey a general who knew my name, yet my horse had already proven to be under the authority of the creator God. His response to my commands was to sprint, and I was tempted to urge him on.

Clearly, this general's horses were also thoroughbreds, as his garrison quickly drew alongside Theo.

"Are you Saul of Tarsus?" he called out.

There was no point in pretending otherwise. "I am!"

"I am General Decimus Calidius Balbus, ordering you to halt in the name of the emperor!"

Again I pulled on Theo's mane and shouted, "Whoa!" And again my horse ignored me.

I smiled apologetically at the general and shrugged. He did not appear amused. "Stop that horse or you'll both suffer the consequences!"

I went through the motions again, to no avail.

The general drew his sword and swung mightily at my neck. I ducked, and the blade caught Theo just below his left ear, drawing blood, making him skid to a stop, wheel around, and rear, front hooves flailing at the general, whose own horse whinnied and shied while the others surrounded us.

"You're under arrest!" General Balbus shouted, and I resisted the urge to respond, *It doesn't appear so.*

Theo continued to thrash until he spied an opening in the circle of armed horsemen and dashed away again, the Romans in pursuit. I merely hung on, shrugging at General Balbus' threats as he and his men stayed a few feet off Theo's heels for nearly twenty more minutes. I reached to feel the wound above the patch of drying blood only to find no opening in the skin. I caressed the coarse hide and the blood flaked away.

As had been the case since we'd left Damascus, Theo never slowed. Occasionally I peeked back at Roman horses foaming with sweat, mouths agape and gasping. Gradually the soldiers fell off the pace, drifting farther and farther back, the general's voice growing fainter, though his threats sounded no less passionate. Theo edged closer to the water where he kicked up wet sand and gentle waves covered our tracks.

When I no longer heard hoofbeats behind us, I looked to find that Balbus and his men had dismounted and huddled in a circle. But the general did not appear the type who would give up the chase for long.

With Theo still rolling on, all I could do was thank God and leave the endpoint and the outcome to Him. When my fear subsided I was content to reflect. Not so many days before I had been what my new friend Ananias had so eloquently called "dead in trespasses and sins," so deeply entrenched that not only did I not see them as such, I also thoroughly believed in my own righteousness. It had taken a miracle to blot out the old and make all things new. I had gone from a life of fully believing I was serving God by tormenting and even killing people who believed Jesus was the Messiah to being converted by Christ Himself. I had traveled to Damascus as one person, arrived there as someone else entirely, and now fled to I knew not where to become I knew not what.

If this stunned people who knew me only by reputation, imagine what it was like for me to have planned to barge into temples to harass believers in Jesus, only to arrive there and proclaim that He was indeed the Messiah.

Would I ever be able to return home? If I was cursed in Damascus, I was anathema in Jerusalem. I longed to meet the original disciples of Jesus, to sit at their feet, hear their stories, learn from them, serve with them. But would they believe I'd become their brother? Would I get the chance the convince them? All I wanted was the privilege of trying.

Clearly, that was not where God was sending me now. And also clearly, I would not be without opposition.

4

STILL SMALL VOICE

ARABIA

GOD HAD USED THE threat on my life to send me to a vast wilderness, but why?

Terrifying as it had been to have my new Lord and Master reveal Himself to me as a blinding light and speak aloud to me, in the days since, I had longed to hear His voice again. Yet somehow when it came to me once more, it was not the piercing clarion call of the One I had once persecuted. No, this time, as the sun rose in a cloudless sky that should have forced me to cover my legs and head, I sensed a still small voice deep within my heart and soul.

As Theo rumbled through the desert sand, I felt God the Father gently urge me to relax, to sit up, to ease my grip on the horse's mane, to rest my palms on my thighs. Despite the unexplainable ride and the miraculous escape from the Roman cavalrymen, still I was hesitant to obey. Yet as soon as I did, I found myself as comfortable and confident as I had ever been, even when I'd enjoyed the security of a saddle.

Without shade or breeze, except for that caused by the speed, my thinning hair wafted and my face was refreshed, and I felt no need even to squint into what should have been a blinding sun. Yet I had been in the Arabian desert for hours.

The same zeal you brought to your former life you will dedicate to the gospel of My Son.

"Yes, Lord!" I shouted. "I will proclaim Him for as long as You give me breath!"

You will be My witness—

"Yes, Lord!"

But suddenly, by His silence, I felt a deep rebuke. Now I fell silent and lowered my head. I dared not even beg forgiveness. I had interrupted the very God of the universe, the God of Abraham, Isaac, and Jacob. He had said He would use my zeal, but had that fervor already offended Him? I wanted to leap from Theo and prostrate myself, hiding my face in the sand. What was wrong with me?

He had to know this! I knew from my memorizing of the ancient Scriptures as a child that He knew my innermost being! A sob rose in my throat, and desperate as I was to return to a right relationship with Him, I dared not speak. Had I ruined everything? I would never be impudent with an earthly ruler! How could I with God the Father? I felt as bad as I had on the floor of Judas' house.

As my horse raced on, I rocked along, head bowed, weeping, aching for another word, anything from my God. I would never speak in His presence again if only He would forgive me. All my life I had been desperate for a walking-and-talking interaction with God like the ones enjoyed by biblical heroes of old. Christ Himself had confronted me and now God had spoken to me. But in my exhilaration I had overstepped my position.

I determined that from now on I would speak to God only in spirit. I would be open to Him always, listening. *Mercy. Mercy. Mercy.*

You will no longer identify yourself by your Greek name.

Oh, praise God, He was speaking to me again! And though I was confused, I would merely listen. I would obey, of course, but if I was no longer Saul, who was I? And identify myself to whom? Where was I going and to whom would I be speaking?

By your Roman name.

When it was to my advantage I used the name Paul, but growing up a Pharisee and in my role with the Sanhedrin I had always been Saul. I could not have been more puzzled or curious, but I had always been a fast learner. I was not about to pester my Lord God with questions. Nothing sickened me more than His silence, and clearly He had something in mind for me.

For as long as I could remember, I had been filled with purpose—an early riser, busy all day. How I longed to devote that vigor and passion to my Lord, if only He would tell me what He wanted me to do.

I knew nothing more than to be prayerfully silent and listen. This I did as patiently as I knew how for the rest of the day, finally so confident of my balance on the broad back of the great beast Theo that I folded my hands in my lap and sat straight up, back rigid, hood hanging loosely about my neck, eyes closed.

Still aware of the moist air, the sound of the sand beneath my horse's hooves, and the warmth of the sun on my scalp, I alternately dozed and hummed praises to God—trying to be patient. This I found nearly impossible as the sun reached its zenith, then arced out over the Red Sea and began to wane.

The miracle of riding a speeding horse for hours on end without pain or fear or hunger or fatigue had lost its novelty—how long could this go on? Would Theo take me to the ends of the earth? What did my Lord have in mind? I determined that I had been aboard this animal for almost twenty-four hours and could well have covered as many as nine hundred miles. No one in his right mind would believe it. I wouldn't have myself had I not been the foolish-looking man perched atop the magnificent stallion.

As the sun flattened and broadened and its hues began to change from yellow to orange, suddenly both sky and sea seemed to burst into flames of color painted just for me by God Himself. I was captivated, mesmerized, overcome. How many times must I have seen this before without ever giving it a second look? As I spread my arms to gather it in, God spoke deeply to my soul—making me wish I had parchment and quill—but I would never forget one syllable.

My Son is the very image of Me, the firstborn over all creation. For by Him all things were created that are in heaven and that are on earth, visible and invisible, whether thrones or dominions or principalities or powers. All things were created through Him and for Him. And He is before all things, and in Him all things consist. And He is the head of the body, the church, who is the beginning, the firstborn from the dead, that in all things He may have the preeminence.

For it pleased Me that in Him all the fullness should dwell, and by Him to reconcile all things to Himself, by Him, where things on earth or things in heaven, having made peace through the blood of His cross.

At this I lowered my face into Theo's mane and sobbed. Would that God would speak to me this way and that I would have the unspeakable privilege of sharing it.

My horse thundered on as my tears streamed, but I was soon startled by a break in his gait. He hadn't slowed, but something had caused him to miss a step. I sat up and peered into the distance. In the fading light a rising cloud of dust could mean only one thing: a caravan.

Giving not a hint of slowing, Theo would in a matter of minutes overtake the plodding camels and carts. But I feared we would also spook the massive security detail that protected the precious goods—silk or spices and incense, perhaps ivory. And there was the matter of the Roman garrison, no doubt still in dogged pursuit. Did I dare give them a chance to make up ground?

Had it been up to me, I would have steered clear of the caravan, shambling along about forty yards east and maybe half a mile ahead of us. A gentle breeze carried back to me clear aromatic evidence of its cargo, reminding me afresh of the miracle of my sated appetite. At any other time, particularly when I had gone an entire night and day without a bite, the pungent fragrance of cinnamon, pepper, onion, garlic, and the like would have sent me on a course toward warm bread, sizzling meat, and an appropriate libation.

Now it merely piqued my interest, kindled my imagination, and made me nostalgic for faraway places and long-forgotten friends.

It was too much to hope for that the caravan guards would ignore an enormous black stallion with a tiny, bald, middle-aged man on his bare back, racing madly past them along the shore of the Red Sea. By the time we pulled to within a couple of hundred yards of them, three of their black-clad guards peeled off and galloped over to intercept us.

As we drew near, I could see from their dark countenances and turbans that they hailed from the Far East. One eased his mount directly into Theo's path and casually raised a hand in a not-unfriendly manner, as if to request I stop for a chat. As Theo had had a mind of his own since I had leapt astride him a full day and night before, that decision was out of my hands. I merely smiled and shrugged as we flew by, and the guard's steed skittered back as the man quickly unsheathed his weapon.

The three lit out after us, shouting in a language I did not recognize, and they were soon joined by at least a half dozen others. Though they were all no doubt well trained and their horses fresh, fit, and fed, they were no match for a mount and rider already tested to their limits for twenty-four hours and empowered by the God of the universe.

By the time Theo finally, strangely, bore hard to his left and made me reach desperately for his mane again, our pursuers had disappeared. At long last, it appeared we had reached some sort of a destination. The great animal slowed to a gallop, then to a trot, then to a walk. He eased across the trade route past a sign I would not have been able to read at the speed we had been going: Jeddah 185 miles.

He slipped behind a tall rock outcropping and down a ravine that led to a shallow dip unlike anything else I'd seen in the Arabian desert. He stopped on a rocky plateau that overlooked a cluster of dwellings that appeared to comprise a shabby Bedouin settlement. It reminded me of a bleak city of refuge I had seen years before. And had my horse not followed this unlikely path, I would have seen not a bit of evidence of it—nor could anyone else. In the middle of the vast Arabian desert, it was the perfect spot to hide a dwelling place.

And so, Lord?

I slid off Theo's back, expecting to feel tight, cramped, weary. If this was not a dream, if I really had traveled from Damascus to 185 miles north of Jeddah from sundown to sundown on horseback, I could not imagine ever doubting or questioning God again for as long as I lived. What must He have be planning for me?

Is this where I am to reside, Lord?

"You?"

I jumped and whirled at the sound of an ancient voice, instinctively reaching to my waist for a weapon that wasn't there. An old man stood watching me in the fading light, holding the hand of cherubic dark-eyed boy not more than four years old.

Remember.

God had reminded me of how I was to identify myself. "*You* what?" I said.

"*You* are the one the Lord told me of in a dream?"

"Not again," I said.

"This is common for you?" the old man said.

"It has happened before."

"Not to me, stranger." He turned to the boy, who looked scared. "If he tells us the correct name, Corydon, we will know he is the man of God."

"My name is Paul," I said, thrusting out my hand. "Where am I?"

The man gasped but did not take my hand. He gathered the boy close to him and said, "Could he have come so far, so fast? Does his horse look tired? And where is his saddle?"

"You're saying the Lord told you where I was last night?" I said.

The man nodded solemnly.

"If I tell you where that was, will you shake my hand and tell me where I am?"

He nodded, but his fingers trembled.

"Damascus," I said.

He took my hand but fell to his knees, causing the boy to burst into tears and cry out, "Grandfather!"

"It's all right, son," I said. "Corydon, is it?" The boy fought to stop crying, pressing his lips together. He nodded. I helped the man to his feet. "And you, sir? Your name?"

"Alastor. And you have arrived at Yanbu."

I knelt so I was eye level with the boy and showing deference to his grandfather. "Sir, you have plainly walked with God much longer than I. But am I to gather that below us is an enclave of followers of The Way?"

The old man nodded. "We have all been driven many miles from our various homelands."

"As have I."

"We are to take you in."

"Who else knows this?" I said.

"No one."

"Will I be accepted or suspected?"

It was nice to see Alastor smile at last. "If I were you, Paul, I would not tell the story of your journey."

That made me chuckle. "I barely believe it myself, sir."

"The Lord told me you would come to us with nothing, but that we were to offer you food and lodging in exchange for your trade."

"My trade?"

Alastor nodded. "We are to leave you alone so He can meet with you in the wilderness in the mornings, and you will ply your trade in the afternoons."

"Did He say what my trade was to be?"

Alastor shook his head. "You must understand, Paul. I did not know it was really the Lord until you confirmed what He told me. Forgive me, but you do not look like someone He would have sent."

"Coming all this way so quickly—"

"And without a saddle. Or sunburn."

"I understand," I said. "But as for my trade, I—" *Do not reveal your training.* "—I, ah, don't know what I can offer."

"Paul, if you do not know, I certainly don't either. But for now I must obey the Lord. Are you thirsty, hungry, tired? Let's water and feed your horse and wash your feet, have my daughter set another bowl at the table—"

"Oh, I'm not—" *Accept.* "I would be so grateful. Thank you, sir. And Corydon, I am eager to meet your parents. Tell me—"

"The lad has recently lost his father, sir."

"I'm so sorry."

"And his mother is still in mourning, so—"

"I understand. Don't put her to any trouble."

"She likes to keep busy."

I asked Alastor if he and the boy would like to ride down to the settlement while I led the horse. He looked to Corydon who nodded, and I helped them both up onto Theo.

Curious eyes met us as we approached the commune, but the unsmiling people only nodded and kept to themselves.

A cluster of nine unwieldy tents lay hidden about a mile from the trade route and another quarter-mile from the sea. The dwellings consisted of crude, rectangular sections of woven dark sheepskin and goatskin sewn together and supported by wood poles anchored to the rocky ground by wood pegs. A glance told me my father, a master tentmaker, would have been horrified at the workmanship. Frayed edges and gaping holes clearly allowed in wind, dust, dirt, rocks, and whatever chill the night winds brought. It dawned on me what trade the Lord intended for me to barter here.

Alastor gestured toward the largest tent, set at the far left end of the compound, and handed Corydon down to me. The lad quickly wriggled from my grasp and ran inside calling, "Mama, a man!"

I moved to help Alastor, but the old man assured me he was all right and deftly slid off Theo, bellowing a strange name. A young man of ruddy countenance came running from another tent, bowed to me, and was introduced as Nadav.

"Our guest is Paul of Damascus. Bring him water to drink, wash his feet, take his horse to the trough, and let the elders know all will meet him tonight at second watch."

"Yes, Rabbi," Nadav said. He turned to me. "Welcome, Paul of Damascus." He looked at Theo and turned back with a puzzled expression.

"He'll follow you," I said.

Nadav made a clicking sound and Theo followed him to the middle of the compound.

"You didn't tell me you were a rabbi, Alastor. Your name—"

"Is not Hebrew. My family is Hellenistic. But yes, I am a lifelong student of the Scriptures."

Do not reveal your training.

"Interesting. As it happens, sir, while I appreciate your hospitality, I am not thirsty, nor are my feet—"

"You have come a long way, Paul. And don't deprive the young man the blessing of serving you."

"Very well."

"Ah, my daughter, Taryn."

I could barely make out the lithe, veiled figure just inside the opening of the tent. She stood motionless, seeming to protect Corydon, one dark hand around his shoulder, peeking out from the shadows, the waning sunlight revealing long slender fingers that somehow portended a certain gracefulness.

It was not my practice to greet unbidden a married woman, let alone a widow, but her own father introduced us. Her entire being seemed hesitant, even unwilling. How fresh must be her grief? Alastor laid a hand gently on my shoulder and nudged me toward her.

"Taryn, our guest is Paul, a brother in Christ from Damascus."

She offered a nod and flashed a glance at her father. Annoyance? Panic? Frustration?

"I regret any inconvenience," I said.

"Not at all," she said, but her tone and eyes betrayed her.

"Nadav will refresh him. Do I smell stew?"

She nodded, eyes cast down. "Just broth with vegetables and bread. Then some figs."

"I don't want to be any extra work," I said.

"We have plenty," she said, backing away. "You are welcome."

Somehow I didn't feel welcome.

"Taryn, please," Alastor said in a tone more disappointed than scolding, "I have more to tell you."

"Forgive me, Father," she said, turning back.

"I'll be back for supper. Please prepare the room for an elders' meeting at second watch."

"Very well."

Nadav arrived with a cup of water for me to drink and a bowl to wash my feet. Taryn and Corydon had disappeared behind the curtain that separated the two main sections of the tent, and I heard them whispering as she worked. Presently, the boy reappeared and watched intently as Nadav dried my feet. Corydon removed his own sandals and put his tiny feet into mine then amused himself by padding around in them.

I made a great show of pretending his sandals were mine and trying to force my feet into them. I stood as if I didn't notice that my toes barely fit through the straps and the heels stopped before the middle of my feet. I strolled to the front of the tent as if to gaze out at the horizon, which made Corydon laugh aloud and call for his mother to "come and see the funny man!"

"I'm not washing your feet again!" Nadav said.

Taryn pulled back the curtain slightly and peeked out, shaking her head at Corydon in my big sandals. I raised the hem of my tunic a few inches so she could see his little ones on me. It warmed me to see her put a hand to her mouth over the veil as if to keep from laughing aloud.

When she went back to her work, I kept Corydon giggling by acting as if I were shocked to have just discovered that we had on each other's sandals. I began a long process of trading him one for the other where we kept ending up with one large and one small sandal each. He found this endlessly entertaining, and it dawned on me that I had not played with a child since I had been one myself.

Nadav said he needed to get back to his family as he would be coming back for the elders' meeting. I asked if I could chat with him as he walked, telling Corydon to tell his mother I would be back. "Can't I go with you, Master Paul?"

"Not this time, son. I'll be back soon for supper. You tell Mama, okay?"

As the boy ran back, Nadav whispered, "I believe she was pleased that you amused him."

I asked him all about the place, the elders, the well, who did what, where they got their fabrics, their clothes, their tools, everything. He told me of their communal garden, livestock, and how much of their diet consisted of fish from the Red Sea. "I'm sure Rabbi Alastor will explain much more tonight."

Back at Alastor's tent, I was hesitant to enter, given that his daughter was alone with the child. I lingered outside as the sky blackened. Pulling my mantle off my shoulders, I gathered it at the neck against the cool breeze and gazed into the heavens to see what stars had begun to appear. Silently I said, *This is where You would have me meet You in the mornings?*

Not a temple, not a forest, not a meadow. A desert. A wilderness.

Whether Corydon heard me or just noticed me when he came from the back to play, I do not know, but he immediately squealed, "Master Paul!" He knelt, slipped off a sandal, and came running, waving it over his head. "Look! Look! I found your shoe!"

"Indeed you did!" I said, taking off one of my own. "And I found yours!"

Leaping into my arms, he nearly bowled me over. "Corydon!" his mother called, appearing from behind the curtain. "Don't bother our guest. Grandfather will be here soon, and it's time to eat."

"It's entirely my fault, and he's no bother. He's a delight."

"Thank you," she said quietly. "Corydon, come now."

When the boy made no move, I set him down and nudged him toward his mother. Alastor startled me when he clapped me on the back and said, "How good of you to make him obey! She'll appreciate that. I don't do enough of it."

The four of us sat on mats across from each other, Taryn and the boy on one side, Alastor and I on the other, with the bread and steaming pot of stew between us. Corydon begged to sit next to me, but when I began to assure his mother it would be all right, Alastor stopped me with a touch, pronounced a blessing over the food, and changed the subject.

The bread was nearly as warm as the stew, and while I was not hungry from what should've been an arduous journey, I found the repast more than satisfying. Taryn sat nearly motionless except to help her son, and she and Alastor kept the lad quiet the entire meal, though it was clear he very much wanted to talk.

As soon as we were finished with the dessert of figs, Taryn excused herself to put the boy to bed. He protested only briefly and giggled when I told him that in the morning he must help me find my sandals. When I began to help clear the eating area, Alastor shook his head and led me into the front section of the tent where he drew out a Scripture scroll, cradled it in his lap, and suggested we talk about what to expect from the meeting of the elders.

I was frankly more concerned with where I was to spend the night. The miracle of my sojourn had left me with no question that I was where I was meant to be and that no human—elders or otherwise—would have the power to turn me away, whether I succeeded in persuading them of my value or not. God had already told Alastor of my coming, so it seemed the rest was simply a matter of details.

Nadav and five others made up the remainder of the elders, and around the beginning of the second watch, they arrived in ones and twos. When they were situated, Alastor opened the scroll, read a psalm, prayed, and introduced me by name as "the man I spoke to you about. I am welcoming him as a guest in my home, and I would like you to acquaint yourselves with him so you may make him feel welcome as well."

A beefy man who looked not much younger than Alastor and who bore a stony visage said, "You welcome a stranger and expect us simply to do the same? If you feel that by having him sit here in our midst will keep us from speaking our minds, you are mistaken."

Alastor raised a hand. "Zuriel, surely you know me better than that. That is the reason for this meeting. All things are to be revealed openly. Ask this man anything you want. Tell him anything you want. Satisfy yourself completely."

"And if in the end I am not satisfied, what then? Do we send him on his way?"

"Trust me, friend," I said, "you'll find that unnecessary."

"Excuse me, sir," Zuriel said. "I am not your friend. At least not yet. For all I know you could be a spy, a Roman, an agent of the Sanhedrin."

"I assure you I am a follower of The Way."

"And because you know a phrase meant to set my mind at ease, I'm to welcome you with open arms."

"Brother, I believe God wants me here and that eventually He will make that plain to you."

"What leads you to believe God wants you here?"

Below the curtain separating the sections of the tent I noticed Taryn's sandals and the fringes of her mantle. What must she be thinking of all this?

"He sent me here—that's all I can say."

"What drove you from Damascus?"

"Frankly, my fellow Jews. I think some wanted to hand me over to the Sanhedrin and Jerusalem. Some of my friends believed others actually wanted to kill me."

Zuriel narrowed his eyes at me and glanced at his fellow elders. "For what charge?"

"I was teaching at private gatherings of followers of The Way. And I was speaking in synagogues, preaching Christ."

At this, Zuriel fell silent. Someone else said, "Do we know anyone from Damascus who can vouch for this man?"

"Enough with this!" Alastor said. "I am your rabbi and I vouch for him. Is that not enough?"

"No! It is not!" It was Zuriel again. "You tell us you met this man just hours ago, yet—"

"I told you God has given me peace about him."

"And that should give us peace?"

"Absolutely."

The others began to murmur and someone suggested getting word to the brethren in Damascus to try to corroborate my story.

"If you know the brethren in Damascus," I said, "you must know—"

Do not name Ananias or Judas.

Alastor leaned forward and spoke softly. "We all come from various cities, towns, and villages. Some of us are familiar with the leaders of The Way in Damascus."

"Tell us who you know there, Paul," Zuriel said.

"I am not at liberty," I said.

"There! You see? And why not?"

Zuriel laughed derisively, but Alastor held up a hand to quiet him and said we should discuss my role in the community.

"His *role?*" Zuriel said. "It will not be a part of this body, I can tell you that, because that requires a unanimous vote, and he will not have mine."

"My friend," I said, "I am not in the least qualified to be an elder. I am very new to the faith."

"And yet you would have us believe you were chased from the synagogues in Damascus for preaching Christ? You are a madman."

"You are not the first to think that," I said, smiling.

Zuriel was clearly not amused.

"Paul is a new believer," Alastor said, "full of passion and zeal, and upon whom I believe God has His hand. I will personally see to it that he carries his weight here. He will have mornings to himself, will apply a trade in the afternoon so he can afford food and lodging and clothes, and he will take his turn with both the fishing detail and the night watch."

"What is your trade?" someone asked. "We have no need of a preacher, especially a new one."

This caused the others to chuckle and Alastor to break in to explain that I had not yet determined my trade, but I interrupted him to say, "I am a tentmaker. And frankly, from the looks of things, there's enough repair work here to keep me busy."

Again I had apparently surprised everyone. And again Zuriel broke the silence. "Your hands do not look like those of a tentmaker. More like a cleric's."

"I confess it's been a while. But I'll develop my calluses soon enough, and your dwellings will evidence my handiwork."

"Start with mine," the burly man said.

"All I need are the tools and a place to work."

All the elders save Zuriel spoke cordially to me and welcomed me before they left. Nadav held back and told me where Theo was corralled and could be watered and fed every day. "He's a fine-looking animal."

I nodded. "You look as if you have something on your mind."

He signaled me outside with a nod. "Forgive me, it was none of my business."

"What's that?"

"I hand-fed him some grain, just a little, when I was watering him before, and I got a twig in with it. He let me remove it, and I noticed the marking inside his lip."

"Did you?"

He nodded. "That's not a private horse, is it? At least it hasn't always been."

"That's right."

"How did you come by him?"

"He was issued to me, and that's all I care to say about it."

"He's yours now, though."

I was silent.

"You wouldn't risk bringing a stolen horse among us, would you, Paul?"

"Nadav, I have to ask you to trust me to handle my own business. There are things I cannot speak about yet. Now, leave Theo to me, and

I hope I can trust you not to trouble the others with your questions about him."

"But I have only just met you, sir. We are risking our lives and our families, and—"

"And I am doing the same, I assure you. Any risk I expose you to would expose me as well. Believe me, my friend, God seems to have led me here for a purpose even I don't yet understand. But I am learning to trust Him. I pledge to you my fidelity in doing everything I can to maintain your safety. Will you trust me to handle my private affairs?"

Nadav seemed to study me and consider my request. Finally he reached for my forearm and we shook hands. He offered a tight-lipped smile. "Perhaps my confidence might earn me the next place on your repair list after Zuriel? My tent is the farthest north."

"I've seen it. It's in the worst repair."

"Do you really have tentmaking experience?"

"I don't mean to boast, but in a few days, you will know."

As Nadav disappeared into the night, I turned to find Alastor waiting just inside the tent, laden with the mat he and I had shared at supper, along with a heavy fur blanket. I apologized for putting him out and asked if I really needed so thick a covering.

"You might be surprised."

He told me he had scolded Zuriel for his treatment of me and had also informed him that before I started repairing his tent, I would fashion my own lodging quarters. "For tonight you will sleep right here, but by tomorrow night you should have your own area around this side."

Alastor led me out and showed me in the moonlight where I could add on to the side of his tent an eight-foot overhang, enclosed at the back to accommodate a sleeping mat, and open at the front except to block the sun, where I could work in the afternoon. "By the time you return from the wilderness, I'll see to it that you have all the equipment and tools you need. We will all be glad to give up this odious chore, at which none of us bear any skill."

"That is clear."

"I'll thank you not to continue to emphasize that."

Alastor started back inside but I lingered, having more questions and not wanting to bother his daughter or grandson. I asked him how I might earn actual money in the event I had debts, and how I would send money out of Yanbu. He told me of an elaborate scheme he and the others had devised that included their Red Sea night-fishing parties bartering with occasional caravans, and sometimes sending someone on a long journey to get messages to families and loved ones they had left.

I wondered how I would send payment to the Sanhedrin for my horse without revealing more about myself to these people than I cared to. I saved the question for another time.

Before we retired, Alastor whispered, "Taryn asked me to thank you for your kindness to Corydon. He has few playmates, and few adults pay him any attention."

"Oh, she should think nothing of it. I find him amusing. But tell me, is she too shy to speak to me on her own?"

"She is in pain, Paul. And I'm sure she wonders about propriety. Give her time to get accustomed to having you around. It was insensitive of me to give her so little notice. I did not tell her of my dream because I was unsure of it myself, and then Corydon and I simply arrived with you, saying you would be staying with us."

"How long ago did she lose her husband?"

"It has been only this year."

Alastor's voice caught telling me that, which should have slowed me, but I asked, "And how did he die?"

He looked away and sighed. "We, ah, find it difficult to talk about yet."

"Forgive me. You were close to him too."

"I did not live with them, but he wanted me to. Taryn's mother has been gone for many years, but I am healthy, and I wanted to allow them time to themselves. Now I wish I had accepted his offer. He was such a wonderful man. I didn't know if we would ever smile again. Taryn told me you had the lad laughing."

"I was just teasing him."

"It humored her too. So good for her."

"Well, I'm glad."

We stepped back inside the tent and I spread out the fur covering. Alastor bid me good night, but just before he reached the curtain he returned. "Tell me something," he whispered. "Were you really in Damascus yesterday?"

"I mounted Theo at first watch."

The old man shook his head. "And I thought *I'd* had an experience when the Lord spoke to me. I don't know how you'll sleep."

"I'm finally tired. I'm curious, though. I have no idea what I am to do in the morning. You say I am to meet God in the wilderness. I don't even know where that is."

Alastor put one hand on his belly and another over his mouth and wheezed, clearly trying to keep from laughing. "You have been in the wilderness since you reached the Red Sea, my friend! All you have to do is leave the tent and head east and you'll have all the wilderness you want. But don't you think the God who got you here from Damascus in one day's time can get you where He wants you tomorrow?"

5

THE PRESENCE OF THE DIVINE

THE ARABIAN WILDERNESS

I SLEPT THE SLEEP of the dead and woke before dawn to a most unusual mixture of pungent odors. Next to my head sat a small table draped with a striped cloth, on which lay a loaf of warm bread and a shallow bowl of olives, which appeared to have been tossed with grapes.

I crept near the curtain to listen for whether anyone would join me, but I heard the old man's snore and nothing of the boy or his mother.

"Thank you," I said quietly.

"You are welcome, sir," came Taryn's whisper, in a tone implying that I should not wake the others. She extended a cup of wine around the curtain.

"I don't usually eat this early," I said. "But I'm grateful."

"Father said you were going into the wilderness this morning," she said dismissively. "You need something."

I found her voice captivating, but it was also apparent she wished I would not make too much of her gesture and that she didn't care to commence a conversation.

The combination of sour olives with sweet grapes and the warmth of the bread made me close my eyes and sigh, and I silently thanked God for every bite. I considered returning the bowl and cup to Taryn, but not wanting to cause her any discomfort, I merely slipped out of the tent in the darkness and headed east through the communal area.

There the sand had been packed hard by daily life. I smelled the livestock and heard the horses nickering before I was confronted by the man on watch. He stepped into my path and I heard the faint scrape of blade against scabbard.

"Friend?" he said, tension in his voice.

"The new man, Paul," I said. "Greetings in the name of Christ."

"And to you, sir. If you're looking to relieve yourself, you'll find the easement area to the northwest about a quarter-mile."

"Thank you. And might you have a lamp? I want to check on my horse."

"A moment."

He trotted away and returned to kneel and scrape a flint twice before a torch erupted with a hiss. "Yours is the big black stallion then?"

"He is. I call him Theo."

"Well, Theo's been hungry, Paul. There's all that's left of his second bale."

I held the light where I could see that my horse barely seemed to notice me as he chewed.

And God spoke to me. *Fuel for a long journey.*

"Oh, Lord, no."

"You don't want him eating that much?"

"Sorry, no, it's fine," I said, handing back the torch. "I'm off."

Beyond the easement area I reached the softer, windblown desert sands that quickly filled my sandals. With no idea how far I was to go or what I was to do when I got there, I turned west again, my eyes on the horizon, waiting for the sun to rise behind me and lighten the sky.

Frustrated with myself for having responded aloud to the Lord's message about Theo, I determined again to speak to Him only in my spirit. Silently I said, *I believe You, I trust You, I am here. I will obey. But the steed has been so faithful to me. Must he—?*

Do you seek to please Me or to please men?

I stopped.

Do not stop.

I continued, but what a question! In my past I thought I pleased God by being zealous for Him, but I *had* craved the praise of men. I lived for the approval of my superiors, the priest Nathanael, who served as the vice chief justice, and the high priest, Caiaphas. Yet even then I was not serving God as much as I was serving the Law.

I no longer want to please men, Lord. I want to serve You and You alone.

You must become a bondservant of Christ.

A bondservant. Bound to serve without wages. A slave. All my life I had been superior to everyone else, at least everyone my age. I had been the best, the brightest, the fastest, the most accomplished, the most revered. Many considered me boastful. I couldn't deny it. I hadn't cared. I'd had much to be proud of. Surely the last thing anyone would have expected of me was to be a slave.

Yet now, as soon as I pledged myself to serve God alone, He asked me—no, commanded me—to become a bondservant of Christ. And strangely, nothing appealed to me more. *Yes, Lord! Anything!*

My Son appeared to you to make you a witness of the things you have seen and what I will reveal to you. I will send you to open the eyes of the Gentiles in order to turn them from darkness to light, and from the power of Satan to Me, that they may receive forgiveness of sins and an inheritance among those who are sanctified by faith in My Son.

I wanted to say, *Yes, Lord* again, but I could not find utterance, even silently. I merely trudged on as a pinkish hue spread in the sky.

Make your way to the plateau before you.

It appeared about a half mile away, and I prayed God would not remain silent as I increased my pace. I gathered my mantle at my thighs so it would not restrict me, and sand flew from my sandals as I broke into a trot. I felt as if I were racing into the very presence of God and couldn't get there fast enough. My breath became short and I wondered why He could not have prompted me to ride Theo.

The pink in the sky gave way to orange and then yellow and finally a cloudless blue, and the sun warmed the skin above and below the hair that rimmed my head. Sweat trickled down my neck, and I slipped out of my mantle, draping it over my arm as I ran on across the desert.

When finally I reached the plateau, I was spent and thankful beyond measure for the perfect breakfast I had enjoyed, without which I would not have been able to endure that run. But now I had to climb ten feet of steep, slippery rock, my throat parched, and spread my mantle across the broad boulder at the top so I could prostrate myself there in prayer.

I draped myself over it, planted my elbows, and rested my head in my hands. *Lord, I thirst.*

Thirst for Me.

I do.

And as my panting slowed, my physical thirst disappeared.

Prone there in the early morning sun, I might have dozed had I not been so expectant. Who else anywhere had been awarded such a privilege?

Should I have brought parchment and quills? On the other hand, could anyone forget anything told him by God Almighty?

He had to be amused at the very sight of me. What must the desert creatures have thought of the crazy man racing through the sand to the point of exhaustion, without food or water, now stretched out like a lizard in the sun?

Yet I had the sense I was where I was supposed to be, and I would wait there all day for another word from on high. It wasn't long before I wondered if I might have to. I lay there in an attitude of prayer for about an hour before my back stiffened and my joints ached and I found myself constantly shifting to take the pressure off my bones. Finally I sat up and crossed my legs. What a contrast to the comfort I'd felt on Theo's back as he hurtled hundreds of miles throughout night and day to get me to Arabia.

Was this a test? Did the Lord require something else of me? I would have done anything. But being sovereign and omniscient, He knew that. It began to dawn on me: I had never been a patient man. God had brought me to this remote, desolate wasteland to free me of the distractions of life. He had stripped me of all but the clothes on my back and the sandals on my feet and left me dependent on an old man, a widow, a child, a trade I hadn't plied since childhood, and a horse that didn't even belong to me and of which He had already implied He was about to deprive me.

Now He was forcing patience upon me. But had He not told me that He would use the same zeal, the passion that I had misdirected against Jesus, now to make Him known, yea, even to the Gentiles? Had He not planned since eternity past to make me both Greek and Roman and a Pharisee of Pharisees, to give me such a fervor for life that I would do anything for His cause? Would not my singular restlessness be of benefit to Him if I were to become a bondservant to His Son?

So young in my faith, so new in my rapport with God, and yet here I was already trying to shape the nature of how we should work together.

The silence of God is a harsh discipline, especially when you have known the sweet, rich fullness of His voice. I found myself suddenly overcome with emotion, conscious of His presence but also of my unworthiness. So unclean, so undeserving, so lacking in merit was I that even my conversion had been the result not of my repentance from sin, but entirely His doing. Jesus had, in effect, attacked me, forced His way into my heart and life and soul.

I had not sought Him. I'd even had to ask who He was! And when He told me, I had no choice but to surrender to Him!

Sitting on the unforgiving plateau in the hot sun under the unrelenting stillness of God, I bowed my head, wishing myself capable of wholly hiding from Him. It was as if the sun embodied Him now and my sin, all of it, was exposed. When He had merely impressed upon my heart that Theo had eaten nearly two bales of feed because he had another long journey ahead, my first response was to say no.

Well, of course it was, in my flesh. That animal had become almost human to me. But *no*? *That* was my response to God Himself? *That* was the attitude of a man who said he would become a bondservant and do anything? Did I not trust the Creator of the universe—the One who had miraculously delivered me to Yanbu from Damascus in one day—to provide for me without a horse? Did I not trust Him to get Theo all the way back to Jerusalem, to the Sanhedrin stables, to Nathanael himself, thereby clearing my debt?

Was my plan better? To eke out some sort of cash from this tiny band of refugees who had fled the same persecution I myself had inflicted on the followers of Jesus throughout Judea, and then risk exposing their whereabouts to the authorities by sending payment for my horse to the precise ones looking for me and for them?

God should have been silent toward me for my stupidity alone.

And then there was my sin. Oh, the agility of the conscience! I had asked forgiveness for the heinous acts I had committed against so many innocents, and I believed God had pardoned me. But how had I been able to sleep? How had I been able to live, to move about, to converse, to eat, to do anything with the blood of human lives on my hands?

I told myself I had merely watched the coats of the men who stoned that young deacon, the one whose face had shone when he looked to heaven, the one the followers of The Way now referred to as their first martyr. Yet I might as well have dropped the last millstone on his chest for what I did to coax that mob into action. When I couldn't distract my conscience with activity I was unable to force from my mind's eye the distinct memory of inciting the ire of the crowd to drive that brave orator out of the assembly to where they could kill him. I badgered and cajoled and demanded to know how long they would put up with his blasphemy, and then I conveniently stepped aside and allowed them to do their duty.

That I had thrown no stone made me no less proud of the work I had done that day, and now it did nothing to salve my conscience. I wept bitterly atop that plateau.

When the sun reached its zenith and I grew faint with hunger, sweat pouring, I reminded myself that if there was a lesson here for me, I would learn it, whatever was required. If God wanted me to nearly starve to death, so be it. But I would not worry about dying, because I believed Jesus, and He had told me my role on the road to Damascus, that I was to be made a messenger not only to my own people, but also to the Gentiles.

And then the Lord sent Ananias to me to tell me that I was a chosen vessel to bear God's name before Gentiles, kings, and the children of Israel, and He was going to show me how many things I must suffer for His name's sake.

Had God been a man, I would have told Him that if He was not going to kill me, then either teach me or tell me what to do. But if I had learned nothing else, I knew I didn't want to be the reason for His silence. Over my many years as an expert in the Law, I had grown so frustrated at my inability to elicit any response to all my prayers that there were seasons when I wondered even whether God existed.

Well, now I had no doubts, but neither did I want to be the cause when our conversations stopped.

I raised my head and dried my eyes, taking comfort in the fact that Alastor had said God told him he was to leave me alone in the mornings because I was to ply my trade in the afternoons. That meant I was not to be out here all day. If I was gone too long, wouldn't the old man worry and come searching for me?

When you return, water your horse thoroughly and loose him.

Deep sadness swept over me, and I wanted to ask the obvious, but I dared not. I would not see Theo again, would not be responsible for him. God would take care of him, I knew, and in the process, take care of me and my debt as well. I would cling to that in my grief over seeing the horse leave.

But surely He had not led me all the way out here for only that word. Unquestionably, to Him that was just a detail He wanted out of the way first. Whenever He spoke to me anew I was thrilled afresh, and it didn't matter if it was about things that seemed trifling to Him or about preaching the gospel to the ends of the earth. Nothing could be unimportant to God.

The gentlest of midday breezes cooled the sweat of my brow, and I shivered. I turned to face the sun, which forced my eyes shut, and still sitting cross-legged, I opened my hands, palms up, in my lap.

In a unique and most mysterious manner, I was able to distinguish the Father's voice from the Son's. As I sat motionless, the sun bathing me now, Jesus Himself spoke to the depths of my soul.

The truth you will preach will not be according to man, for you neither received it from a man, nor were you taught it. It came to you when I revealed Myself to you.

It pleased My Father, who separated you from your mother's womb and called you through His grace, to reveal Me in you, that you might preach Me among the Gentiles. Resist the temptation to confer with flesh and blood or to seek out My apostles, but remain here until My Father has taught you and equipped you to carry My gospel to every creature. For you have been saved and called with a holy calling, not according to your works, but according to His own purpose and grace that were given to you in Me before the creation of the world.

For as long as I lived I would never cease to be amazed at the eternality of God's plan. How puny I felt in the face of His majesty and how I longed to be used in any way to advance His kingdom.

Many will turn from idols to serve the living God and to wait for Me, whom He raised from the dead.

I could not stop the tears from coming again. *May it be so, may it be so.*

God has approved you, entrusted you with the gospel, and He will test your heart. Never resort to flattery, telling men what they want to hear or seeking their glory. You will be My apostle to the Jew and the Gentile, but never make demands as one of status. But be gentle and affectionate, imparting to all not only the gospel, but also your own life so you become dear to them. In this way you will be remembered and beloved, toiling night and day that you not become a burden to any.

Remain devout and just and blameless, acting uprightly among those who believe. Exhort and comfort and charge all, as a father does his children, that they walk worthy of God who calls them into His kingdom.

How I knew my time with the Lord had ended for that day I cannot say, but I knew. It was not as if His Spirit lifted from me, for I felt so full of Him I could have floated across that wasteland and back to the encampment. Rather I slowly stood atop the rocky plateau and turned in a circle, scanning the expanse of the Arabian desert that would never again look the same to me. *Thank You, Lord, thank You, Lord, thank You, Lord.*

I wiped the sweat from my face and beard and ran my hands over my scalp and through my thinning rim of hair. I shook out and donned my mantle, covering my arms against the blistering sun. Getting down proved trickier than going up, though I prided myself in my athleticism for a man in his mid-thirties.

Despite being in a hurry to get back to Yanbu, I resisted the urge to run. My mind, my heart, my soul were full and I needed to reflect upon the most sacred moments of my life. I set off at a deliberate pace, knowing the rest of my day would be full of mundane chores but unable to give them a thought. My mind was bursting with the things of God.

Nothing could compare to the moment Jesus revealed Himself to me on the road to Damascus, but that had been a shock, an ordeal nearly unto death. My life had altogether changed from darkness to light in an instant.

But this, today, this unspeakable privilege! To sit in the presence of the Holy One! To hear His voice! To be taught!

Already I had repented of my notion that I would not need quill or parchments. True, I would not forget what I had just heard, but neither did I want to miss the joy of putting it in permanent form. And who knew how long this would continue? Alastor said the Lord had told him he and the others were to leave me alone "in the mornings." How many mornings? How much did the Lord have to teach me before He sent me to the Gentiles? I was ready to go now!

It was no wonder He had already needed to teach me patience through His silence. What more could I tell the Gentiles than what I had testified to the Jews in Damascus, that Jesus was the Christ, the Messiah, the Son of the living God? That He had died on the cross for the sins of the world and had been resurrected on the third day and now sits at His Father's right hand, interceding for His own?

To me that was enough. It was the truth.

But plainly, God had more for me to learn before He sent me out. Who could understand Him if they had eternity to study Him? I had read and memorized His laws and doctrines and precepts since childhood—yea, I had even learned to read from the ancient Scriptures—yet I understood little. I had yearned to talk not just *to* God, but *with* Him for my whole life, and yet I had not recognized the Messiah when He came. In fact, I saw Him as an imposter, the opposite of the Divine. I opposed Him, reviled Him, persecuted Him, was glad when He was executed, and went on terrorizing His followers—until He Himself confronted me.

So perhaps what He had to teach me was less about Himself than about me. I was beginning to see His ingenious design, giving me my unique background and upbringing in order to make an apostle of me to the Gentiles. But only He could make me an apostle. Those already known as Jesus' apostles had encountered Him personally before He had ascended to heaven. They had seen Him in the flesh, heard Him speak and teach, seen His miracles, performed miracles themselves in His name.

After His death, burial, and resurrection, I had seen Him on the road, and the very experience had blinded me for three days.

Now He had miraculously delivered me here, and I was hearing Him speak and teach.

Would I also perform miracles in His name? I felt so unworthy.

How interesting that He had counseled me to resist the temptation to seek out His apostles, because there was little I would rather have done than crept into Jerusalem straightaway for that very purpose. I would have to evade the Sanhedrin, of course, not to mention all the victims who had much against me. Then there would be the matter of convincing the apostles that I was now their brother in Christ. Who would believe that? I had been their chief enemy! I couldn't blame them if it took years to convince them. But how I wanted to revel in their stories of daily life with Jesus Himself. It was likely I would try their patience, keeping them up all hours of the night, begging them to repeat everything they had seen and heard and experienced of Him.

When the compound finally shimmered into sight through the heat waves over the sand, my thoughts turned to where I would find writing supplies. Surely someone there must have something I could use. Who marked wood for the cutting of tent poles? How did people make lists?

As fortune would have it, as I came upon the livestock pen near the corral, I espied Taryn at the well and Corydon playing with two other children nearby. A breeze lifted her veil while she was transferring water from the bucket to her pitcher, and with her hands occupied she was unable to adjust it. She tried to turn her face from me, causing her to spill some water.

"Allow me," I said.

"I can manage," she said, clearly knowing I had seen her.

"Please," I said and busied myself taking charge of the process.

She stepped aside, unmistakably embarrassed. I prayed for another zephyr to reveal just one more hint of her olive complexion. Not even the abject sadness of her countenance could hide her loveliness. But I was touched by her humiliation and wanted to assuage that at all costs.

"May I call you Taryn?" I said, keeping my eyes on my work.

"Of course."

"I am in need of two things, if I may impose."

"Certainly, sir."

"I need a trough to water my horse, and—"

"Corydon!" she called out, and as soon as he saw me he came running. "You and your friends drag that trough over for Master Paul."

"That's my friend!" he shouted as he recruited them.

"Pardon me," she said. "And?"

"And I need parchments and something to write with."

I handed her the pitcher, which she hefted to her shoulder. "I'll see what I can do." Taryn hesitated, watching her son.

"How about I bring him back with me when I finish with the horse?" I said.

"Thank you."

The children watched and giggled as I filled the trough, unhitched Theo, and led him to it. They begged to sit on him, but I told them to wait till he'd had his drink. As if he knew what lay ahead, he slowly emptied the entire vessel. I held in one hand the rope that had tethered him to the corral fence all night and used the other to swing each of the children atop him. He stood immobile except to snort and shake his head at an insect on his nose, which caused the children to squeal. I spread my feet and put both hands on the rope, but to his credit, Theo did not bolt.

I shushed him and lifted the children down, telling them to stand behind me, then lifted the rope from around his neck and tossed it aside. His ears perked and I caressed his heavily muscled jowl as I swallowed a sob.

The children stared at me and I urged Corydon's friends to run along. The boy waited shyly as if puzzled.

I had fought my whole life to overcome embarrassment about my short stature. Now it just irritated me because I wished I could face the towering Theo at his level. All I could do was awkwardly wrap my arms around his neck, pressing my head into his shoulder. Theo actually gathered me in by lowering his throat to the top of my head and nuzzling my back, exhaling through his nose.

"Farewell, friend," I whispered, hating to pull away when he nickered softly. He stamped and seemed to set himself.

Let him go.

I am not stopping him, Lord, I said silently.

Send him.

Must I? I said, immediately regretting it.

Paul.

How dare I question my Lord God? Before I could talk myself out of it I retrieved the rope and snapped Theo sharply on his thigh. He whinnied sharply and moved slowly toward the tents. I kept an eye on him as he cleared the row of dwellings.

"Where's he going?" Corydon said.

"Home," I managed.

"I don't want him to go!" he whined, and he couldn't know he was speaking for me. "Will he be back?"

I shook my head. "Say good-bye, Corydon."

He called out his farewell.

The horse cantered into the ravine, then broke into a trot as he climbed the incline. By the time he reached the overlook he was galloping, and before he disappeared I recognized the magnificent sprint I assumed would carry him all the way to Jerusalem and the Temple stables.

Maybe tomorrow I would smile at the bewilderment this would bring to Nathanael. No doubt word had spread of my theft. The authorities knew that when they found the steed, they'd find the horse thief—and the turncoat.

Corydon looked curiously at me. "Well," I said. "I have work to do, but I can't imagine you're big enough to help me."

"Yes, I am!"

"But I need someone who can hand me supplies and tools."

"I can!"

I began walking toward his tent. "Oh, I think I had better find your grandfather to help me, don't you?"

"No! He's too old! You need me!"

Alastor was waiting near a pile of rough-hewn narrow tent poles and dried, dark-haired goat- and sheepskins. He had set out a bench and a low-slung table with needles and threads of varying thickness. "Perfect," I said.

"And so?" the old man said.

"I have much to tell you."

"I'm helping Master Paul!" Corydon said.

"I need you to come with me," his mother said.

When he protested, I said, "When you get back, I'll be ready for you," and he ran off.

Alastor proved remarkably agile, steadying the poles while I anchored them and then standing on the table to drape the coverings overhead. In little time we had shaded one side of the dwelling so I would have a place to work and could set about sewing together the hides and skins to enclose my sleeping area.

By the time Taryn and Corydon returned—she with a welcome supply of parchment and quills—I was seated beneath my new canopy and at work with various tools laid out next to me as Alastor watched.

"I wanted to help!" Corydon wailed.

"I'm ready for you," I said. "Sit right here and I will tell you which tool to hand me."

I pointed to an awl or a length of thread or whatever device I needed and traded it for the one I finished with. As I suspected, it didn't take the child long to tire of the job, and he was soon off playing again.

Presently his mother reappeared with a tray containing two cups of water and a bowl of cheese and figs. I tried to thank her in such a way that she would linger and talk, but she hurried away.

"Give her time," Alastor said.

"She has such grace," I said, studying the redness already rising on my fingertips. "She moves with ease and silence."

Alastor nodded, chewing. "My son-in-law often remarked about that very thing. He said her beauty reflected her character. That she was as handsome inside as out."

"I was speaking more of her elegance."

He nodded. "She comes by that naturally. Her mother had that same comeliness. But the light has gone out of Taryn." A sob seemed to catch in his throat. "She lived for Stephanos."

The cheese went dry in my mouth and I quickly sipped water. "And they came here from where?" I managed.

"Judea," he whispered, shaking his head and holding up a hand as if he had again said all he cared to. "I'm sorry. Forgive me. It's too raw."

Of course it was, but I had to know.

I stood and my legs pushed back the bench. I leaned over the table, resting my weight on my palms.

"Paul, are you all right?"

I nodded. "I just want to finish. Let's get this done so I can start on Zuriel's repairs tomorrow."

"He'll be glad for that!"

"He can be glad?" I said.

That made Alastor smile, which was a relief. I had trouble breathing.

I set about sorting the untreated hides and told Alastor that in the future I would like to select the sheep and goats that would provide the same. "And when they are harvested, I want to oversee the boiling and dyeing and drying so we get uniformity and eliminate warping and shrinkage."

"This really is your trade, isn't it, Paul?"

"Well, you couldn't tell it from these blisters, but it was my father's, and he was widely revered."

"It appears he taught you well."

"We'll see. What we have here will serve well as the walls of my bed-chamber, but let's set aside and stack the best choices for our friend. I'll be his pal by sundown tomorrow."

"You do believe in miracles," Alastor said.

6

REVELATION

THAT EVENING, OVER A supper of dried fish Taryn had mixed into a stew of legumes, I could not bear even to look at her. The four of us sat on the floor around a mat with the steaming bowl in the middle, into which we dipped our bread. I forced myself to say something polite about the meal, for she had creatively added a side dish of baked grains seasoned with honey. I mentioned that I had never before enjoyed that as part of a supper, but my voice emerged so flat that I noticed her glance at me with what appeared surprise, and if I wasn't mistaken, even her father shifted uncomfortably.

Corydon's constant jabbering and begging to sit or play with me occupied Taryn, who scolded and apologized for him. But he was only a child, speaking and acting like a child.

After the meal I tried to entertain him, but my heart wasn't in it. I was troubled in spirit, desperate to ask where in Judea Taryn and her husband had lived and what had been his profession. But did I really want to know? Or was it better to assume it would be too great a coincidence that I would ever have crossed paths with the late Stephanos?

I confess I learned something about children that evening, or at least about that child. I had so little experience with young ones—in fact, none—that it would have been folly for me to assume it applied to all. But I was struck by how perceptive Corydon seemed to be.

With his mother's permission to play with me for a few minutes before he went to bed, "or for as long as Master Paul has the patience for it," he seemed full of vigor. He ran and jumped and showed me little things he played with and told me all about them. I asked about his friends I had met that day, and he told me all about them too.

But after climbing up my back and over my head and asking where my hair had gone, then sliding into my lap and onto the floor and running around to take the same route again, he settled in my lap. He reached to cradle my cheeks in his palms and turned my face so he could look into my eyes.

"Your beard is scratchy," he said.

"Is it?"

"Yes, and you're not listening to me."

How did he know? I thought I had responded adequately enough to feign interest. Was Corydon unusually smart for his age, or was this typical? I had long ago abandoned the idea of marrying and having children, and my work had not exposed me to any except in passing, so I was largely ignorant on the matter. Some of my colleagues in the Temple were charged with teaching children, but when they began their stories about particularly precocious—or problematic—youngsters, I could not pretend to remain engrossed. I had nothing against children. They were simply of little interest.

That had changed in two days with this fascinating little person, but now doubly so with his ability to magically judge the level of my engagement. Shaken by his perception, I decided to put in abeyance my misgivings over his departed father and give Corydon my full attention.

"You know," I said, turning to look behind me, "I was certain there was just a little boy back here, but now I don't see him anywhere."

"That was me!" he said, scampering back there as I turned to the front again.

"Now where did he go?" I shouted. "He was right here in my lap!"

He poked his face around to show me where he was, but of course I was wrenching around to look behind me again. "I can't find him!"

We kept at this until he grabbed my face again and planted his nose on mine, and I affected great surprise to discover him, to his great glee. And then it was time for him to go to bed. When Taryn came to fetch him, she lifted him from me and hesitated. "Thank you, sir," she said softly. "Thank you very much."

I looked away and nodded, unable to speak.

As Taryn put Corydon down and then busied herself baking bread for the next day, Alastor and I sat chatting.

"Are you all right, Paul?"

I shrugged. "Long day. Used new muscles, you know."

"Certainly a return to tentmaking wasn't the pinnacle of your day."

"When I get a little time tomorrow I'll write it all down and let you read it."

"You can imagine my curiosity. I mean, I can't even imply it's any of my concern, except that the Lord did tell me of your coming."

"No, I understand. I don't mean to be so mysterious."

"You're obviously troubled, Paul. Just assure me it proved an enriching experience."

"Oh, it was, yes. In some ways it was an ordeal. But 'enriching' would be putting it lightly."

"I'll force myself to wait until I can read about it, then. Ah, there is another matter."

"There is?" I fought to maintain my composure. Did he know who I was?

"Do you know how to fish?"

I laughed, a little too loudly. "I would not be mistaken for a fisherman, no."

"Still, you must take your turn tomorrow night during second watch. Naturally they go at night so as not to attract attention or give away our location. Four others will go with you. They will have all you need and show you how to use it. The next time you will be expected to act on your own."

"Willing to do my part."

"One more thing. Zuriel heads tomorrow night's party. But given that you said he will be your best friend by sundown . . ."

After Alastor retired and Taryn come in from the ovens, I strolled out to the easement area. On the way back I tried to occupy myself with thoughts of my tent work, playing with the boy, fishing the next night, even when I would take my turn as night watchman. But I couldn't crowd from my mind the dread that had taken up residence ever since Alastor had mentioned his son-in-law.

Stephanos.

It couldn't be, could it?

As I reentered the amalgam of dwellings I came upon Nadav, on watch under a torch set in a stand near the livestock pen.

"I'll have to get you to teach me all I need to know before I take my turn guarding the camp," I said.

The ruddy-faced young man chuckled. "This is all you need to know," he said, patting the short sword in an ornate scabbard at his waist.

"May I?" I asked. "I've never carried one."

He slid the sword out and turned it, handing it to me grip-first. "Others have their own weapons, but this is the official one wielded by the man on duty."

"A Roman gladius," I said, hefting the weighty piece, just under two feet long. "Where did it come from?"

"You won't believe it. Zuriel claims a Roman legionnaire left it at the foot of the cross at Jesus' crucifixion."

I was dumbfounded. "Zuriel was there?"

Nadav nodded. "He says a few of the armed guards tossed things in a small pile, sort of as a silent tribute, as the Master's body was being taken away. When the gladius was still lying there at the end of everything, Zuriel took it. And now we use it to protect our little base of refuge."

"Astonishing."

Nadav nodded as he replaced it in its sheath. "I don't see your horse, Paul."

"I couldn't afford him. I sent him home."

"Oh? Where's that?"

"We agreed not to talk about it."

Nadav's countenance fell in the flickering shadows. "That's curious."

"I asked you to trust me and keep my confidence."

"That you did."

"I can only assure you, friend, that your faith in me in well placed."

Nadav crossed his arms. "I confess it's not faith just yet, sir. Let's say I have no choice but that I hope you are all you say you are."

"I'm saying I am your brother in Christ, Nadav. If I am not, I am despicable beyond measure for even claiming that."

"My feeling exactly."

I lay on the thick mat that separated me from the floor and intertwined my fingers behind my head. Yanbu was windless that night, and only if I strained could I hear the occasional bleat or baa from the livestock pen or Nadav as he made his deliberate passage between tents.

My body craved the relief of the previous night's sleep, if not more desperately, but my mind was so full I could not imagine where one thought ended and another began. For the brief season I had been in Damascus I had reveled in my marvelous new relationship with God. I had become an entirely different person and awoke with wonder every day, eager to ponder and discuss the richness of God's love and forgiveness.

Then came danger and flight and the miraculous escape, discovering this enclave of refuge, the precious little family, my encounter with God, the return to tentmaking. And now this, this peculiarity of identical names. But was it anything more than concurrence, or had I simply concocted it?

Nothing should have kept me from quickly descending into a deep slumber—nothing but the raging thoughts cascading through my head. Try as I might to steer them to the most pleasant events of the last two days—meeting with God, the delightful child, his beautiful mother finding me writing supplies—all that reminded me of her father mentioning her late husband. And when I finally did surrender to unconsciousness, I was immediately transported to that tumultuous day in Jerusalem not so long before, when the man I felt was so brash, brazen, and nervy was given his chance to address the Sanhedrin—and would not stop.

Now converted and with a new understanding, I viewed him in a fresh light as courageous, a hero, a martyr to the ultimate cause. But on that day, to me he had been vile, audacious, the symbol of everything I hated. He was an enemy, *the* enemy, representing a so-called messiah whom I knew to have been a charlatan by the very fact that he was dead! Dead! Who worships a dead god? A dead king? A dead messiah?

This man did.

That night in the desert he inhabited my dream, tormented my sleep, railing against me and my revered colleagues. We were known, admired, respected! People nodded, sometimes even bowed to us as we passed them in the streets. Yet his man spoke to us as if we were recalcitrant ruffians.

Even at full volume, the man spoke eloquently as he recited our own rich history and demanded: "Which of the prophets did your fathers not persecute? And they killed those who foretold the coming of the Just One, whom you have betrayed and murdered."

"*You* are betrayers and murderers?" I shouted to my cohorts. "How dare he? He comes into our domain and accuses *us* of such heinous deeds?"

The assembled gnashed their teeth and rose up as one, rushing him. In my dream I was suddenly next to him at the dais—why, oh, why had we honored him with such a place of prominence when it was he who was under indictment? He turned and looked fully into my eyes as if he knew me. Then he gazed up as if through the ceiling of the great arched chamber.

"Look!" he said. "I see the heavens opened and the Son of Man standing at the right hand of God!"

"Blasphemer!" I screamed, and the council cried out, covering their ears. Then they surrounded him and dragged him away. I ran ahead, leading them to a plain strewn with rocks, and urged them to stay away from any pit and to use no stones large enough to crush him. I shouted, "This

must not look like an execution, but merely a punishment gone awry!"
As they forced him into the open where he could not hide, I took their
cloaks and pointed them to the piles of rocks. Nearly seventy men began
throwing at him. First one, then another thudded into his belly and chest,
and he called out, "Lord Jesus, receive my spirit!"

He knelt and cried, "Lord, do not charge them with this sin!"

Now, in my dream that had become a nightmare, he lay dead in a pool
of blood. I raised both fists, then congratulated the men as I returned their
cloaks. They, we, I had done a righteous thing. Each grinned broadly at
me and said, "You murdered Stephanos."

When it had actually happened, I believed it had been a great day and
that I might be lauded within the Temple for my role in it. That night I
had slept soundly for the first time in months. But now, in my dream,
everything was askew. Suddenly I didn't want the credit, didn't want the
attention, was puzzled by those who had thrown the rocks now praising
me, nay, accusing me, not of having justly executed a blasphemer but of
having murdered him.

Though the stone-throwers had numbered fewer than six dozen, in
my dream the line seemed to go on forever as I handed them their cloaks,
yet the pile of garments never grew smaller. My smile and enthusiasm
waned as I fought to get them to stop congratulating me and calling
it murder. "No!" I said over and over, "not me, you! And not murder,
justice!"

Suddenly the next man in line was Alastor, small and hunched and
fifty years older than I knew him to be. His scraggly beard had been
bleached pure white, blown by a dry wind to reveal a face pale and drawn
and wrinkled. I was pierced by his gaze and tried to evade it. He refused
his cloak, refused to shake my hand, and solemnly shook his head. In a
voice hollow and ethereal, and pointing a shaky, bony finger, he rasped,

"You're not Paul of Damascus at all. You're Saul of Tarsus, and you murdered Stephanos."

"No! No, Alastor! I—"

But in an instant he had become a slender young woman dressed in black from head to toe, a veil covering her face, an angelic boy on her hip staring at me with eyes so large and deep and dark that I knew he saw past his fun new friend to the very soul of an assassin.

As I opened my mouth to plead with the woman, her veil disappeared to reveal such beauty and pain that I could not utter a sound. "You murdered my Stephanos," she said with a lilt, as if it had just dawned on her.

The boy lowered his chin and said, "You killed Papa."

I found my voice and reached desperately for mother and son. But she was backing away! "Wait!" I cried. In an instant I saw only a lone figure remaining, dressed in gleaming white with his back to me.

Only one cloak remained at my feet, and when I stooped and draped it over my arm I found it blood-soaked and it stuck to my sleeve.

"Sir!" I called, and the man turned.

The cacophony had ceased, all others had vanished, and now it was just the two of us in the punishing heat of day. I had to shield my eyes, not against the unforgiving sun but rather the severe glow of his countenance. The man seemed to look upon me with compassion, and when he reached for the gory cloak, I tried to keep it from him. Despite my objections he peeled it from my arm and pulled it on over his pristine tunic.

"I'm sorry," I whispered, throat constricted. "Forgive me."

"I do not charge you with this sin," he said.

With a gentle smile, he straightened and smoothed the blood-caked cloak, then carefully lay at my feet, crossed his hands over his chest, and closed his eyes.

"No!" I howled, falling to my knees over him. "No, Stephanos! No!"

I was suddenly awakened in the darkness by the wails of a little boy, the snorts of an old man, and the frightened murmurings of a woman.

"It's all right, Corydon!" Taryn whispered urgently. "He's just having a bad dream."

I found myself on all fours, sobbing.

"Check on him, Father. He said 'Stephanos.'"

"Surely not."

"He did!"

I coughed and cleared my throat as I heard the old man groan, rising.

"Forgive me, please!" I said. "All is well. It was just a dream. I am so sorry to have disturbed you."

"You scared me, Master Paul!" Corydon said.

"I'm sorry, little one."

"Do you need anything?" Taryn said. "Water?"

"I'm fine. Just embarrassed. Please pardon me."

I heard a whap on the wall of the tent and Nadav's tense voice. "Everything all right here?"

"We're fine, son," Alastor said. "Thank you. What of the night?"

"Nearly fourth watch, sir."

About two and a half hours later I awoke from a sound sleep—thankfully with no more incidents—covered against the chilly predawn. What roused me now was Taryn again quietly placing a light breakfast out for me, this time a cluster of plump grapes, a bowl of roasted grain, a warmed piece of flatbread, and a cup of water.

In the faintest light from the other side of the curtain where she had apparently lit a small lamp, I noticed she had not bothered to apply her veil. That touched me, because while it was common for a woman to eschew her veil in her own home before her family, this meant she had already accepted me, if not as family at least as familiar. I assumed I had won this consideration by the kindnesses I had shown Corydon.

I also noticed she didn't rush from my presence though she knew I was awake. I thanked her for the food as I raised up on my elbow to reach for the grapes. She knelt beyond the small table. "You so appreciated the roast grain, and there was a bit left."

"Wonderful," I said, careful not to scare her away. "And again, so sorry about disturbing you in the night."

"Think nothing more of that. But are you aware of what you said?"

"What I said?"

"Excuse me, but I couldn't make out much, and I know it was just a dream. But you clearly said 'Stephanos.'"

Fortunately I had just filled my mouth, which gave me time to think. I held up a finger and took a sip of water. "I know that is—was your husband's name. Your father mentioned it yesterday. It must have stayed in my mind."

"I see," she said, rising. "Just curious. Do you need anything else?"

I shook my head. "You have been more than kind."

"It's nothing, sir."

Suddenly I felt as if I hadn't slept at all. Eager as I was to commune again with the Lord, I did not look forward to the walk across the desert or the short, treacherous climb.

Given the new proximity of my sleeping quarters to where Taryn labored most of the day, plus the implicit permission she had given by not fleeing from my presence, I arranged the cup and bowl on the table and carried it outside. Setting it near the tent wall on the other side of her work area, I quietly announced it was there. To my delight she quickly opened the flap and thanked me, actually smiling.

I couldn't pretend I didn't detect pain and grief in her eyes still, but her panic in my presence seemed to have abated. How I prayed her Stephanos and Stephen the Martyr were two entirely different people. If they were not, how would I ever bring myself to tell her?

Few outside the Sanhedrin knew my role in that stoning.

I had known nothing of Stephen beyond what I considered his blasphemy. I could not have told you whether he was married or had a family, and now I hoped that he had not. *Hoped* was not even the word for it. Had anyone been in the crowd to support him that day, I would have known of it. Even fellow members of The Way had fled when it became obvious what was to become of him. Of course they had their own loved ones to think of.

Now as I hiked across the Arabian sands again, I had to wonder whether it was possible God would meet me at the same place in the wilderness every day and teach me the unsearchable riches of His Son, yet not tell me that He might have sent me nearly a thousand miles to sleep within feet of the widow of the very martyr I had put to death.

It couldn't be!

And I didn't dare ask. It seemed so obvious He would tell me. Surely this woman's husband was only coincidentally named the same and from the same region. Surely.

Facedown before the Lord on the plateau, I emptied myself of all distractions save that one—which I found impossible. I wanted to ask, nay, I wanted to demand. But who was I to question the creator God? The woman who had immediately enchanted me with her shyness and grace—then her beauty and elegance—until that very morning had done all she could to avoid me. Now, captivated as I had been, I knew I should be evading her, just when she finally seemed to be softening.

The nightmare had been such a close call. I would have to watch every word I said while awake, and hope I didn't blurt out anything again in my sleep. What would she and her father think? What would Corydon make of it? I could not shun him! That would be entirely unfair and impossible to explain.

Again, I worked to put it all out of my mind and concentrate on what God had for me that day. I was amazed at my capacity to be diverted from the import of such a privilege. Would anyone else be able to think of anything but the prospect of communing with God? Yet here I was worrying about a slight possibility and its ramifications, just when the Lord Himself was to speak to me.

I lay before Him, face buried in the crook of my arm, vainly trying to rid myself of anything but openness to His voice, and I was miserable. All because of an old man's utterance of one word, one name: Stephanos.

I was desperate not to do anything to cause the Lord's silence again, but this was not the result of anything I had said or done. I was powerless to control my response to it. The more I tried to separate myself from the bonds of it, the tighter they wrapped themselves around my spirit until I thought I would go mad.

But God knew. He had formed my innermost parts. I need to tell Him, ask Him, nothing. Whatever I needed, He would give me. All He asked of me was to be a vessel willing to be filled. And I was.

Jesus spoke to my heart: *This is the will of God for you, your sanctification. You are to abstain from sexual immorality. Maintain yourself sanctified and honorable, not in lust or passion like those who do not know My Father. He is the avenger, and He calls you to holiness.*

Was this instruction for my calling? I had not lusted after this woman. I had just met her and hardly knew her. I had merely been intrigued by her. But I would accept this counsel from the Lord no matter how it was intended. It was doubtful He had led me so miraculously to this place for some purpose other than to teach me about Himself, especially if He had a specific calling for me. Apostle to the Gentiles. I couldn't deny He had been preparing me for this since my birth.

Now concerning those who die trusting in Me, there is no need to sorrow as others who have no hope. For if you believe I rose again, then believe My Father will bring with Me those who sleep in Me, for this you may say confidently by My word, that those who are alive at My coming will not precede those who are dead. For I Myself will descend from heaven with a shout, with the voice of an archangel, and with the trumpet of God. And the dead in Christ will rise first. Then those who are alive and remain shall be caught up together with them in the clouds to meet Me in the air. And thus they shall always be with Me. Therefore comfort everyone with those words.

But concerning when this will happen, that day will come as a thief in the night. Watch and be vigilant. Put on the breastplate of faith and love and the helmet of the hope of salvation. For My Father did not appoint you to wrath but to salvation through Me, who died for you.

So comfort the fainthearted, uphold the weak, be patient with all. Don't return evil for evil, but pursue what is good both for you and for all. Rejoice always, pray without ceasing, give thanks in everything, for this is My will for you. Do not quench My Spirit. Do not despise prophecies. Test all things and hold to what is good. Abstain from evil.

He who calls you is faithful and will bring all this to pass.

I responded, *Yes, Lord.*

I will require of you patience and faith, for you will suffer persecutions and tribulations in your work for Me. This will give evidence of the righteous judgment of My Father, that you may be counted worthy of His kingdom. Be assured He will repay with tribulation those who trouble you, and He will give you rest when I am revealed from heaven with My mighty angels and in fire take vengeance on those who do not know Me and on those who do not obey

My gospel. These will be punished with everlasting destruction, banished from My presence and from the glory of My power.

I wondered, *Can I know and proclaim when the Day of the Lord will be?*

That day will not come until the man of sin is revealed, the son of perdition who exalts himself above God and is worshiped, sitting as God in the temple of God, proclaiming himself to be God. That lawless one will be revealed, and I will consume him with the breath of My mouth and destroy him with the brightness of My coming.

The coming of the lawless one is the work of Satan, who will deceive all who perish, because they did not love the truth so that they might be saved. For this reason My Father will send them strong delusion, and they will believe the lie, and they all will be condemned who did not believe the truth but took pleasure in unrighteousness.

Though the Lord fell silent, I sensed He wanted me to meditate on what He had revealed to me. I remained there in the Spirit, unmoving, reflecting. How long this reverie lasted I cannot say, but when He spoke again I was aware the sun was much higher than when He had last spoken.

I am not sending you out to baptize but to preach My gospel, not with wisdom or eloquence, lest My death should be made worthless. For the message of My cross is foolishness to those who are dying, but to those who will be saved it is the power of My Father. It is written: "I will destroy the wisdom of the wise, and bring to nothing the understanding of the prudent." Where is the wise? Where is the scribe? Where is the disputer? Has not My Father made foolish the wisdom of this world? It will please Him through the foolishness of the preaching of His gospel to save those who believe.

Jews ask for a sign, and Greeks seek wisdom. You preach Me crucified, which to the Jews will be a stumbling block and to the Greeks foolishness, but to those who are called, both Jews and Greeks, I am the power and the wisdom of My Father. God's foolishness is wiser than men, and God's weakness is stronger than men.

I will not call many wise, mighty, or noble. But My Father has chosen the foolish things to put to shame the wise of the world, and the weak things to put to shame the things that are mighty of the world; and the base things and the things that are despised of the world My Father has chosen, that no flesh should be proud in His presence. But you are in Me. As it is written, "He who glories, let him glory in the Lord."

So don't worry about excellence of speech or wisdom when you declare the testimony of My Father. You need know nothing except Me and Me crucified. You may be weak and fearful, even trembling, and your preaching may not be persuasive. But in My Spirit and with power, My Father will be manifest through you.

It is written, "Eye has not seen, nor ear heard, nor have entered into the heart of man the things which God has prepared for those who love Him." But My Father will reveal them to you through His Spirit. For the Spirit searches all things, the deep things of God. No one knows the things of God except the Spirit of God.

The natural man does not receive the things of God. They are foolishness to him, because they are spiritually discerned. He who is spiritual judges all things, yet he himself is rightly judged by no one. For "who has known the mind of the Lord that he may instruct Him?"

Some you will have to speak to not as spiritual people but as carnal, as to babes. Feed them milk and not solid food until they are able to receive it. Where there are envy, strife, and division, people are carnal and behave like mere humans.

As a wise master builder, lay the foundation and let another build on it. But let each take heed how he builds. For no other foundation can anyone lay than the one that is laid, which is Me. If anyone builds on this foundation with gold, silver, precious stones, wood, hay, or straw, each one's work will become clear, because it one day will be revealed by fire, and the fire will test what sort it is. If anyone's work endures, he will receive a reward. If anyone's work is burned, he will suffer loss; but he himself will be saved, yet as through fire.

You are the temple of God, and the Spirit of God dwells in you. If anyone defiles the temple of God, My Father will destroy him. For the temple of God is holy.

I knew the instruction for that day had ended, and I felt a profound change in me. As one might imagine, hearing the very voice of God humbles a man to the point where he feels like a worm, lower than low. All the while I was in communion with God I felt the depth of my unworthiness, of my sin, of my wretched lostness.

Yet in the silences that followed, even in the silences He allowed between revelations to me, it was as if my Creator knew me—as David of old had exulted about Him—and knew my frame and remembered that I was dust. In those moments He warmed me, filled me, comforted me with His presence. I was overwhelmed by His love and forgiveness.

I, of all people, had no right, no claim to His endless, immeasurable mercy. I had been the chiefest of sinners, a murderer, and I had not seen myself for who I was, had not shown remorse, regret, or sorrow. I had not repented when He showered me with grace—only when was I faced with my depravity and could do nothing more than receive His righteousness.

I had read the ancient Scripture without understanding, and now it was as if God's own light of truth shone on it from heaven and made clear as crystal for me the meaning and the object, about whom this had been written: "All we like sheep have gone astray; we have turned, every one, to his own way; and the LORD has laid on Him the iniquity of us all."

Enraptured by the truth that there was nothing I could have done about my sin and that God had laid upon Jesus *my* iniquity, all I could do was lie in the sun and weep. Unable to frame words, I merely praised my Savior until my eyes were dry.

When I reached my work table an hour later, trying to refocus on things temporal, I prayed God would soon tell me specifically what He wanted me to preach in His name. Where was I to go, to whom was I to speak, and what was I to say?

7

TRUTH

THE RED SEA

I ENDURED THE DIRE consequences of a conflicted mind. Thrilled with the majestic truth that rolled to my spirit from God and Jesus on high, I longed to be launched like a great ship on the vast ocean of Gentiles in need of the redeeming message of the gospel of Christ. Yet in the routine of daily life I was tormented with the fear of being found out. Had I been the agitator, the instigator behind the murder of the head of the household where I now resided?

If Stephanos, the late husband and father, was Stephen the Martyr, I was!

So vexed was I by the very uncertainty that I came to believe that learning the awful truth would be better than not knowing. That illogic alone should have proved I had not thought through the consequences, for what would I do with the truth revealed? No outcome I could imagine would assuage my guilt without injuring anew the bereaved.

As Alastor—and even Corydon when the mood struck him—aided me in fashioning repaired sections for Zuriel's ragged tent, the old man apparently felt compelled to encourage me for what I had brought to the wounded remnants of his family.

"Moving is always fraught with strife," he said, as I busied myself stitching together great rectangles of dark wool and Corydon scampered here and there. "But frankly, the long journey here was miserable. Taryn was useless, and I couldn't blame her, poor thing. No woman deserves to lose a husband that way."

I stopped working and looked up at him, hoping my full attention would elicit a detail that would illumine me. But as before, the mere mention of his son-in-law and whatever way he had passed suddenly overtook him. Alastor pressed his lips together and shook his head as if to steel himself against whatever was rising in him. He waited until Corydon skittered out of earshot. "And this one, naturally he did not understand where Papa was and kept begging for him."

Now the old man could not speak again. I went back to my work and tried to take the burden off him while at the same time angling for more information. "Lost in a battle, was he? A military man?"

Alastor breathed deeply through his nose and wiped his forehead and beard with a hand. He shook his head, and his voice came pinched and labored, as if he were ready to burst into tears. "He was valiantly fighting for a cause, I'll say that."

"Oh? A worthy one, I'm sure."

He held up a hand and turned away. "The worthiest," he whispered huskily. "I'm sorry, I can't."

"He sounds like a brave, wonderful man."

I had pushed too far. With that, Alastor stood and left the table. Corydon came bounding over and leapt into his chair, announcing, "Now I will be your helper!"

"Oh! My helper must hand me, let's see, that piece right over there."
I had selected the largest untrimmed section of goat hide, covered
with thick, dark hair—something I would not even have asked of his
grandfather.

Corydon's eyes widened and he stood on the bench, seemingly eager
to show me he was up to the task. He gathered the hide, spread his feet for
leverage, and began to lift, but the raw material must have weighed nearly
as much as he did. Once he had it off the table, it shifted and pitched him
backward, and he would have tumbled had I not caught him.

"I had no idea that goat was still alive!" I said, which caused him to
squeal with delight and want to try it again. I told him we would have
to save playtime for later, before I went fishing, because I had to finish
Master Zuriel's tent very soon.

As I replaced the hide, Corydon rested his elbows on the table and
planted his chin in his palm, making his head bob when he talked. "I
know him."

"You do?"

"Um-hm. He knows Papa."

I was sorely tempted to work the lad for more information but I knew
that was unfair. No doubt Corydon had been protected from the details
of how his father died. Wasn't it enough that these people were followers
of The Way, that they had fled Judea—as apparently so had Zuriel—and
that the man's own father-in-law had said he'd fought for the worthiest of
causes?

Soon Alastor returned with apologies and engrossed himself in the
work again. Taryn sought Corydon's help in bringing us a light repast, and
then we were off to Zuriel's tent. It didn't surprise me to find him in the
same sour mood he had exhibited at the meeting of the elders. And as I
had deduced from a cursory scan of the dwellings the day before, his was
the shabbiest of the lot.

This he did not deny. The thick, jowly man prowled the dusty area outside, squinting at the gaping holes in the walls of his tent, pointing out the worst. His pleasant, soft-spoken wife, introduced as Kaia, looked enough like him to give me pause. She said, "Oh, some gaps are worse than others, but none are acceptable when the winds blow."

One of the openings revealed an ancient woman sitting cross-legged on a mat, staring out and smiling blankly. Waiting for an introduction and getting none, I said, "Fear not, I have the remedy for all."

Three trips between Alastor's tent and Zuriel's delivered enough material, and by the eleventh hour of the day—with everyone else handing me the pieces I pointed out and me crawling, climbing, and dangling from poles while I stitched and stretched—Zuriel and Kaia's tent soon looked like new.

They seemed pleased. She smiled and he appeared to try. But I had misjudged my ability to make a friend of him so easily. He said, "Don't think this gets you out of fishing duty. I'll see you at second watch."

When Alastor headed back to his own tent, I lingered. "You knew Taryn's husband," I said.

"He did," Kaia said. "A wonderful young m—"

"He was speaking to me, woman," Zuriel said, not unkindly, but this sent his wife trundling inside.

"What can you tell me about him?" I said.

"Nothing. He's not your business, and besides, you're unworthy of him."

"I'm sure that's so. I'm just curi—"

"Why don't you ask his family then?"

"They're still grieving, sir. They find it difficult to—"

"Well, so do I. Newcomer asking questions, especially in a place like this, it doesn't look good."

"I apologize."

He nodded and went inside, leaving me standing there.

After the evening meal that night I played with Corydon and tried not to think about the awkwardness of fishing under Zuriel's supervision later. Right about the time Taryn told Corydon it was time for bed, the four of us looked up in surprise at a quiet "Hello!" Kaia stood at the entrance to the tent with an empty bowl and asked Taryn if she had a few figs she could borrow.

When Taryn invited her in, they whispered briefly, then Taryn took Corydon and Kaia sat shyly next to me. "I can stay only a moment," she said, so quietly I had to lean close. "I sense you were earnest in wanting to know more of Stephanos."

"I was. Thank you."

"Let me say only this. The woman you saw in our tent is Zuriel's elderly sister. Stephanos was so kind to her that he will always have a special place in our hearts. She was of no benefit to him, yet he served her faithfully in the name of the Lord."

"In what capacity did he do this, ma'am?"

She was rising, ready to leave. I leapt to my feet to help her up.

"I must go," she said. "I came here for figs, you understand, not to speak to you."

"I do understand. May I walk you?"

"Just to the back corner of the tent. And please thank Taryn again for me."

I assured her I would.

Kaia spoke quickly. "Zuriel and I felt strongly—and we weren't the only ones—that the Greek widows among our number in the church were being neglected in the daily distribution of food and other necessities. We didn't want to make trouble, but it was apparent that the Jewish widows were favored. We had no problem with their getting whatever they needed, but it did not seem fair that our women were slighted.

"When Zuriel raised the matter—and I was proud that he did it peaceably—the apostles called together the greater multitude of disciples, of whom Stephanos was one, and said that it didn't make sense for them to stop teaching and preaching and take care of the widows. So they asked that the disciples seek from among themselves seven men of good reputation, full of the Holy Spirit and wisdom, whom they could appoint over this business. That way, the apostles could continually give themselves to prayer and ministering the word while these seven did this worthy work."

"And Stephanos was one of those?"

"Yes, he was well known as a man full of faith and the Holy Spirit, as were the other six. We remember well the apostles laying hands on them and praying. Soon after that, the word of God spread, and the disciples multiplied greatly in Jerusalem. Stephanos performed wonders and signs among us all.

"Now I really must go. Zuriel will come looking for me."

"Ma'am, please. How did Stephanos die?"

"Oh, he became a threat to the Pharisees. He was charged with blasphemy and stoned."

"Kaia!"

"Coming, Zuriel. I have your figs!"

I moved stiff-legged back to the tent and tried to make small talk with Alastor and Taryn. Whether I hid my turmoil, I do not know. I felt as if guilt were written all over me. How long was I expected to stay here, and what was I to say?

It would have been folly to deny this was God's plan when He brought me here, but why not just tell me? He was meeting me in the wilderness and teaching me the deep things of Himself, and yet He arranged for me to learn the macabre truth this way?

I asked Taryn for a lamp and for the small table to use upon my return from the fishing expedition. Knowing I would be unable to sleep until I collapsed from exhaustion, I planned to write until then or until the oil ran out.

The fishing proved much different from what I expected. The other men, of whom Nadav was one, were not intimidated by Zuriel. They obeyed his few sparse commands, and the only thing he said to me was that the entire activity would take less than an hour. It took nearly half as long to get to the Sea as it did to work in the shallow water. We tied our tunics at our waists and waded out, some working rudimentary nets, others with poles and lines and hooks.

Few spoke to me other than to teach me the tricks and techniques, but I was touched by Nadav's simple prayer of thanks when the catch was separated into baskets for several to carry back. But just before we looked up from the prayer, Zuriel spoke in an urgent whisper. "No one move. Remain right where you are."

"What is it?" Nadav said.

"If I'm not mistaken, horsemen stopped on the trade route could be Romans."

"How can you tell?"

"Just from their silhouettes in the moonlight. They must have seen us. We must let them assume us locals and remain here till they're gone."

Another of the men said, "Could they have seen our tracks from the enclave?"

"Not likely in the darkness," Zuriel said. "But we'll be wise to cover them when we do return. They would never stumble upon our outpost by accident."

I could barely breathe. "How many are there?" I said, not daring even to turn and look.

"Four," Zuriel said. "Not more than five. Why do you ask?"

I shrugged. "In case we are forced to engage them."

"We'd be in pieces inside a minute!" he spat. "Are we to counter their swords with fishhooks? You're the smallest among us. You ought to see if you can get close enough to hear them, see what they're about."

"Don't be foolish," one of the older men said. "You were right in the first place. Wait them out. Let them leave."

"He's the most expendable," Zuriel said. "What's the risk?"

"Only our lives. And our families."

"I'm not afraid," Zuriel said. "I'll go myself."

"Don't be insane!"

"Shh!" The wind had shifted and we could hear the horses' hooves on the stones of the trade route, then bits of conversation. The water seemed to grow colder when I distinctly heard one of the soldiers refer to General Balbus.

The others glanced at each other. "That's all we need," Nadav said. "He's quite a reputation, that one does."

"You can bet they're not around here looking for us," Zuriel said.

"How can you be sure of that?"

"Because I helped find this location. No one knows where we are."

Was it possible Theo had been spotted coming from this area?

We waited nearly an hour before the Romans trotted off and disappeared.

Upon our return Nadav showed me how to clean and gut the harvest, rinsing the carcasses in saltwater and hanging them on a line to dry in the sun the next day before the community shared them.

Nadav was largely silent and curt when he did speak, though he allowed that I had acquitted myself well as a new member of the fishing party. I responded casually, hoping to draw him into more pleasant conversation, but it was clear my hesitance to be more forthcoming about my horse had either offended or made him suspicious.

"Many are still undecided about you, Paul of Damascus," he said, with careful emphasis on the latter. "I and my wife, Anna, included."

I had the impression that forcing the issue would be to my detriment. "I appreciate your forthrightness. And I welcome your scrutiny."

It was as close as I'd come to lying since I had arrived. I had evaded the whole truth and omitted details when necessary, but I did not want to render myself unworthy of what God had entrusted to me. If He was to continue speaking to me, far be it from me to become a bearer of false witness.

What might true scrutiny reveal about me? That I was Paul of Damascus, yes, at least of late. But that I was also Saul of Tarsus and had been responsible for people like these—in fact for some of these—to flee to a place like this. What might Nadav do with such information? Any progress I had made in persuading him of my authenticity as a brother would be ruined by this fact alone—that I had not been open about my past.

After that first night of fishing I had found myself too exhausted from the delay and the fear to write as I had planned. In fact, it was several weeks later—after having felt no freedom from the Lord to reveal my connection with Stephen to Alastor or Taryn—before I finally felt the urge again and came back from an evening in the sea and wrote and wrote, exhausting three quills and two inkwells, nodding off several times before hearing the watchman call fourth watch.

To my great embarrassment, when I awoke the sun was up, as were all three members of the family. My lamp had burned out and my quill lay atop my pages, which had been moved slightly to make room for the light breakfast Taryn had provided. The olive juice had coagulated in the bowl and the bread was cold, and I could hear her insisting that Corydon be quiet until I had risen.

I ate quickly and thanked my hostess, telling the begging boy I couldn't play until evening but would see him around midday. After hurriedly scanning my pages to remind myself what I had written and to be sure there was nothing that might embarrass me if Taryn had seen it, I carefully wrapped and stored the parchments.

Rushing into the wilderness, I chastised myself for the fatigue of a short night and tried to clear my mind for whatever God had for me. All the way to the familiar rendezvous spot I pleaded with Him, as I had done for a month, to tell me what to do. *Why here? Why them? What would You have me say? Am I to compound their grief by revealing myself? It requires all the faith I can muster to feel Your forgiveness! How would I ever elicit theirs and know it was genuine?*

I couldn't tell if the silence was due to my impudence for demanding an answer, because I was late, or because this was part of an elaborate test—the very reason He had brought me here from Damascus. Perhaps this was about more than preparing me for ministry.

Lest there be any doubt about my heart's posture before my God, I slipped out of my mantle at the base of the plateau and left it on the ground. When I reached the apex I knelt, my bare knees painfully supporting my weight. And I waited.

I died for your sins according to the Scriptures. I was buried, and I rose again the third day according to the Scriptures, and I was seen by Cephas, then by the twelve. After that I was seen by over five hundred brethren at once. After that I was seen by James, then by all the apostles.

Then I revealed Myself to you also, though you persecuted the church of My Father. But His grace toward you was not in vain, for you will labor more than anyone, yet not you, but the grace of My Father which will be with you.

Some will say there is no resurrection of the dead, but if that is so, then I am not risen. And if I am not risen, then your preaching will be empty and your faith also. You would then be a false witness of God, testifying that He raised Me—if in fact the dead do not rise. For if the dead do not rise, then I am not risen. And if I am not risen, your faith is futile; you are still in your sins. And if in this life only you have hope in Me, then you, of all men, would be the most pitiable.

But I am risen from the dead! And I will deliver the kingdom to God My Father when I put an end to all rule and all authority and power. For I must reign till I have put all enemies under My feet. The last enemy I will destroy is death.

Behold this mystery: you shall be changed—in a moment, in the twinkling of an eye, at the last trumpet when the dead will be raised. What is corruptible must put on incorruption, and what is mortal must put on immortality. Then shall come to pass the sayings: "Death is swallowed up in victory."

"O Death, where is your sting? O Hades, where is your victory?"

The sting of death is sin, and the strength of sin is the Law. But thank My Father who gives you victory through Me. Remain steadfast, immovable, always abounding in the work of the Lord, knowing that your labor is not in vain.

Again, with all the guilt and turmoil that plagued me, I felt unworthy of such divine encouragement. But I accepted it with the gratitude of a man in the desert for life-giving water.

I brushed away specs of blood from my knees as I put my mantle back on and began the long trek back to the refuge, but this time as the tops of the tents appeared as great dark spots in the distance, I found myself on my knees in the sand again. *Lord, please! Just give me a word! What am I to do? I cannot live a lie of silence before these dear anguished souls. I know the lad is too young to understand, but in my flesh I would divulge the truth to his mother and grandfather as soon as he's asleep this very night. But is that selfish, only to relieve me of this weight? Is it fair to force them to some action for which they are not prepared nor might take if their grief was not so raw?*

In due time.

At that I fell prostrate in the sand. *Thank You, Lord! Though I still dread that day when the truth reveals me as the opposite of their new friend, I will trust You and rest in Your infinite wisdom.*

Rising and brushing myself off, I hurried to my new home and what would become my routine for days and weeks and months, and—to my great surprise—years.

Part Two

SET ASIDE

8

LOVE

YANBU

Day after day as the weeks and months passed, I woke to the light, nourishing, delicious breakfast prepared so kindly by my hostess. Taryn grew more and more familiar with me until we were able to converse as friends and then almost as brother and sister. Gradually I got her to smile and occasionally even to laugh. Then the day came that she chuckled like Corydon at some foolishness we perpetrated at the expense of Alastor, and he played along.

My mornings in the wilderness evolved from tense forays of wonder to fascinating journeys into the heart of God Himself. The contrast between the desolate walk across the sand and ascent to the plateau and the sweet fellowship I enjoyed while being taught for hours made me look forward to these meetings the way I looked forward to heaven at the end of my days.

My fingers had quickly callused from the tentmaking, and the old craft came back to me, making my afternoons meld into one another. I was never bored, and as more and more Christ-followers joined the little city of refuge, my work merely increased. If I wasn't creating a new dwelling, I was repairing an old one, and even skeptical Nadav, his comely wife, Anna, and the curmudgeon Zuriel had seemed to reluctantly loosen their reins on me.

Evening meals became more than routine as Taryn came to welcome me into the tent the way she did her father and often asked what I would like her to prepare. It became common for her to sit up talking with me long after Alastor and Corydon had gone to sleep. Occasionally she put a hand on my arm to emphasize a point, and eventually she even leaned or rested her head on my shoulder.

Things changed between us when she grew comfortable enough to speak to me of her Stephanos. That made my mouth dry, but I believe she thought I was merely being respectful and letting her talk. The old guilt returned when she told me of his demise and how the news had come to her in their small dwelling in the City of David. How grateful I was that neither she nor her father had been present when it happened. Still, I rued the day when the truth would come out. I could only hope Taryn had come to trust me and care enough for me by then that my long silence would not prove to be too much of a betrayal to forgive.

It took several weeks for her to exhaust her stories of her husband, and though I found myself developing deep feelings for her, I strangely found myself not only not jealous of Stephanos but rather wishing I had known him. Oh, to be a man like him, known for his devotion to Christ and to the service of others!

Taryn was most impressed with my knowledge of the Scriptures and my willingness to help Alastor teach Corydon to read by using the scrolls.

"As moved as I have always been by your playing with him, I am so deeply touched by your care for his soul."

It had been ages since she had worn her veil inside the tent, and in the low lamplight of the evening she caught me staring at her. When she did not look away, I mustered my courage, held her gaze, and reached to lightly caress her cheek. To my delight and thrill, she did not pull away. I wondered how long it would be before she would permit a kiss.

Taryn began waiting up for me on those nights I had fishing duty. And often when I took my turn as watchman, she would silently hand me a cup of something to eat or drink.

When Corydon reached the age of six, I noticed less fleshiness in his face, more definition, more awareness in his eyes. With his rudimentary reading skills came questions, youthful and naïve at first, but sometimes insightful. I came to appreciate and enjoy his mind.

On my walks across the desert every morning, I thanked God for my new family and allowed myself to speculate on whether He might bless me by making it truly mine one day. Was it possible that fit the plan He had for me?

I had misgivings, for He continued to make plain that I would suffer for my calling. Clearly there would be much travel, hardship, and persecution. Would it be right to subject a wife and child to such a life, willing as I was to take it on? And what of her father?

On these questions I found God silent.

9

THE DISCOVERY

YANBU

THE PROPHETS OF OLD had intrigued me since I had begun reading them as a child. But now, though I was beginning to understand the unique privilege I enjoyed of God's making me an apostle of Jesus, though I had never seen Him before He had ascended to heaven, I comprehended that prophecy—at least of the foretelling nature—was not to become one of my gifts.

I could only imagine the terrible responsibility of knowing what was to come, for two and a half years into my odyssey, a sense of foreboding came over me. It wasn't as if I was wholly unaware of what caused it. Though pessimism had never been part of my character, I was enough of a realist to know that a man's life cannot sustain solely joy and happiness for long. Especially when lurking in the back of his mind—and often at the forefront of it—lay two inescapable realities.

The first was that I had clearly been called to a life of suffering. God had made that manifest from the first. So this idyllic season was only that, a season. A man could expect to enjoy such delight for just a while.

Second, if my love for Taryn—and yes, that is what it had blossomed into—was reciprocated and became what I had come to long for, the truth would have to emerge. There was no longer any hiding our feelings for one another. First her father had noticed, and then he had consented to allow us time to stroll alone occasionally under the stars.

Then came the awkward day over supper when Corydon blurted, "Are you to become my new papa?"

Before I could devise even an evasive response, his mother said, "Would you like that, son?"

I stopped mid-chew and noticed that Taryn and Alastor stiffened as well, waiting for the verdict of this near-seven-year-old, upon whose opinion it seemed all of our futures hung in the balance. He appeared to think deeply about the prospect.

Then he shrugged, dipped his bread in the communal bowl, and said, "I like this, Mother. What is it?"

She laughed. "Just vegetable broth with a bit of animal fat."

Corydon looked puzzled at our grins and shaking heads.

Nothing could have deterred me from my calling, no matter what I faced. One morning I assured Him, *I have given up everything and would give up anything in my future to remain your bondservant.*

Anything?

Anything, Lord!

Anything?

Hurt that He made me repeat it, I wondered if my Lord did not believe me. Did He question my devotion, my resolve?

Anything?

Lord, please! I don't know how else to say it, to show it. I will never be ashamed of Your gospel, for You have taught me through Your mercy to me even when I was dead in my sins, that it is the power of God to save all who believe! I am willing to be poured out for You, to die for You! Yes, anything!

Anyone?

How could I have been so blind? Was Taryn my test, my trial? Would she determine the true measure of my devotion? Had I mistaken her for yet another divine gift when His entire elaborate construct was designed only to make her my Isaac? Was I willing to sacrifice a life with her on the altar of my faithfulness?

Lord, don't ask this of me.

Only the night before, Taryn and I had finally allowed ourselves to talk seriously of our future. For months others in the refuge had noticed the difference in her. She appeared outside her tent without her veil, looked radiant, conversed more, was quick to smile and often to laugh. She even chuckled at good-natured teasing about me.

Alastor told me he had raised at a meeting of the elders the question of whether it remained appropriate for me to lodge with them. The consensus was that as long as he trusted me and that she and I were never there alone, until such time as there was a betrothal, the matter of propriety was his judgment to make.

"You're saying that if I ask for her hand, I will need to find somewhere else to dwell until the marriage."

"Did you say 'if'?" he asked with a twinkle.

"When."

"But you're not asking yet?"

"Not quite yet."

"I am not a young man, Paul."

"I would not be marrying you, Alastor."

"Oh, I am afraid you would be!" he said with a laugh.

He and I talked long into the night about the things God was telling me and how hard my life would be. To my great relief, Alastor did not take this lightly. "You are wise to ponder the ramifications," he said. "And it is only fair she knows the reality."

That last pierced me, of course, because there was so much she did not know.

Taryn and I had taken to walking arm in arm during our nighttime strolls and often praying together. After a week or two of loving embraces at the ends of these evenings, out of view of the curious eyes of whoever was on watch, we kissed. In the weeks that followed we shared life stories, and I told her almost everything. I could tell she thought nothing of my leaving out the name of my native city but referring only to the region. And naturally I did not use my Greek name.

We joked about *Paul* meaning "small," and she said she had never seen me that way. "Not even the day we met," I said, "when you knew nothing about me? I'm not much taller than you, love."

She cocked her head and seemed to study me. "Truthfully, that day I was wary of you. Without warning, Corydon announces a man, and there you stand with Father, next to a black stallion that dwarfs you both. And yes, now that I think of it, I was struck that you were short."

"Yet you found me handsome, with my bald head and Roman nose. I tried to stand tall and hide my bowed legs."

"You don't have bowed legs! What I noticed was that you seemed unaffected by whatever journey you had endured to reach us, and the closest town is miles away. I was in mourning, protective of my son and my aging father."

"But you just said you never saw me as small."

"Only then. As soon as you befriended Corydon and revealed your character, you grew in stature."

"And so how tall do you see me now?"

"Oh, you could look down on the Colossus at Rhodes."

I drew back to stare at her. "You know of the Colossus?"

"Don't insult me, Paul. My father taught me everything he would have taught a son. I read the scrolls. I read history. Why do you think we were among the first to recognize Jesus as the Messiah?"

"You were among the first?"

Taryn nodded. "Father, being a rabbi, was skeptical in the beginning, but he was there when Jesus fed the multitudes. He saw Him restore a man's sight. When Stephanos and I took Corydon, not even a year old, to hear Jesus, the Lord had children in His lap and was blessing them. His disciples scolded the people for bothering Him with children, but Jesus immediately corrected them and asked for more to join Him. I was standing at the edge of the crowd, shading Corydon's face from the sun, when Jesus noticed and caught my eye. He lifted His chin, I can still see it, and gestured almost imperceptibly that I should bring my baby to Him."

Taryn's face contorted and she pressed a finger to her lips.

"When I handed Corydon to Him, Jesus cradled him so gently that the other children immediately quieted and leaned in to see the baby's face. Jesus whispered, 'He's sleeping,' but just as He said it, Corydon awoke with a gurgle and grabbed the Lord's finger. The Lord chortled—I don't know how else to say it—and that made the children giggle, and the baby smiled."

Again she was overcome and had to gather herself.

"Then He looked at me with a smile of such joy that I will not forget it as long as I live. He put His hand atop Corydon's head, the tiny fingers still wrapped around His, lifted His eyes toward the sky, and said, 'Father, bless this child.'"

That night I wrote until the wee hours again, eager to make a record of every detail. "What must she have thought," I wrote, "when not long after that, Jesus was crucified and her own husband was stoned?"

I hadn't had the heart to ask if she had shared that story with Corydon. While he was now at an age where he would enjoy it, it would raise questions about the nature of God and what kind of blessing rested upon him if his own father had been brutally murdered. I wrote several pages on my own crushing inner turmoil, agonizing over when and how I could tell the love of my life of my role in the death of her husband.

As the days progressed and we told each other more and more of our stories, Taryn shared how her father had persuaded her and Stephanos to examine the Scriptures with him and to see how Jesus fulfilled the ancient prophecies of the Messiah. "We risked everything, sacrificed everything, and became believers, followers of Jesus and The Way. When Jesus was crucified, we were devastated and terrified, yet Stephanos was among the first to believe the report of His resurrection. He became more like Jesus than anyone else I have ever known. I feared his boldness could cost him his life, but I did not expect it to happen so fast."

That night I wrote that I was concerned my uneasiness showed when we kissed each other good night. Taryn had come to know my moods and expressions and asked what was troubling me. I told her I felt I had almost come to know Stephanos through her memories and that I wish I could have met him. "I mean, I wish I could have known him." (As for meeting him, in a manner of speaking I most certainly had.)

She said, "And you shall, at the resurrection."

The following day in the wilderness I pleaded with the Lord anew for permission and for the words. *I don't know how long I can endure this deceit, for that's what it feels like and that is what it will appear to her.*

In due time.

I couldn't tell my God that His answer was not enough.

That was also the day He taught me: *The just shall live by faith. The wrath of My Father is revealed from heaven against all who suppress the truth in unrighteousness, because what may be known of Him He has shown to them. Since creation, even His invisible attributes have been clear and can be understood by the things that are made, even His power and eternal Godhead. So people are without excuse. They knew Him, but they did not glorify Him, nor were they thankful. Their foolish hearts were darkened. Thinking themselves wise, they became fools and changed the glory of the incorruptible God into images like corruptible man, and birds and animals and creeping things.*

Therefore, My Father gave them up to the lusts of their hearts to dishonor their bodies among themselves, those who exchanged His truth for lies and worshiped and served the creature rather than the Creator.

He gave them over to debased minds to do things that are not fitting. Filled with unrighteousness, sexual immorality, wickedness, covetousness, and maliciousness, and full of envy, murder, strife, deceit, and evil-mindedness, they are whisperers, backbiters, haters of God, violent, proud, boasters, inventors of evil things, disobedient to parents, undiscerning, untrustworthy, unloving, unforgiving, and unmerciful. Knowing the righteous judgment of My Father, those who practice such things are deserving of death, along with those who approve of those who practice them.

My Father will render to each one according to his deeds: eternal life to those who continue doing good, seeking glory, honor, and immortality; but to those who are self-seeking and unrighteous and do not obey the truth, their lot will be His indignation and wrath, tribulation and anguish.

Now I was confused. Could men somehow earn their salvation by continuing to do good? No. No one was capable of that.

My Father made you alive when you were dead in trespasses and sins, living according to Satan, the prince of the power of the air, the spirit who now works in the sons of disobedience, among whom also you once conducted yourself in the lusts of your flesh, fulfilling the desires of the flesh and of the mind.

But My Father, who is rich in mercy, because of His great love, even when you were dead in trespasses, made you alive together with Me and will make us to sit together in heaven. That is your message to the Gentiles, that in the ages to come My Father might show the exceeding riches of His grace and kindness toward men through Me.

For by grace you have been saved through faith, and that not of yourself. It is the gift of God, not of works, lest anyone should boast. For you are His workmanship, created in Me for good works.

You are no longer a stranger or a foreigner, but a fellow citizen with the saints and members of the household of God. Built on the foundation of the apostles and prophets, I being the chief Cornerstone, the whole building, being fitted together, grows into a holy temple.

Walk worthy of My Father, fully pleasing Him, being fruitful in every good work and increasing in His knowledge, strengthened with all might, according to His glorious power, for all patience and longsuffering with joy, giving thanks to Him who has qualified you to be a partaker of the inheritance of the saints. He has delivered you from the power of darkness and brought you into My kingdom, and in Me you have redemption through My blood, the forgiveness of sins.

I am the image of the invisible God, the firstborn over all creation. For by Me all things were created in heaven and on earth, visible and invisible, whether thrones or dominions or principalities or powers. All things were created through Me and for Me. And I am before all things, and in Me all things consist. I am the Head of the body, the church, the Beginning, the Firstborn from the dead, that in all things I may have the preeminence.

For it pleased My Father that in Me all the fullness should dwell, and through Me to reconcile all things to Himself, whether things on earth or things in heaven, having made peace through the blood of My cross.

It had been my practice to walk deliberately back to the slowly expanding campground of refuge each day, meditating on everything the Lord had impressed upon me and allowing Him to sear it into my soul. But this day I felt filled to overflowing. When would He send me out? When would I get to preach? When would I be able to proclaim His truth to the world?

I had submitted myself to divine counsel and training and instruction. I knew the importance of preparation, especially because my message would be welcomed by only those few the Spirit drew to see their need. Others would hate it and me for spreading it, but that had long since stopped mattering to me. If it were up to me, I would have said I was ready. As Samuel of old had offered, I wanted to shout from the rooftops, "Here am I, Lord! Send me!"

And so it was that I could not keep myself from rushing back. Taryn was always busy with her chores and with Corydon, and so while we would greet each other, smile warmly, and extend kindnesses to each other throughout the day, we generally kept to ourselves and looked forward to time together in the evenings.

This day I wanted to find her immediately and steal her away from whatever seemed more important at the moment. I wanted to give her just a taste of that with which God was blessing me and tell her that perhaps it was time to get serious about our future. Maybe the Lord wasn't ready to send me out quite as quickly as I planned, but I sensed He was building toward something. He was certainly no longer spoon-feeding me the milk of His word. I was being steeped in doctrine and the knowledge of men's hearts more deeply than in any lecture I had ever sat through—even from the great Gamaliel himself. I had the feeling that my first audience, whoever and wherever it might be, would get the loudest, heaviest, most vigorous dose of preaching they had ever heard. How would I contain myself?

My first hint something was awry came when Corydon was nowhere to be found in the open area around the well and the livestock pen. With the expansion of the refuge, this had grown as new tents had been constructed in a vast circle around it, maintaining a wide berth for animals, children, and women fetching water all day. Daily Corydon would break from his dusty playtime with others and run to welcome me as I entered the area.

Not today.

One of the original tents that backed up to this common area was the rather large dwelling of Zuriel and Kaia. Their tent's repairs served as a model to newcomers of how they wanted the tentmaker to craft their abodes. It was common for me to come upon Kaia and Taryn—and sometimes a few others—talking or fetching water or baking or planting. Each day had become a new opportunity for someone to joke about Taryn and me. I would respond with some rueful statement about how she showed no interest in me, or she would claim her father was looking for a wealthier suitor, and all would laugh.

Today, no Taryn either. In fact, the few people busy in the common area appeared unwilling to look at me. I noticed a stony Kaia standing rigidly behind her tent, almost as if on guard. When she saw me she stepped between tents and called to the front, "Zuriel!" Then she returned and resumed her post.

I greeted several people I knew but elicited no more than a nod. I approached Kaia, who looked as if she had been given an assignment she didn't want. When I searched her eyes, they darted everywhere but at me, and the hard line of her mouth made her look more like her husband than ever.

"What is it, my friend?" I said. "Where is my beloved today?"

"That is not for me to say," she said, her voice quavery. "You might want to ask Alastor."

"And where might I find him?"

"In his tent."

"Kaia, we're friends. Is something wrong? Is everyone all right?"

"Go about your business."

Zuriel would tell me. He wasn't warm with anyone, but I had won him over somewhat with my work on his tent, carrying my weight on his fishing party, and even saving a couple of his goats from a jackal one night on my watch despite the noisy scuffle that had wakened many—including him. The next day Kaia had delivered a dessert of raisins and honey, whispering, "He won't admit it, but this was his suggestion and his way of showing he's grateful."

I told her, "Tell him I said thanks."

"I'll do nothing of the kind."

And we had laughed. But that was then.

Now I headed to the front of their tent to find Zuriel standing sentry and scowling at me with fierce, dark eyes. "Didn't she tell you Alastor was waiting for you?"

"She did, friend, but surely you can tell me what's happened."

Before I could flinch, let alone elude him or defend myself, the older man clutched my mantle and tunic in one meaty fist and yanked me close. Exhaling what smelled like decades of garlic and leeks and fish, he growled, "Are you from Tarsus?"

"Originally, or—"

He shoved me away with such force that my sandal caught and I slid on my seat in the hard-packed sand. "You're Saul of Tarsus!"

I felt like a worm, struggling to my feet and dusting myself off. "Not anymore," I said. "That was a previous life."

"Well, your previous life has come home to roost, *Saul*." He spat my name with such disgust that it sickened even me.

Then it hit me. They were guarding their tent against me. "Are Taryn and Corydon here?"

"You'll have to kill me to find out. Now move along."

I closed my eyes and sighed, desperate to get a message to her. But what? Neither Zuriel nor Kaia seemed in a mood to speak for me. And what could I say, especially through an intermediary, that could persuade Taryn to delay any rash decisions, to allow me at least to explain?

"I love her," I said.

"You have a strange way of showing it," Zuriel said, waving me off as if he could no longer stand me in his sight.

I lumbered to our tent, or to what had been our tent—I couldn't imagine calling it that again, and came upon Nadav out front. "He's here, sir," he called. Turning to me with knowing eyes, he said, "I guess we've solved the mystery of your horse, at long last."

"I hope it puts your mind at ease."

"No one's mind is at ease here anymore, Saul."

"It's Paul now, Nadav."

"As you wish. You just concoct any reality that suits you, sir, and let Anna and me know what we should believe."

"Enough, Nadav!" The young man started at the fury in Alastor's voice, and I realized I had not seen the old man angry before myself. "Send him in and return home!"

"Are you sure you don't want me to stay and—"

"You heard me!"

I slipped inside as if approaching the gallows, wondering if any of my future with this family was salvageable. And naturally, I was curious beyond measure how I had been found out.

Alastor sat on the other side of the low table with his head in his hands, looking older than I'd ever seen him. My foot-high stack of parchments lay facedown in a ragged pile on the table before him, and he pointed to a stool across from him.

"I was not unwise to let Nadav go, was I, Paul? You're not going to stone me, are you?"

I hesitated and hung my head. "First," I muttered, "thank you for calling me by my Roman name. And second, if you know me at all, you know you are safe with me. Old things are passed away—"

"*Do* I know you? I thought I did."

"I don't know how much you have read, or why, but I have written the truth. I did not know who you were when God sent me here, and when I discovered it, I could not risk saying anything. When finally I knew I must, I did not feel freedom from the Lord—"

"I read that much, Paul. The damage, the tragedy here, is that it was the lad who found your writings."

"Oh, no!"

"As you know, he's an accomplished reader. You have helped make him so. There was much he didn't understand, but when Taryn discovered him with the pages, she scolded him and put them back where you had stored them. Then Corydon said you had worked in the Temple in Jerusalem. She could not help herself. I had no sons, Paul. Forgive me, but I taught her to read, and she read. She showed me. And she left."

"I know where she is."

"She cannot abide you just now, certainly not living in the same tent."

"I understand. Does Corydon know—"

"Your role in the death of his father? No."

"Thank God."

"Taryn said you told her you had been raised a Pharisee and that you studied under Gamaliel."

I nodded. "I told her that until Christ found me, I was an enemy of believers."

"But Paul, you must know she had no idea the extent—"

"Of course I know. Does she believe I did not know who she was when I arrived?"

"She wants to, but she is having a terrible time. She loves you, Paul. She has given you her heart."

"And now?"

Alastor sounded weary. "Put yourself in her place. The first man she loves is sacrificed to a cause she believes in. Despite her pain, she somehow draws strength from his memory and the depth of his character. Thinking she would remain a widow the rest of her days, she feels blessed of God when you find each other. And now the second man she loves is not who she thought he was. In fact, he may as well have personally taken the life of her first love. Paul, it's too much to bear."

"Hurting her," I said, "and the prospect of losing her, is too much for *me* to bear. Alastor, I have come to admire and respect you, to love you. Can *you* forgive me? Do *you* believe me, and can you tell me what to do?"

"Bring your chair over here," the old man said, and I rolled the stool to where I faced him on the other side of the table. He rested his palms on my shoulders. "I believe God found you. I read your account of what happened to you on the road to Damascus, and I have never heard anything like it. Clearly, you have been chosen.

"I don't know what to make of your choices since you have been here. It's difficult to say what I would have done had I found myself in the same predicament. As for me, yes, I believe I do know you and your heart. And I do forgive you. But I cannot speak for my daughter, and frankly, I would not hold it against her if she could never accept becoming your wife."

"That's my fear."

"Imagine it. How long would it take for her to think of anything else anytime she lays eyes on you, you talk to her, touch her, embrace her?"

"I know. I feel as if I might die if I don't see her."

"It's too soon yet."

"When?"

"That is for her alone to say."

"What am I to do in the meantime?"

"Plan."

"Plan what?"

"Plan what you will say when she grants you an audience." Alastor seemed to stifle a smile.

"What could possibly be humorous right now?"

"The boy. In many ways, he will be your ally."

"How so?"

"Corydon knows only what he understands. He doesn't know why they are staying away from home. He won't know why you are not visiting when his grandfather visits. He's going to want to see you, and he'll pester her until it happens."

"I pray you're right."

"Of course I'm right. But while you're waiting, use your gift to prepare your thoughts."

"My gift?"

"The gift that has thrust you into this mess. I couldn't believe how much you had written since you have arrived here. And praise God, what He has been telling you in the wilderness! That, too, is your ally, Paul, because it is hard for Taryn to separate the man God has called, and in whom He is confiding so much, from the man who for some reason has kept this terrible secret."

"I should write to her."

"That's what I'm saying."

"And you'll see that she gets it."

"Yes. But I can't make her read it, and I can't tell her how she is to respond."

"Am I still allowed to dwell in your tent?"

"You are if you will do me a favor from now on."

"Name it, Alastor."

"You will bury your writings where the lad can't find them."

10

THE VISION

YANBU

For the first time since Christ had forgiven and redeemed me, my old nature come flooding back. I was terrified it could wash away the newness of life the Lord had borne in me. I wanted to pray, needed to, but could not. I stood, I paced, I sighed, I talked to myself.

Legs crossed and arms folded, Alastor tilted his head and studied me as I rushed about the tent. "I am about to go mad," I said, half the time facing him, the other spinning toward the opening and looking to the west. "You tell me to write to her, but what am I to say? Jesus arrests me, God calls me, sends me here, makes me an apostle, allows me to fall in love with the widow of a man I sentenced to death, doesn't allow me to tell her, and yet now I feel no liberty to use Him as an alibi for my silence! I must own my unexplainable guilt."

"Paul, Paul," the old man said, "you are the very embodiment of Isaiah!"

That stopped me and I turned to face him. "What on earth are you talking about? Isaiah?"

Alastor rose and reached around the curtain for one of the ancient Scripture scrolls. He tucked it under his arm while carefully sliding my cluttered parchments out of the way. Unrolling the spool before him, he said, "Come, look. When Isaiah is called to be a prophet, Yahweh reveals Himself. You know the text."

"Yes, on the throne, high and lifted up, the train of His robe filling the temple, the seraphim crying 'Holy is the Lord,' the earth full of His glory, the smoke . . ."

Alastor traced the text with his finger. "Here Isaiah says what you are feeling now: 'Woe is me, for I am undone!'"

"Come now, Rabbi," I said. "I am distraught, but Isaiah had seen God, the Lord of hosts."

"Yes, but then God has the seraphim touch Isaiah's lips with the coal and purge his sin, and the Lord asks, 'Whom shall I send, and who will go for Us?' And how does Isaiah reply?"

Finally I sat and my shoulders slumped. "'Here am I! Send me.'"

Alastor slowly rerolled the cylinder, set it down, moved behind me, and dug his fingers into the muscles on either side of my neck. "You've already answered the call, son. Just write to Taryn so you can get on with your task."

My head lolled as he kneaded my shoulders. "But will she understand? And forgive?"

"Only God knows," Alastor said. "You must do what you must do regardless. If she does not, will your course change? Will you not follow your calling?"

I covered my face with my hands and wept as the man I hoped would become my father-in-law prayed for me.

I took a stool and table to my sleeping area, found fresh parchments and a quill, and filled both an inkwell and a lamp. I was puzzled when Alastor left the tent, until he returned shortly with a digging tool. "Don't make an old man do this work for you," he said. "And do it now, before you begin writing."

I nodded, resigned. It wouldn't take long to dig a hole large enough to store my parchments. "Can I trouble you to find me a dry hide?" I said. "A square yard or so should be all I need."

I had dug a two-foot square by the time he returned. My parchments would stay clean and dry wrapped in the hide if I could find a suitable covering when I finished my letter. "I must hurry," I said. "I fish tonight and am on watch tomorrow night."

"Oh, no, I'm sorry, Paul. I was to tell you that you have been relieved of both obligations for the time being."

"I have?"

He nodded. "The entire compound knows who you are—who you were. Do you suppose anyone does not worry about the implications?"

"But they know me, Alastor! I have been here nearly three years!"

"Most know you. But many don't. Not really. When you arrived we had how many tents—a dozen?"

"Nine. I repaired them all."

"You see? We're at two dozen now. That new family, with the prematurely balding husband—"

"The dark one everyone says looks like me, except for that missing little finger on his left hand."

"Yes, Brunon. He will take your place fishing and on watch."

"And I am under suspicion."

Alastor shrugged. "Among many, certainly. Naturally."

"So my persecution has begun."

The rabbi grunted. "If that is the worst you ever face, consider yourself fortunate. I doubt the suspicion of those in this little enclave is what the Lord has been warning you about. Now get to work."

My precious Taryn,

I hesitate to employ that endearing term I have felt bold enough to use only recently with you, knowing what you must be thinking of me just now. Yet you are precious to me.

I can only assure you, beloved, that anything you read in my parchments is the truth. For all the sins of my former life, dishonesty was not among them. That is of little virtue, for you now well know the depth of my depravity. But to whatever extent I knew myself, I was truthful to the point of offense. Many suffered under my self-righteous judgments.

But as God is my witness, where my journal first records my morbid connection to you, that is precisely when I became aware of it. And my anguish over keeping it from you is, if anything, muted in that account. I pleaded with the Lord to know when and how to reveal it to you, and further, how to explain the delay.

My most wretched fear is that even if you can somehow absolve me of my guilt, you could not abide sharing a life with me without it daily defiling me in your mind's eye.

I can do nothing but leave that to you and to God.

Taryn, I plead with you to understand me. Entirely apart from my unabashed desire for you, strictly from one human being to another, I am without excuse. I am unequivocally guilty. I was wrong. I am sorry, and I beg your forgiveness. My actions robbed you of your loving, godly husband and the father of your child. I undeservedly cast myself upon the sea of your mercy.

Painful as it is to admit, I recognize I am asking something that may be beyond your capacity to bestow. You would be justified to refuse ever to see me again. And while I cannot fathom the desolation of that loss, worse would be missing my last chance to tell you how much I love you.

God has taught me that when I am finally loosed to preach in His name, love must be my sole theme. He has made clear that even if I speak with the tongues of men and of angels, if I don't have love, I will become like sounding brass or a clanging cymbal. And even if I have the gift of prophecy or understand all mysteries and have all knowledge, and though I have enough faith to move mountains, if I don't have love, I am nothing.

Even if I give all my goods to feed the poor and give my body to be burned, if I don't have love, it profits me nothing. Love is long-suffering and kind; love is not envious; love does not boast, is not puffed up, is not rude, does not seek its own way, is not provoked, doesn't think the worst, does not rejoice in sin, but rejoices in the truth.

Love bears all things, believes all things, hopes all things, endures all things. Love never fails.

Prophecies will fail; tongues will cease; knowledge will vanish. When I was a child like Corydon, I spoke as a child, I understood as a child, I thought as a child; but when I became a man, I put away childish things.

There are faith, hope, and love, but the greatest of these is love. And I love you. Forgive me.

Your devoted Paul

As exercised as I had been, getting my thoughts down had put my mind somewhat at ease. I reread the document several times, trying to imagine

Taryn reading it. Would she be eager to receive it, read it immediately, or be busy with Corydon or still too upset? Would her father stay with her, read it as well, discuss it with her?

These were the kinds of things I had never pondered as an official of the Sanhedrin. I had a reputation with Nathanael for tracking every detail of his schedule as vice chief justice of the Sanhedrin, but certainly that never concerned matters of the heart.

Though Alastor had but fewer than seventy feet to walk to deliver the missive, I carefully rolled it and sealed it with wax. I found him tidying my pile of parchments, apparently in preparation for my burying them. They remained facedown as he arranged them in a crisp stack. I was alarmed, however, by his grave expression.

"What is it, Rabbi?"

"Nadav is missing."

Missing? If there was one rule in an encampment of refuge it was that everyone knew where everyone else was at all times. While I enjoyed my solitude from just before dawn until just after midday, not a person over the age of twelve in Yanbu had a doubt about my location. Some may have had to search to find the exact rock outcropping where I stationed myself, but it would never have taken longer than half an hour to fetch me.

"What is Anna saying? He couldn't be far."

"He took a horse, Paul."

"He doesn't own a—"

"He took one of the new men's horses."

"Meeting a caravan? Buying or bartering?"

Alastor shook his head. "This is entirely unlike him. He's always been suspicious, but he understands our rules. He's never been any trouble."

"Anna?"

"Some of the elders are questioning her, and she's crying."

"Because she's frightened, worried? Or because she knows something and is not saying?"

"I fear the latter. But Zuriel will get it out of her."

"You should be there, Alastor. He can be overbearing."

"Perhaps he needs to be."

"Anna and I have always gotten along," I said. "Perhaps I could—"

"Oh, Paul, no! You dare not show your face just now. Many fear this may be about you."

"About me? You don't think—"

"I don't know."

"Nadav hasn't trusted me from the beginning."

"I know. But I'd sooner think he'd rally the others to cast you out than seek help elsewhere that could expose us."

"Rabbi, you need to be there."

"You're right," he said, rising. I must have looked worried about my letter. "I haven't forgotten," he added, reaching for it.

Suddenly, strangely, drowsiness overtook me. With so much on my mind, I couldn't explain it. I had my parchments to bury in the hide Alastor had provided, and now I needed a covering of some sort for the hole I'd dug—while avoiding curious and perhaps hostile eyes. Plus I was desperate to know when Alastor would deliver my message and when Taryn would read it, what she would think, when she would respond, what she would say. And hovering over all this like a fresh storm cloud churned the matter of whatever Nadav was about.

I carried the parchments to my sleeping area and wrapped them snugly in the hide, setting the package deep into the hole. When I ventured outside for something to fill it that would be easy for me to remove each time I wanted to access the pages, I felt as if I were wading in deep water and longed to lie down.

Trying to ignore the raised voices coming from the common area, I perused my workbench, gathering scraps of wood left over from the hide-drying frames I had fashioned. I also collected scraps of hide and fur too small for tent repairs. These nicely camouflaged the hole without making my parchments hard to retrieve. But once I had finished, the fatigue that had begun nagging me now overwhelmed to the point where I could barely move. I made my way to my sleeping mat and sat, hoping the feeling would pass.

My eyes fluttered and closed and I couldn't resist stretching out on my back. I wasn't aware of falling asleep, but I found my mind a mix of everything that had occurred that day, interspersed with the account of Isaiah seeing the Lord on His throne, high and lifted up.

The ambient noise of the camp faded to silence, and suddenly it was just me lying in the stillness, unmoving. No wind, no tent flaps, no footsteps, no animal noises, no conversation, no insects, no birds, no crackling fires, no water sloshing. Nothing.

I felt transported, and though I knew—or believed—I still lay on my cot, it was as if I flew silently through the roof of the tent and into the sky, past the slightest wisps of clouds and toward the sun itself. Yet even my flight created no sound.

Below lay the symmetry of the twenty-four large tents I had built or repaired, hulking black mounds on the desert floor, encircling the common area comprising the well, the livestock pen, the corral. Children played, women talked, men worked, and a crowd, headed by the elders, milled about the entrance to Nadav and Anna's dwelling. How was it possible that the cacophony that had to be rising from all that activity had not reached my sleep chamber—where I had the distinct feeling I still lay? Nor did it reach my ears as I winged my way above the sun, which felt every bit as real.

Had my unexplained weariness been of God for the very purpose of this ethereal journey? Of one thing I was suddenly certain: I was not napping. I did not know then, and neither have I been able to determine since, whether I was in my body or out of it, but this was clearly God's doing. He was transporting me, at least my soul, somewhere to show me something. I was no longer tired, no longer vexed, no longer worried about Taryn or Corydon or Alastor. I did not fret about my calling or the warnings of persecution I would face when He sent me to the Gentiles.

I felt a peace as vast as the heavens.

Wherever God was leading, whatever I was to experience, I sensed it was for my edification and that I would be back with plenty of time to engage again in earthly pursuits. For now, however, they did not matter. Body and soul or just soul, I didn't care, my being now majestically rose above the sun itself. I found myself among the stars, dazzling in their sheer whiteness against the blue blackness of the unending immensity of the heavens.

On I soared, for how long and how far I have no reference point or memory. All I know is that I had transcended the earth and sky where the clouds and sun resided and now fearlessly sailed—I don't know how else to express it—not upon the sea but through the star-strewn inkiness of the heavens. What made me consider that my soul had left my body was that I felt no wind, no heat, and no cold, and in that immeasurable darkness, illumined by only the dazzling orbs, I should have been shivering.

For whatever interlude I spent traversing the colossal canopy of the night skies, I suddenly left it and found myself thrust into a brightness so infinite that no description of its colors could ever do it justice. That I was able even to keep my eyes open against its brilliance was all the evidence I needed to know this was God's domain.

Unable to speak aloud, in my spirit I said, *Lord, what would You have me—*

Be still.

Obedience was the only option.

All I dare say is that I saw a door standing open in paradise, and there before a throne lay a sea of glass like crystal. On the throne sat One more beautiful than precious gems in a rainbow, surrounded by the thrones of many others in white robes and crowns of gold. And I saw lamps of fire and lightning and heard thunder and a voice like a trumpet making utterances in a language I had never heard but that I immediately comprehended to the depths of my soul and knew that I would never be permitted to repeat.

While I have never been tempted to speak of what I heard that day, the mere experience entirely removed from me any semblance of doubt about the existence and nature of God Himself.

Having been granted a glimpse of what awaits those who trust in Christ and His work on the cross for their salvation, I felt fortified for whatever lay ahead—regardless the task, obstacle, or hardship.

How could I worry about things so banal as what might happen to me at the hands of men on earth when I knew what awaited me in heaven? If God Himself was for me, who could be against me? The One who did not spare His own Son but delivered Him up for all of us, how would He not with Jesus also freely give us all things?

Who or what would I ever have to worry about again? Who could separate me from the love of Christ? Could tribulation or distress or persecution or famine or nakedness or peril or sword? In all these things I would be more than a conqueror through Christ who loved me.

Neither death nor life nor angels nor principalities nor powers nor things present nor things to come, nor height nor depth, nor any other created thing, would be able to separate me from the love of God in Christ.

Awestruck, I realized that God's preparation of me was nearly complete, for I no longer feared for my life. I had been willing to be His slave since the day He had found me, but a bondservant unafraid to die for his Lord is a weapon to be reckoned with.

Wherever I was, in whatever form I was, however long I had been gone, and whenever I would return for the task to which I had been called, I felt imbued with unshakeable courage and power. I viewed myself as an eternal being, ready to be used up and poured out in the service of my Lord. To me, to live was Christ, and to die was gain.

I was suddenly back on the mat in my sleeping chamber in Alastor's tent. How long I had lain there, I could not tell. But it was dark, so it had been hours. I smelled food, yet I was not hungry. And all the normal earthy sounds had returned: the wind, tent flaps, sand hitting the walls. Animals. Footsteps. Conversation.

Light from a lamp flickered on the curtain that separated my quarters from the rest of the dwelling, so I assumed Alastor was back. What was the news of Nadav? Anna? Taryn? My letter?

I wanted to rise, to make my way out, but I could not move! Neither could I open my mouth to call out. Somehow this did not alarm me. It all seemed part of the experience God had bestowed upon me. Was I to have no say in my own life anymore? Would He raise and move me at His will? Was that the kind of full surrender He required of me? I was willing, but was it necessary?

I was more curious than worried, but I confess I was relieved when I heard a visitor arrive and recognized Zuriel's voice.

"I trust Nadav more than Paul or Saul or whoever he is, Alastor," he said. "But we must be prudent. I say we amass all our arms and prepare to defend ourselves."

"I don't know," Alastor said. "The strength of our location is also our weakness. We are low so we are hidden. If the Romans know where we are, they know the force required to overwhelm us. We would be indefensible."

"Nadav would not do that to us. He may be foolish, but he is not suicidal."

"I don't know what he thinks he's doing," Alastor said. "But he has never trusted Paul and no doubt thinks he is doing the right thing."

"By doing what? If he wants Paul out, he should have brought the matter to the rest of us for a vote. He might have been surprised at the support he found."

"Not from me," Alastor said.

"Even now, Rabbi? If you're still for him, you'd be opposed by your own daughter."

That pierced me. Did Zuriel know that, and was it indeed Taryn's sentiment even after reading my letter? *Lord, spare me this torment so that I may serve You unfettered.*

My grace is sufficient. My strength is made perfect in weakness.

Was I to boast in my infirmity that the power of Christ would be manifest in me? Would this lost love, this reproach, be part of the persecution, the distress I would suffer for His sake? I prayed not.

My grace is sufficient.

From the other side of the curtain Alastor and Zuriel agreed that three watchmen be assigned that night. Zuriel left, saying, "I would have one keep an eye on Anna. She knows more than she is saying."

Alastor's silhouette filled the entrance to my sleeping area and he whispered, "Are you awake?"

I still could not speak, and apparently in the darkness he could not see me staring wide-eyed at him. But perhaps he detected a difference in my breathing, for he moved into the main area and soon returned and hovered over me with a lamp, lighting my face.

"Are you all right, my friend?" I was relieved to realize I was not totally paralyzed, for I was able to press my lips together and make a face at him. He quickly set the light down and helped me sit up. "Can you speak?" I shook my head. "Are you ill?" I shook my head again. "Just mute," he muttered. "I'll get you some broth."

I wanted to decline, as I was still not hungry, but I needed his company. He rushed back in and handed me the bowl and a chunk of bread. When I did not reach for it, he asked, "Are you paralyzed, too?" I tried to affect an apologetic expression but am afraid I looked merely sheepish. He sat and fed me, dipping cold, dry bread in the tepid soup.

I chewed slowly, breathing deeply, not nearly as concerned as Alastor looked. I was certain I was feeling the aftereffects of my encounter with the Lord, which I did not feel at liberty to talk about, even if I had found my voice. I was, however, desperate to know how things had gone with Taryn.

Yet when words came, accompanied by deep emotion, I was as surprised as Alastor by what I said. "I miss the boy."

The old rabbi laughed heartily and set the food aside. He embraced me and said, "So do I! And he asked about you."

"What did you tell him?"

"I didn't know what to say. I looked to his mother. I didn't want to make promises I couldn't keep. Taryn just shrugged. Now what is the matter with you? Why couldn't you talk, and why couldn't you move?"

"I don't know, Alastor. After I buried my parchments, a great weariness overtook me."

"When I returned you were sound asleep and slept for hours. I worried about you, but you must have needed it." He lifted my hands and flexed my arms. "Do you feel that? Can you push against me?"

"I can feel your touch, but it is as if I have been drained of all strength."

"The food will be good for you, but if you can stand, you should. We should take a walk before you sleep again."

"Give me a few more moments."

Alastor told me of the increased security and of the failure to coax any more information from Anna. "Some speculate that Nadav is giving us away. Others, myself included, give him more credit. He would never do such a thing, especially with his own family to think about."

"Then where do you think he is?"

"Trading, buying, I don't know. But he will be removed from eldership upon his return, regardless the reason. He has taken a reckless course of action. Even if he had a valid reason, going without telling anyone is inexcusable. It's a bad example to the newcomers. We must have discipline or we'll have anarchy, and then all will be lost."

I felt tingling in my legs and the urge to stand, so I asked Alastor to help me. Though I was wobbly, we were able to make our way to the common area, where more people than usual were out after dark in small groups. They fell silent and stared, some glowering as we passed on our way to the easement area. Alastor hung back and faced the camp as I relieved myself and rejoined him.

By the time we reached the flickering ring of light from the torches, I had full use of my limbs and felt better, though inside I still glowed from my vision. I had to write of it before I slept again, and I looked forward to the next morning's fellowship with God.

I was saddened as we passed Zuriel's tent, knowing Taryn and Corydon were within. "Do you know whether she has read—"

"I merely gave it to her, Paul." Alastor said. "I didn't press her."

"She knew it was from me?"

He looked at me in the low light as if I'd asked a ridiculous question. "Who else would be writing her? You are the only person here who can't approach her."

"Of course."

"And I'm sure she saw your mark."

"She examined it?"

"I didn't mean to imply that."

"You didn't see her break the seal?"

"Paul, please. If you must know, I saw her *not* break the seal. She set it aside."

"She didn't discard it."

"She did not. But now you know as much as I do, so you may stop asking."

"I apologize."

"I understand your curiosity, but this is between the two of you and I'd rather not become the mediator."

"May I trouble you for one more answer?"

Alastor stopped between our tent and the one next to it and sighed. "One."

"Did she fix our supper tonight?"

"In a manner of speaking."

"She did?"

"That's two."

"Yes, but I mean, did—"

"She and Kaia baked this afternoon, and she sent me home with a bit. There was enough for you, though she didn't make it obvious she had done that on purpose."

"But you think she did?"

"I did not think about it."

"Think about it."

"I don't think she thought about it either. She's been in the habit of cooking for four, and there was plenty."

Inside the tent he lit a lamp. "I'm ready to retire. You slept much of the afternoon."

"I won't be up long. I will have to find something to eat before I leave in the morning."

"No." Alastor pulled the curtain aside and pointed to a basket of grapes and a damp cloth. He pulled aside a corner of it to reveal a lump of dough. "The bread can be fried quickly atop the oven there."

"She sent that for me?"

"I did not say that. And neither did she."

"But clearly—"

"Don't make more of it than it is, Paul. Assume she's looking out for me."

"You can think what you want, Alastor. And I will think what I want."

"I'm sure you will."

I wrote for an hour, doused the lamp, slept more soundly than I expected, then before dawn proved less of a baker than even I expected. But telling myself the breakfast was a gift from a woman who could have entirely shunned me, I enjoyed the light repast nonetheless and headed out.

All three watchmen made a point of stopping and questioning me, and it was obvious they had conspired to delay me this way. They all asked the same questions and warned me of the same dire consequences if I were to betray the trust of the commune. I felt the color rise in my neck, and my old nature made me want to lash out and resort to condescension and sarcasm to show them they didn't even have the intelligence to insult me properly. But I refrained, praying silently that God would give me the strength to stake out the higher ground.

I was nearly to the easement area when I turned back and approached the third watchman who had stopped me. "Was there an incident?" I said.

"An incident?"

"Did something happen in the night? I'm just curious why all of you felt it necessary to interrogate me."

He eyed me in the faint light of the gathering dawn. "It happens that there was. What do you know of it?"

"Nothing. I just want to give you the benefit of the doubt."

"We need no benefit, sir. We take seriously the well-being of this camp and don't apologize for being vigilant."

"Nor should you. What happened?"

He hesitated, and was joined by another watchman, and told him, "He wants to know why we're being so cautious."

"I wouldn't wonder."

They seemed to look at each other knowingly and the second man shrugged. "Tell him. If he's part of it, he'll live to regret it. Or die."

"Think about it, brothers. If I meant this place harm, I could have accomplished that long ago. I assure you, I'm part of nothing but you."

The first beckoned me off to the side with a nod. "You know we've got a man unaccounted for."

"I heard."

"He was supposed to be fishing last night."

"Right. So was I."

"Brunon replaced you. No one replaced Nadav."

"Oh?"

"The party fished by the light of the moon."

"As usual," I said.

"They were watched."

I flinched. "By whom?"

"Four on horseback."

Again? My mind traveled back to my first night fishing when we'd heard a small contingent of Roman soldiers mention General Decimus Calidius Balbus.

"No one travels the trade route by night," I said.

"Zuriel kept them in the water till late. He made them all act as if they hadn't seen the horsemen, and they just waited them out. They couldn't risk leading them back here. If they were caravan guards, they had to assume our fishermen were local Bedouins and lost interest."

"There are no local Bedouins," I said.

"You and I know that. They don't. Guards would be just looking out for their own. But what if they were Roman soldiers again?"

"What are the chances?"

The man cocked his head at me. "For all we know, they could be here looking for you. Put up to it for some reward by the man we can't account for."

I shook my head. "Now you're inventing stories."

"Do you have a better idea?"

"Why would he risk his own family, leading the Romans to us?"

"Maybe sparing his family is part of his price."

"Nadav has to return," I said, "if for no other reason than to gather his wife and children."

"He's lost face here, man, lost trust. Who's to say what the elders will do with him, to him, what the rest of us will do? Most of us barely escaped our homes with our lives as it is. How dare he expose us to such danger again?"

"On the other hand," I said, "we can't hide from the world out here forever, can we? How will the world ever hear the good news that way?"

"They don't want to hear the good news! Look what they did to Jesus. And to Stephen. And the authorities in Jerusalem have flogged the apostles and thrown them in jail, threatened with worse."

"But Jesus told us to go into all the world and preach the gospel and make disciples, baptizing them in His name."

The watchmen looked at each other, then at me. "How do you know this?"

I could not tell him that Jesus Himself had told me.

"Is this not just a temporary outpost?" I said. "A place to heal and grow so you can—"

"No! It is a place of refuge! I don't believe God expects us to risk our lives again. This is where He has chosen to protect us."

"Oh, my brother, don't you want the world to know of Jesus? He is alive! He is risen! He is the Savior! Every day we are here we must be preparing to leave, to take His message—"

"Feel free, Paul! If you have a death wish, *you* go, and go with my blessing."

The sky was growing lighter and I did not want to delay any longer. The Lord reminded me I would face much worse opposition than this when representing Him to the Gentiles, and He also impressed upon me that my time to leave Yanbu was imminent.

My greatest desire was to reunite with my love, to put behind us the misery that had come between us. I wanted to make Taryn my wife, to have a companion and helpmeet, to adopt her son and make her father my father-in-law and official counselor in the things of God. It would not be an easy life, I knew that. But imagine the things God could do, Jesus could accomplish, what could be done in the name of the kingdom through us if we were together.

I could hardly wait to get to the place of solitude.

11

ASSIGNED

YANBU

THE MESSAGE JESUS SHARED with me that day in the wilderness took less time than my walk to the plateau.

The ministry I am entrusting to you will be birthed soon, not in joy but in pain. Under persecution and tribulation, the mystery hidden from generations I have revealed to My saints, you will make known among the Gentiles. The riches of this mystery are the hope of glory. Warn everyone, teach everyone that you may present them perfect before God only through Me.

By the deeds of the law no flesh can be justified in God's sight, for the law reveals only the knowledge of sin. As my servant and a steward of the mysteries of God, you are required to be found faithful. You will both hunger and thirst, be poorly clothed, beaten, and homeless. But being reviled, bless; being persecuted, endure; being defamed, preach.

For My Father's kingdom is not in word but in power. Woe to you if you

do not preach My gospel. For I am entrusting you with a stewardship. Make of
yourself a servant to all that you might win more. Become all things to all men
that you might by all means save some. Do this for My gospel's sake.

Those who run in a race all run, but only one receives the prize. Run in
such a way that you may win it. Do it to obtain an imperishable crown. Run
with certainty.

Blessed be God My Father, the Author of mercy, who will comfort you in
all your tribulation so you may comfort those in any trouble.

I had gone to the rock looking for direction, for marching orders, and for solace for my soul in the midst of my own turmoil. Rather I was admonished and reminded that God would reassure me so I could reassure others. It wasn't what I expected, but He always knew better.

Somehow I anticipated coming back to some degree of encouraging news. Might Nadav have returned with a reasonable explanation of his whereabouts? Or could Taryn have realized I had been thrust into an impossible quandary no mortal could have navigated? Perhaps God Himself had visited her and bestowed upon her some supernatural grace to cope with the situation. Or perchance I would happen upon Corydon, so overjoyed to reconnect with me that his very bliss would soften his mother's heart toward me. I even imagined Alastor had become my advocate, my distress and the sincerity of my heart causing him to champion my cause and persuade his daughter I was a worthy suitor.

Alas, I had missed the mark on every count. The camp dwellers were no more hospitable than they had been the day before. I faced the same tight-lipped expressions and sentry stances, no sight of the object of my adoration or the youngster I missed almost as painfully, and not even the welcome of the one man who stood by me.

Nadav was still missing and Anna had donned a veil, apparently to hide a devastated visage. But nothing could cover the redness of her tormented eyes. She confined her children to the limited area in front of her tent and had taken to decorating her dwelling with a bewildering collection of mismatched swatches of colored cloth bearing images of eagles and dragons.

Anna explained she just wanted it to look nice "for Nadav upon his return."

Maddeningly, Alastor volunteered nothing when I arrived, nor after we had worked together almost all afternoon. Finally I had to ask, and I couldn't hide the anger in my tone. "At least tell me the seal has been broken and there's some evidence she has read my letter."

"I wish I could," he said, shrugging. "I haven't seen it since I gave it to her. I don't know where she put it."

"Or even whether she still has it?"

"That either."

"And you haven't asked."

"No, Paul," he said evenly, as if speaking to Corydon. "I haven't asked and I will not. It is not my concern."

"Well, *I* can't ask her, Alastor! I am not allowed even to see her. Can you tell me whether she is all right?"

"She's fine."

"Does she ever leave the tent?"

"She walks with me in the morning."

"When I am away from the compound. And the boy. How is the boy?"

"He misses you, asks for you."

"You could have told me that."

"I just did."

"You know what I mean."

"I don't want to encourage you unnecessarily, Paul."

"Why? What does Taryn say when Corydon asks about me?"

"I told you, I'm not going to do this."

"Just tell me what she says!"

I had pushed him too far, had taken my frustration out on the innocent party. The rabbi shoved his equipment and work pieces aside and stood. "I should start planning our evening meal."

"Alastor, I'm sorry. Forgive me. It's not your fault. I am at the end of myself."

He moved toward the tent, then stopped and turned. "The truth is, Taryn usually says nothing. Sometimes she weeps. Sometimes she looks angry. Sometimes she shakes her head and tells Corydon to stop asking. To her credit, she does not say anything bad about you."

"I suppose that's something to hold onto. Does she think of me at mealtimes? Ask about me?"

Alastor shook his head. "She sends food and tells me how to prepare it. She keeps it simple, knowing I am not the cook she is."

"You don't need to tell me that."

"Oh! A dagger to my heart."

I waved him off and tried to smile. How could a man who heard the voice of God every day and sat on the cusp of a divine appointment find himself so upset by the things of this world? *Forgive me, Lord*, I said silently.

The next three days were indistinguishable from each other, to the point I was convinced that I was losing my sanity. Even my optimism on the way to the wilderness was the same. The brevity of the Lord's message.

The eagerness to get back, knowing, just knowing this was the day things would change for the better. And being wrong.

I began to despair that Taryn would ever budge. I realized I may have actually lost her to my future. I did not understand why. Why would God have allowed this, brought me to her, let me fall so deeply in love with her, envision all the possibilities, only to see my hopes dashed? No one could concoct a test like the King of kings, and if that's what this was, I wanted desperately to prove worthy. But if He determined my success by whether I survived this wretched disappointment as a better man, I was going to be an utter failure.

Then, a glimmer of hope.

My morning in the wilderness seemed to portend I was close to the end of my preparation. The Lord intensified His admonitions as my time with Him grew shorter but more urgent.

In all things commend yourself as a minister of My Father. With patience, in tribulation, distress, in prison, tumult, labor, sleeplessness, and fasting, with purity, knowledge, longsuffering, kindness, by My Holy Spirit, love, the word of truth, the power of God, and the armor of righteousness, you will be both honored and dishonored.

You are the temple of the living God. Cleanse yourself from all filthiness of the flesh and spirit, perfecting holiness in the fear of God. Wrong no one, corrupt no one, cheat no one. Godly sorrow produces repentance leading to salvation, not to be regretted; but the sorrow of the world produces death.

As you abound in faith, in speech, in knowledge, in all diligence, and in love—see that you abound in grace also. For you know that though I was rich, yet for your sake I became poor, that you through My poverty might become rich.

Though you walk in the flesh, you will not war according to the flesh. The weapons of your warfare are not carnal but mighty in My Father for pulling down strongholds, casting down everything that exalts itself against the knowledge of God, bringing every thought into captivity.

Remember that you are not at all inferior to the most eminent apostles. Though you are untrained in speech, you are not untrained in knowledge. Stand ready. Your mission draws nigh.

That last made me hurry once again back to the camp, only to find it the same laconic, tense, edgy place it had been for nearly a week since I had been found out and since Nadav had absconded with one of the horses. It seemed we were on the verge of something, but no one knew what.

An hour into our afternoon's work on that sweltering day, Alastor broke a long silence. "I have something to tell you that I need you to take calmly."

I confess I had to feign control, as my pulse immediately thundered and I curled my hands into fists to hide my shaking. "Very well."

"I have a treat for our evening meal."

I nearly stopped breathing.

"At the twelfth hour I am to go and fetch Corydon—"

I gasped, and Alastor held up a hand. "And he and I will carry back our meal. We will enjoy his company until it is time for me to walk him back for his bedtime."

"Oh, Rabbi."

"Paul, I need not remind you—"

"I promise."

"You promise what?"

"I won't say anything whatsoever about what is going on between his mother and me. I won't ask about her, won't—"

"No, you won't. If you did and it got back to her that—"

"I know."

I was like a child myself the rest of the afternoon, working faster than I had in ages. Despite how much I accomplished, the hours dragged on till sundown, and though it had been only several days since we had been together, missing him must have made me think of him as he looked when he was much younger. For when Corydon finally arrived with his grandfather, gingerly carrying a portion of the evening meal, he looked and sounded and acted much older than I remembered him.

Still, he was not yet seven years old, so Corydon remained the delightful child who enjoyed humor and being teased. To his mother's credit, I could tell by the way he begged me to run down to Zuriel and Kaia's tent that she had kept from him the reasons we were apart. Alastor and I traded off changing the subject or inventing reasons that we needed to stay at his grandfather's tent until it was time for him to return and go to bed, and then why I could not accompany him.

In truth I'd rather have spent the evening with Taryn, but I had missed Corydon, and spending a few hours with him warmed me and even gave me hope—though it deepened my longing for her. When they left and I waited alone for Alastor to return, it was all I could do to talk myself out of running over there and insisting on talking to her. My old self would have done just that and forever ruined any hope of restoring the relationship.

While I was able to keep myself from pestering Alastor for news, I'm afraid I did keep him up. Sleep would elude me, I knew. He told me Corydon regaled his mother with a full account of our evening and all the fun he had with me. But the rabbi did not say how Taryn responded, good or bad, nor did he mention whether she had said anything about my letter.

When Alastor finally excused himself, something broke within me. A great sadness came over my spirit, perhaps because the excitement of the evening was over and, enriching as it had been, nothing had been resolved. Tension hung in the air throughout the camp, and not even I, the man who heard from God every morning, had any notion what lay ahead.

With the heaviness pressing on me, I took a small lamp into my sleeping area. As I removed my mantle and sandals and bent to blow out the flame, God spoke to me.

Tomorrow, when you return to the camp, you will set out for Damascus.

Damascus, Lord?

He never repeated Himself. He never needed to. It wasn't as if I hadn't heard him, or that I would forget.

I trust You, Lord. But in Damascus I preached to Jews.

There are Damascenes who need Me.

Am I no longer sought there?

You will not be there long, and I will protect you.

Yes, Lord. And how will I get there?

Take no purse and no provisions. When you return from the wilderness in the morning, make your way to the trade route. I will provide transport.

In the morning. That meant I would not be on the plateau for long.

Yes, Lord. I didn't really want to know, but I had to ask. *Will I travel alone?*

His silence crushed me. So this was what it meant to be a bondservant of Christ's. At long last I was to fulfill the call for which He had been training me, but I would be denied my greatest earthly dream.

I approached the curtain, behind which lay Alastor's bed. "Are you sleeping, Rabbi?"

"No, Paul. What is it?" I heard him rise. "Are you weeping?"

"I'm sorry. The Lord has told me I am to leave tomorrow."

He sighed heavily and came out to sit with me again, the lamp flickering dimly between us. "We knew this day would come. I will miss you." He bowed his head. "Lord, thank You for Your hand of blessing on Your servant. Set a hedge of protection around him. Go before him. And assign a heavenly host as his rear guard."

"I must write one more page to Taryn," I said. "Would you deliver it while I am in the wilderness in the morning?"

"Of course."

"It requires an answer."

"Oh, Paul, I—"

"I will stop back here to see if she has responded. Then I will take my parchments and go."

"Surely you don't expect her to uproot on such short notice and—"

"That is not the response I seek. Just knowing you will get my message to her will allow me to sleep."

I ventured into the darkness carrying the lamp, found a length of hide with wool still attached to a portion of it, retrieved my awl, some thick thread and needles, and brought all this back inside. In about a half hour I fashioned a shoulder strap that fit over my head, the wool protecting my neck from the leather, and sewed it securely to the hide I'd used to wrap my parchments in the hole near my bed. It would serve as a snug satchel for them now.

Before reburying it, I retrieved a fresh page and a quill and sat to write to Taryn. I began by telling her what I had told her father, simply that by the time she read the message, I would be hearing from the Lord in the wilderness for the last time.

On my way to fulfill God's calling, I will stop by your father's tent to ask him whether you have found it within your heart to forgive me.

Because I will never see you again, I want you to know that I love you with all that is in me and will until the day I die. My deepest desire would have been to ask him for your hand, but I am resigned to the reality that it is too late for that.

With my last words to you forever, I plead only to be forgiven.

Paul

I wish I could report that I slept soundly, given the season of travel that lay before me. God had not promised miraculous transport, so I did not expect the journey I had enjoyed three years before. That He had instructed me to get to the trade route implied He had arranged conventional transportation, and the journey to Damascus could take weeks. I took comfort in the fact that such matters were no longer my concern. I was a slave, and from now on I would merely do what I was told and go where I was directed.

At least an hour before I needed to rise, an unusual wind roused me from a fitful sleep. Had I not crafted the tent walls myself, based on the careful teaching of my father, I believe more of the desert floor would have found its way inside. I allowed myself another half hour before I tiptoed about, cobbling together a light breakfast while trying not to bother Alastor. There would be time for a proper farewell on my last pass through the camp. I prayed it would not be doubly sad. Certainly Taryn would take pity on a man she had once loved, knowing she would have no further obligation to him.

Alastor surprised me, however, when he rose as I was finishing eating.

"Sorry if I woke you," I said.

"No. I just wanted to tell you what a precious few years these have been for me."

"How kind of you to say. But we'll get a few more moments when I get back."

"But in the event you don't hear what you wish to hear . . ."

"Well, thank you."

We embraced and he lay his right hand atop my head.

"The Lord bless you and keep you. The Lord make His face shine upon you and be gracious to you. The Lord lift up His countenance upon you and give you peace."

I nodded as I pulled away, too overcome to speak.

As I made my way through the commons in the predawn blackness, I had to hold the hood of my mantle to keep it from blowing off my head. The sand stung my shins, calves, ankles, hands, and face. Had the way to the plateau not been so familiar, I would not have been able to traverse so far with my eyes shut against the piercing granules.

I realized I must have started out even earlier than I thought when I reached the outcropping and began climbing, only to see the sun still had not appeared on the horizon. When I removed my mantle to spread it over the rock, I had to hold one end with a foot while trying to smooth it with both hands. Finally anchoring it with my body but wishing for more protection from the chilling wind, I stretched out before the Lord.

Now He who established you in Me and has anointed you is God, who has also sealed you and put My Spirit in your heart as a guarantee. God will always lead you to victory in Me, and through you He disseminates the fragrance of His knowledge everywhere. For you are to Him My fragrance among both those who will be saved and among those who will not. To the one you will be the aroma of death, and to the other the aroma of life.

Your sufficiency is from God, who is making you a minister of the new covenant, not of the letter but of the Spirit; for the letter of the law kills, but the Spirit gives life. The ministry of death, engraved on stones, was so glorious that the children of Israel could not look at Moses because of the glory of his countenance, so the ministry of My Spirit will be even more glorious. For if the ministry of condemnation bore glory, the ministry of righteousness will bear even more. When one turns to Me, there is the Spirit, and where the Spirit of the Lord is, there is liberty.

Do not preach yourself but Me, and make yourself My bondservant. For it is My Father who commanded light to shine out of darkness, who has shone in your heart to give the light of the knowledge of the glory of God in My face.

You have your treasure in an earthen vessel so that the excellence of the power may be of My Father and not of you. You will be hard-pressed on every side, yet not crushed; you will be perplexed, but not in despair; persecuted, but not forsaken; struck down, but not destroyed, knowing that He who raised Me will also raise you with Me and will present you with Me.

Therefore do not lose heart. Though your outward man is perishing, your inward man will be renewed. Do not look at things seen, but at things not seen. For things seen are temporary, but things not seen are eternal.

If your earthly house is destroyed, you have a building from God, a house not made with hands, eternal in the heavens. He who has prepared you for this very thing is My Father, who also has given you the Spirit as a guarantee. So be confident, knowing that while you are in the body you are absent from the Lord. Walk by faith, not by sight. Be confident that to be absent from the body is to be present with the Lord.

Therefore make it your aim, whether present or absent, to be pleasing to Him. If anyone is in Me, he is a new creation; old things have passed away; behold, all things have become new.

Now all things are of My Father, who has reconciled you to Himself through Me. Go as My ambassador, as though My Father were pleading through you, imploring on My behalf that people be reconciled to God. For He made Me who knew no sin to be sin for you, that you might become the righteousness of God in Me.

Behold, now is the accepted time; behold, now is the day of salvation.

Now. Today.

Though the wind still blew, the sun had risen. I lay with my eyes closed, one cheek on the cloth covering the rock, the other exposed to the warming rays. My restless night caught up with me and I was loath to move.

I loved this place. It had been sacred since the first day, and I couldn't foresee ever returning. The Lord had faithfully met me here and had taught me so much. There was little one would describe as beauty here, but I would remember all of it, the desolate stretches of sand and rock and the occasional stunning sunrises.

Dared I doze? I knew God would prod me to go if He had arranged transport for me that was passing at a specific hour. My breathing grew even and deep and I enjoyed a few minutes of slumber. But that didn't last long, for something invaded. I started awake. What was it?

I slipped on my mantle and scampered down. As I headed back, a pungent bitterness in the air became stronger with each step. When I reached that point where the camp normally came into view, one mystery was solved but another born.

It was smoke that I smelled, black clouds billowing over the camp. But what had caused the colossal orange balls of flame that fueled it?

12

THE HORROR

YANBU

In my youth I had been an athlete. I had outrun friends and enemies in races short and long, even in contests longer than twenty-six miles, named after the legendary run from Marathon to Athens by the courier Pheidippides to announce the victory of the Greeks over the Persians five hundred years before I was born.

Life in the desert had hardened my body, and I did not feel age had affected me as it had others of my generation. But even had I grown soft over the years, panic propelled me that morning when I lit out for the campsite, my mantle flailing behind me and sand flying as I sprinted into the blinding sun.

Had there been an accident, an unattended oven allowed to over-heat? I'd seen a leg of lamb added to a stew for a special occasion and a trickle of grease drip into the flame, causing a flare-up. In the desert, anything nearby served as parched kindling that could be especially dangerous.

Though I ran within a few feet of my daily path, the wind had blown the sand smooth, leaving no trace of my footsteps. The clearer the conflagration came into view, the more obvious it became that the entire compound was engulfed. *Lord God, spare my friends, spare my loved ones! We can start over, we can rebuild, but save the people!*

As the wind rushed at me, the stench suffocating, I listened in vain for shouts, screams, anything that would tell me someone was still alive. Surely some had been able to flee. Or had this erupted before sunrise, catching all unawares?

What about the animals? No bleats, no shrieks, no cries. Had they been overcome, trapped in their pens?

My calves and thighs knotted and I drove harder with my arms to compensate, forcing myself to suck deeper gulps of air. But the smoke sickened me as I panted and strained to blink the sting from my eyes. Two hundred feet from what had been the ring of twenty-four tents, I wondered how long the blaze could keep building! How much more was left to extinguish?

The heat repelled me, but I forced myself to push ahead, desperate for any sign of life. Where was someone I recognized, anyone I could help? I heard nothing but the roar of flames and the crack of tent poles as they disintegrated.

Now a hundred feet from the inferno I peeled off my mantle and held it before me as a shield, fearing my hair would ignite. My limbs glowed red and I was forced to stop and wave the garment to keep the furnace blast from incinerating me. Finally I draped it over my head and peered through the heat and smoke and steam.

What I saw drove me to my knees among the embers.

This had been no accident.

No one was left.

I would have pleaded with God to make this a nightmare, but blisters rising on my skin were nothing I had ever felt in a dream. I wanted to cover my eyes, to turn away, but I could not. What came into focus so revolted me that I pitched forward onto my hands, squalling like a newborn.

Black vertical constructs scattered across the site, which I had mistaken for the charred last vestiges of tent poles and the larger remnants of hide walls. But they were not that at all. No, all but one of the tents I had built or repaired with my own hands over the last three years had been rendered ashes—mounds of chairs, tables, pottery, and, I feared, bodies, strewn within. Just one dwelling near the middle of the camp, the one decorated with crude dragons and lions, stood unscathed.

These ghastly ragged structures then, what were they?

Hastily erected Roman crosses with bodies hanging from them—every one, I was certain, a man I would recognize. As I knelt, wailing in the firestorm and fearing I would never be able to draw enough air for my next breath, I squinted through gushing tears to make sense of what lay in piles between the crosses in what remained of the makeshift village that had been my home for these few years.

Limbs, torsos. Singly and in bloody heaps. And not just horses, sheep, and goats. *Oh, Lord, no.* Women. Children. Families.

A massacre. Friends, loved ones, fellow believers with whom I had sung and prayed, read Scripture, fished, eaten, played and laughed, argued, wept.

I wished I'd been there. There was nothing I could have done, but I should have died with my brothers and sisters in Christ. Why had God spared me? Why had He sent me away and covered my tracks?

I rocked on all fours, unable to stand. What was I to do? I couldn't leave all these people, these bodies, to rot in the sun. But how could I bury them all? *God, help me!* Beyond the heinousness of it, the scope of the task overwhelmed me. I had to make myself face this, search for anyone who might have survived, someone who could tell me anything.

I struggled to my feet and the blood rushed from my head, making me nearly topple again. The black plumes roiled away and the flames tapered, but the heat was every bit as intense because of the unrelenting sun. With only Nadav and Anna's tent for reference, I moved to where I could turn slowly and take stock of the catastrophe. I had long been a man of action and method, breaking my tasks into manageable steps and approaching them with logic and dispatch. It struck me as sacrilege to treat this odious responsibility the way I would have an assignment from my superior at the Sanhedrin just a few years before, but I knew no other way to maintain my sanity. If I allowed myself an instant more to dwell on the awful reality, I would render myself useless.

The livestock pens and the corral fences were fading embers, the manure piles clumps of white ash. Many animals were smoking carcasses. Others had been hacked to pieces, proving the marauders had brandished long, heavy blades.

The well appeared untouched, its rope intact. I shook out my mantle, rolled it up, stuffed it in the bucket, and lowered it to the water. I pulled it up and wrung it out over my head, then put it on and headed to Nadav's tent, calling for anyone who might be inside. It was empty. Of everything.

Why had none of us understood the significance of Nadav's wife's decorations? He had brought the Romans to find me, but they were not to touch the home that bore images matching those on their own banners and flags. Why he would not have told them I would be in the wilderness, I would never fathom. No surprise, I found no evidence of harm to Nadav or his wife or children or their belongings. Not only were they spared, they were also apparently allowed to escape.

I couldn't help but hope our paths would cross someday.

The wind that had begun before dawn finally dissipated, but the sun strengthened, and soon my mantle was damp from only my sweat. I began the grisly business of checking the victims among the children. Pushing to the recesses of my mind the possibility of finding Corydon or Alastor or, God forbid, my beloved, I carefully studied the clothing and sandals and hair and coloring of the little ones who had been so savagely laid waste. I set my jaw and choked back tears as I recognized the faces of many of Corydon's playmates. I dreaded discovering him.

Between the piles of ashes and rubble where Zuriel and Kaia's tent once stood, I found the big man hanging and wondered how many brave Romans it took to pin him aloft. I would have wagered he made them work until he breathed his last, as that old face bore a dogged expression, even in repose.

I fashioned a teetering stair-step from scraps and found a tool with which I hacked away at the spikes in his hands until the thickset body crumpled and hung awkwardly by his feet. When I finally freed him and he dropped in a heap, I wept afresh at the task ahead. While Zuriel was the biggest of the men I would have to remove from crosses thus, I realized I had underestimated the job and would likely be there till sundown.

Not far from Zuriel's cross was that of a smaller man's, curiously festooned with a garish red drape that must have come from a soldier's uniform. Because this was the only victim thus adorned, I moved close to see who it was and found the dark body decapitated. But from the missing little finger of the left hand, I recognized the new man, Brunon. I couldn't make sense of it.

Determined to retrieve his body later, I could no longer put off the inevitable. While in a search of bodies in that area I found poor Kaia. I confess that when Taryn did not appear among the victims I began to harbor hope that she might have somehow escaped. I knew in my heart of hearts I was only imagining it, but in my despair I clung to the fiction.

Finally I dragged my fragile contraption to what was left of Alastor's tent. I had seen the cross looming nearby and knew it had to bear his cherished frame, but now I had to face the reality of it. The raiders had not even bothered to remove the old man's sandals, and as I stood before his death tree, his feet rested near my chest. I placed my hands gently over them. "Oh, Rabbi," I whispered.

I jumped back when one of his feet twitched, and I stared up at him. His long hair covered much of his face, but he appeared to peer at me between the strands. Had the old man raised an eyebrow?

I dragged my step close and leapt atop it, bringing my head even with the crosspiece. I slung an arm over it to steady myself, but the cross wasn't much more secure than my footstool and I feared everything would come crashing down.

When I finally felt stable I swept the mass of tangled hair from Alastor's face and he squinted up at me, a wheeze coming from deep in his throat. "You're alive!" I said. "Let me get you down!"

"No!" he rasped. "I'm used up. Just hear me, please."

"But you can't breathe! Let me—"

"Paul!" he whispered desperately. "I'm almost gone. Come close. I must tell you."

I repositioned myself so my ear was by his mouth, but I heard nothing. The wheeze had disappeared, and I felt no air from him. *Lord, no*, I whined. *Not now.*

"The general," he breathed at last.

"The general? Yes, what?"

"Decimus something. Saw her. Wanted her."

Decimus Balbus? "Wanted Taryn? Didn't kill her?" He managed a slight nod. "She's safe? Alive?"

"She told him no."

"She what?"

"She said, 'Kill me or take my son, too.'"

"She did? And so he took them both?"

"Took them both."

"Oh, praise God! Good for her!"

"Paul, no! It's a fate worse than death."

"Don't say that. As long as she's alive there's hope for her, and for Corydon. Now let's get you down."

"No. I'm gone. Listen to me."

"There's more?"

"The general mistook Brunon for you."

"Oh, no!"

"Yes. He thinks you're dead."

"Poor Brunon. Alastor, listen. Was it General Decimus Calidius Balbus?"

He nodded, gasping, looking incredulous. "You know him?"

"I know of him."

His death rattle had begun. "Inside tunic. Under my arm."

"What, brother? Which arm? Alastor? Rabbi?"

I pressed my ear to his chest, felt his neck, then his wrist. My dear friend was no more.

I held my cheek against his.

Curious as I was, I would not defile him by searching him as he hung there. I reversed the order I had used to detach Zuriel from the wood and found Alastor much more manageable than the bigger man. I carried him gingerly over my shoulder and gently laid him on the ground near where we had spent so many afternoons together.

I found the small spade I had used to dig the hole for my parchments and took nearly half an hour carving a space in the ground for him. I whispered, "Forgive me, friend" and reached up under his sleeve until I found a torn fragment of parchment that had been rolled and folded.

Hands shaking, I opened it.

Forgiven and loved.
    Taryn

I hung my head and wept.

And the Lord spoke to me.

Bury your friend and make your way to the trade route.

But Lord, all the others . . .

Precious in My sight are the deaths of My saints. Leave them to me.

I laid Alastor's body in the ground and covered it, overwhelmed at the simple truth God had tried to teach me just three days previous. *The ministry I am entrusting to you will be birthed soon, not in joy but in pain.* I thought He meant I would face anger, opposition, hunger, poverty, hardship. But by "pain" He meant pain.

Every time He asked whether I was truly willing to become His bondservant, I had assured Him I was. Fortunately, He had not revealed the full measure of the cost.

I walked tentatively through the rubble of Alastor's tent, the meager furniture but ashes now, pottery shards scattered. Charred hardwood ends of the cherished scrolls were all that was left of the sacred Scriptures.

The covering I had created for the hole in my sleeping area had largely disintegrated, but my hide satchel lay unscathed. I slipped the treasured note from Taryn inside, pulled it over my shoulder by the newly attached strap, and remembered I was to take nothing else—neither money nor provisions. The Romans had rendered that instruction moot.

I was to leave to the Lord the saints who had been ambushed. It didn't feel right, but if I couldn't trust Him with that, with what could I trust Him?

I stepped out front of where I had first seen Taryn just shy of three years before, peeking warily at me over the top of her veil with a protective arm around her son. I had won her, lost her, won her, and now lost her again. With every fiber of my being I longed to search for her to the ends of the earth and exact revenge for the lives of my brothers and sisters from General Balbus—not to mention the betrayer from our midst.

But God reminded me that my course had been set. I was a bondservant, sworn to obey my Master.

Vengeance is Mine, and recompense; his foot shall slip in due time. I will avenge the blood of My servants and render vengeance to My adversaries. I will provide atonement for My land and My people.

Bone-weary and oily with sweat, streaked with soot and empty of tears, I labored up to where Theo had delivered me after the miraculous chase across Arabia three years before. Then I had gazed from the overlook upon the gathering of threadbare tents that comprised Yanbu before being startled by the voice of Alastor. Now I looked out upon the smoking ruins of a putrid necropolis.

I felt the stark tension of knowing I was to leave, to begin the next season of my life, and yet I could barely move. I loved God, trusted Him, believed Him sovereign. It warred against everything in me to question Him, and yet I had to wonder at His purpose for allowing so thorough an annihilation of my previous existence. Why did all these people have to die?

You hate the man who betrayed his friends and neighbors.

Forgive me, I do, Lord. I know I am to pray for my enemies, but it is not within me to pray for Nadav or Anna today.

You hate the man who led this attack.

I do, and I know his name.

Such were you.

I never—

Such were you.

—slaughtered women and children. Crucified men. Torched villages.

Such were you. You persecuted Me. You terrorized the people called by My name. You had them arrested, imprisoned, put to death. You stole husbands and fathers from wives and children. You were looked upon the way you look upon your enemy today. You held the cloaks of those who stoned to death an innocent man. Such were you.

Such was I. Forgive me.

Your sins and iniquities I will remember no more.

Forgive me, Lord.

Your sins and iniquities I will remember no more.

I am unworthy.

As far as the east is from the west, so far has My Father removed your transgressions from you. Now observe as He proves He has surely seen the oppression of His people. And now I command you, as I commanded Moses of old, take your sandals off your feet, for the place where you stand is holy ground.

I pulled the bag over my head and off my shoulder and stepped out of my sandals. The cloudless sky that had been sullied by grimy smoke suddenly darkened and lightning flashed. I went from being as hot as I'd been since arriving in the desert to as cold as I'd ever been and gathered my mantle around my neck, hunching my shoulders.

A single lightning bolt struck the middle of the ravaged camp with such power that the earth shook, and the resounding thunderclap came so quickly it deafened me and a heavy downpour began. It had been so long since I'd seen rain, it startled me as much as the lightning and thunder had, and as I stood there it washed me head to toe, black residue collecting at my feet and floating away.

Part of me wanted to turn and run and never look back, but in another way I hardly wanted to blink. I gazed over the tiny outpost I never would have found, had God Himself not delivered me there. So much had happened in the camp that I found it hard to believe it had been real. As the cool, clear water cascaded down my face, I thought of all the friendships, the prayers, the meals, and the daily meetings with the Lord.

Slowly I sat and lowered my head, my tears mixing with the rain. When the downpour stopped, my body, my tunic, my mantle, even my sandals and parchment bag were clean. I checked the contents and found everything dry, but still I sat weeping until I sobbed.

Why, Lord? Help me understand.

Go.

Must I? I knew the answer, of course. Why did I ask? Would I never learn? But could I not have even a moment to grieve, to mourn what I had lost?

As quickly as the sky had darkened it cleared and the sun reappeared, and within minutes, I was dry, as were my clothes. I sat stunned. As usual, God would not repeat Himself. He had told me to go, and were I to wait much longer, I would be disobedient.

I reached for my sandals and they felt new on my feet, but as I steadied myself, the rock shifted as the entire site below me, the place of my abode for the last three years—crosses, rubble, bodies, everything—folded over and under itself as the earth split, rose, and covered it like a massive lump of dough kneaded by expert hands.

All I could do was sit and watch, mouth agape, as the earthquake came and vanished. Finally I stood, my sandals warm and supple from the sun, and took one last look at the barren plain below.

No one would be able to tell there had ever been anything there but desert sands.

Part Three

SENT

13

SETTING OFF

THE TRADE ROUTE

THE INSTANT I REACHED the Red Sea side of the trade route a dot appeared on the southern horizon to my right. It gradually grew into a slow-moving caravan from India, flanked front, side, and back by black-clad, saber-wielding horsemen who nodded pleasantly at me. The man astride the lead camel did the same and held up a hand, a gesture mirrored by several consecutively behind him until the entire convoy slowly ground to a halt. Dozens of dark-complexioned men and women dismounted, stretched, checked wheels and axles, drank from cisterns, chatted, and studied me with what appeared friendly curiosity.

I realized how bizarre this was. I had seen many a cavalcade in my time and never did one stop at other than a way station. Neither had I seen one interact with a foreign stranger on the route without regarding him with utter suspicion. The normal course would have called for a fore-guard of security horsemen to sprint ahead and ensure the stranger was not a decoy or a distraction to allow renegades to attack the procession.

The guards would interrogate and intimidate the stranger, demanding to know his business, satisfying themselves that he was a legitimate local trader or that he was a trustworthy traveler who could pay his own way for transport. The natural questions they should have posed to me? What was I doing in the middle of nowhere with one small bag, and how was it that I showed no sign of wear from traveling? They had to assume I had just come from bathing in the sea, clothes and all.

But no advance party investigated me, and the rest acted as if they had been expecting me—no doubt because they had been. When God arranges one's passage, He takes care of everything. No one even searched my bag.

I quickly deduced that no one in the entire party spoke any of the languages I knew, yet when the man in charge approached and said something in his own tongue, I immediately knew it meant "Greetings."

I responded in Greek, "Greetings to you, sir. Thank you."

He gestured to the back of the second wagon, piled high with bolts of silk, and spoke again in his own language. God allowed me to intuit that he said, "We have food, wine, water, and a place for you to sleep. Our destination is Anatolia, but we will reach Damascus in forty days. You are welcome."

I bowed and thanked him, and it struck me that my compartment also offered privacy, concealment, and safety in the face of any danger. Well, almost any danger. I didn't know what I would do if we faced a Roman checkpoint. But God had called me and assigned me and sent me. I would rest in Him. What else could I do?

While it was clear the Lord Himself had arranged all this for me, nothing dulled the burden of my heartache, which proved more wearying than I ever could have anticipated. I found myself so wounded by grief at the loss of my dear friends that I worried whether I would find my fervor for the undertaking before me. I had joined the caravan before midday, yet as soon as I secured my satchel and settled behind the tiny partition allotted me, my extremities felt weighed down with a burden so great it was as if I didn't have the power to brush an insect from my face. I leaned against the rough wood of the jostling cart and allowed the squeaking, creaking rhythm of the passage to lull me to sleep.

As I dozed off I pledged I would not allow laziness to consume me, regardless how entitled I felt after a lifetime of industriousness. Though I had been dealt a blow I did not think I could endure, I determined not to allow it to defeat me. As soon as enough sleep restored me, I would begin a walking regimen—up to twenty-five miles day and night for as long as I could endure, until I was delivered to the great walled city from whence I had come. In just over a month's time I would reunite with my brothers and sisters in Damascus as fit as when I had left them and with the color of the sun on my skin.

I awoke when the column of horses, camels, donkeys, and cargo carts and wagons rattled into a way station at what I estimated was ten hours later. Despite feeling refreshed, anguish still hung over me like a cloud, and I suspected it would for a long time. I was ravenous and grateful to see someone had laid beside me a meal while I slept, which, while bland, at least revived me. It also allowed me to make good on my promise not to succumb to sloth on my way to Damascus. I began my walking as soon as the company had finished its business and set out again.

Keeping an eye on the distance markers, I began a log that showed I had walked fifteen miles that first night. And that exertion, along with my sorrow, allowed me to slumber the rest of the night, despite having slept so long earlier.

The next day I added a mile and continued thus until I was walking more than twenty miles a day and feeling better—at least physically.

Also, I was mistaken if I thought God had finished teaching me merely because I had left the wilderness. This rugged passage had a wilderness quality to it, and the Lord chose to speak to me often along the way.

Make known that the gospel you preach is not according to man, for you neither received it from man nor were you taught it, but I revealed it to you.

When I send you back to where you persecuted My Father's church and tried to destroy it, even if many of My own distrust you and refuse to meet with you, I will grant you freedom to speak boldly in My name before you face fierce persecution. But for a fortnight and a day you will also find fellowship with the brethren, including My brother and also the one who denied Me.

I was excited beyond words at the prospect of returning to Jerusalem but couldn't imagine being safe there. Yet if the Lord was telling me I would be there fifteen days, I would go with boldness. And to meet James and Peter! I was eager to tell them what had happened to me, but even more I wanted to hear every detail they could remember about their time with Jesus.

It will be many years before I will again send you to Jerusalem, but then I will send you brothers to help and encourage you in the work.

I had not expected that, fearing that sacrificing Taryn relegated me to a lonely ministry for the rest of my life. I was willing to carry out my assignment as the Lord willed, but how heartening to know of this prospect!

When the caravan was about ten days outside Damascus I found myself more eager than ever to get there. I did not know what the Lord had in store for me, but I longed to reunite with Ananias, Judas, and the others. God had not indicated how long I was to be there before He sent me to

Jerusalem, but He had indicated that Gentiles were in Damascus, so I could only assume my ministry would begin there in some form.

On the road late one evening I was praying for Taryn and Corydon, pleading that the Lord give them peace, somehow impress upon them that I loved them, cared about them, and would exhaust every effort to find them. Had General Balbus forced Taryn to marry him? Did she worry I could not forgive that? How could I withhold such forgiveness when she had forgiven so great an offense from me? I was just grateful their lives had been spared.

The Lord was strangely silent with me on this. I knew He had protected them, and I also knew His priority for me. I could not abandon my calling to search for them, but when and where I was able, I wanted to learn as much as I could about their abductor and also try to somehow get word to Taryn that she was not alone in this world.

The Lord made it clear to me where He wanted my focus.

You have been crucified with Me. You no longer live, but I live in you, and the life you now live in the flesh you live by faith in Me. I loved you and gave Myself for you.

Yes. Yes. Thank you, Lord.

The caravan leader hurried back to me that evening as I walked, and he spoke to me in his own tongue, and again God gave me understanding. The man said his scouts had determined that a contingent of Roman cavalrymen had encamped near the next way station, which the caravan was due to reach at dawn. How he even knew I needed to be warned, I do not know.

"Should I hide under the cargo?" I said.

He shrugged.

I walked till I was exhausted, then stretched out atop the bales of silk. When we finally rolled up to the way station at dawn, I was nearly dozing, yet God had still provided no leading about what I was to do. The enormous caravan was delayed more than an hour as the officious guards questioned every person in the vast party, searching them and picking through the carefully stacked and packed cargo.

The slaves appeared to try to mask their frustration at having to reassemble the mess the Romans made.

Lord, what would You have me say? How will I answer? Do I tell the truth about who I am and where I'm from, where I've been, where I'm going? Unless You tell me otherwise, I have no other plan.

Three Romans reached the great wagon upon which I sat and set about questioning the six slaves assigned to it. Each was asked to show his *professio,* consisting of two small, hinged wooden diptychs bearing his inscribed identification, proving he had been approved by the Empire to traverse this route in an official service capacity. The men had these secured around their necks and carefully guarded. I'd had nothing of the sort since I had fled Damascus. I was curious what the consequences would be when my interlocutor discovered this lack.

But when they finished with the slaves, the guards turned to the cargo—in the case of this wagon the stacks of bolts of silks, upon many of which I sat. The Romans seemed to look through me as if I weren't there. I didn't move. How was this possible? Even the slaves looked wide-eyed. One nudged another and pointed.

The guards spent another ten minutes rummaging through the silk, and when they finished and moved on, I helped the slaves restack it, causing them to shake their heads and laugh. This had not been the first miracle I had witnessed, and I couldn't imagine it would be my last. But it was certainly the strangest.

I found it most interesting that the caravan had no business in Damascus. It had stopped at a way station about six miles south of the city, and as it rolled near the first gate in the middle of the morning, it merely slowed to a stop. No one dismounted. I just grabbed my bag, waved to the leader and to the security horsemen, who barely acknowledged me, and they began their trek again. They had simply been used of God and were now on their way.

Crowds bustled in and out of the city. I hesitated as I approached the gate. Would I be searched, asked for identification or what my business was, whom I was coming to see? Would I be recognized, turned away, arrested?

As I stood there, God Himself filled me with His presence. I felt imbued from on high with a boldness from His throne, and never again would I go anywhere with even an ounce of timidity, let alone fear.

I send you out as a sheep in the midst of wolves. Be wise as a serpent and harmless as a dove. You will be brought before governors and kings for My sake, as a testimony to them and to the Gentiles. But when they deliver you up, do not worry about how or what you should speak. For it will be given to you in that hour what you should speak; for it is not you who speak, but the Spirit of your Father who speaks in you.

God reminded me to hearken to the Scripture I had memorized from my childhood, and it came rushing back to me as if I had read it that very day. *For the Lord will go before you, and the God of Israel will be your rear guard. The Lord is my light and my salvation; whom shall I fear? The Lord is the strength of my life; of whom shall I be afraid?*

I straightened my satchel and strode through the gate, and while guards stood with feet spread and hands on their hips questioning everyone else who entered the city, I walked past, again as if invisible, and headed toward the street called Straight.

14

THE CYPRIOT

DAMASCUS

I CONFESS THAT THE earliest days of my mission were ones of confusion, for I made the mistake many before and after me have made. I tried to understand the unfathomable mind of God. I had long worshiped the intellect, believing things were to be thought through and reasoned out. I enjoyed a conundrum, a puzzle. Eventually, careful study should render any matter logical.

But God refused to allow Himself to be understood.

He would speak to me, instruct me, teach me, train me. He would give me all I needed. He prepared my way before me, as He had by getting me from Damascus to Arabia on Theo's bare back, and from Arabia to Damascus by merely impressing upon traders from India that they were to extend hospitality to a stranger.

Why, then, would He not merely visit the apostles in Jerusalem and tell them of the change in me? He had informed me, weeks before I was to leave Damascus to finally meet them, that they would fear me and most would refuse even to associate with me. He could remedy that. God had proved He could do anything. I did not understand Him.

When I dared ask, He would remind me He had been teaching me about Himself since long before I believed in Him. He would bring to my mind passages from the prophets I had learned as a child, before I could fully comprehend their meaning.

There is no other God besides Me, a just God and a Savior. Look to Me and be saved, all you ends of the earth! For I am God, and there is no other. I have sworn by Myself. The word has gone out of My mouth in righteousness and shall not return, that to Me every knee shall bow, every tongue shall take an oath.

As I strode toward Judas' home, knowing the Lord Himself would have told Ananias to be there as surely as He told him to restore my sight three years before, all I could do was exult, *Oh, the depth of the riches both of Your wisdom and knowledge, my God! How unsearchable are Your judgments and Your ways past finding out! For who has known the mind of my Lord? Who has become Your counselor?*

I knew immediately I should not, in the future, anticipate wherever I went the sort of welcome I received at Judas' home. Surely such warmth was not what God had been warning me about daily in the wilderness, predicting persecution and hardship. For not only was I greeted with affectionate embraces and smiles and even adulation from Judas and Ananias about how healthy I appeared, but the same came from a dozen others of the brothers and sisters I so fondly recalled.

"Wherever God called you was good for you!" Ananias said. "You must tell us about it!"

"Yes! Yes!" the others chorused, but Judas quieted them.

"This is not all of us," he said, taking my bag and expressing surprise that it was all I had brought. "This evening more will join us, including many unbelievers."

"Unbelievers!" I said, unable to hide my excitement.

Judas pointed to Ananias. "This one has been listening to the Lord again."

"It's true," Ananias said. "God told me the time has been accomplished that you are to fulfill His call upon you when He met you on the road."

"I have so much to tell you," I said.

I spent much of the afternoon regaling them with the story of all that had transpired since Ananias and the owners of the home on the wall lowered me to freedom in the basket.

"That couple will be here tonight," Judas said, "along with others from their gathering."

I told of Theo, the ride, the enclave, and the family who took me in—even their relationship to the martyr Stephen. But I did not tell that the widow and I had fallen in love.

I recounted much of what God had taught me and of the precious times in the wilderness. They gasped and wept with me at the account of the betrayal and the massacre, and when I told of the kidnapping of Taryn and Corydon, I shared my vow to track down General Balbus, not that I had any indication from the Lord what I was to do then.

As time drew near for the evening meal, we discussed what I should talk about when the greater group assembled later. I told them I would need time alone with the Lord and that He would guide me, but I had but one message: my own story and how it proved Jesus was the Son of God, the Messiah, the Savior, who died to take away the sins of the world.

Ananias and Judas laid hands on me, and most everyone prayed. Then Ananias pronounced a blessing.

Though more than a month had passed since the deaths of so many of my friends, when I was allowed privacy, grief washed over me anew from retelling the awfulness of that day. I pulled from my bag the precious note from Taryn and through my tears prayed God would allow me to set aside my longing, at least for that evening, for the sake of His glory so I could point my listeners to Him. Mostly I thanked Him for the privilege of speaking in His name.

After a quiet supper we sang hymns and prayed for those who were coming, and after dark they began to appear, singly, in pairs, and in small groups. Old acquaintances tenderly hailed me and cordially introduced me to curious newcomers.

When my hosts were satisfied that all they expected had arrived, Judas introduced me by simply saying that he had a guest who had traveled a long distance because he had something important to say.

As had been my custom when I presented addresses on behalf of the Sanhedrin, I had run through my remarks many times in my mind. It had been years since I'd been nervous before speaking. I had always mastered my topic and knew exactly what I wanted to say and how I wanted to say it.

The last time I'd been in Damascus I had spoken with such passion and fervor that I didn't have the time or inclination to worry about my presentation. Now, especially with unbelievers as part of my audience, I began wishing I had written out my address. But God had told me He would give me utterance, even if I were called before kings and princes.

Still, as Judas was introducing me, I could not calm my heart or slow my breathing. "His name is Paul, and he has a most interesting story."

I smiled and tried to appear at ease, but I was certain I was fooling no one.

"Paul is a much different person today from who he was just a few years ago."

I nodded as I began to rise, but the hem of my tunic caught under one sandal.

"I will let him tell you all about it."

As I stood, my tunic popped from under my foot and I had to hop to keep my balance. Those around me thrust out their hands, either to steady me or to keep me from falling on them, and I laughed at myself. I was embarrassed, but as soon as I faced the thirty or so gathered there, I felt as peaceful and at ease as if I were speaking to the Lord Himself. It struck me that this was a divine assignment, that it had nothing whatever to do with me and everything to do with Jesus. I had one task, to lift up His name.

I would tell my own story, because it was the most direct way to describe who Jesus was and how He could miraculously change a person.

"About three years ago," I said, "I was third in line to the high priest at the Temple in Jerusalem." As I told of having studied under Gamaliel, being a Pharisee of Pharisees, a Roman citizen, and eventually a zealot for God who saw believers in Jesus and followers of The Way as enemies of the one true religion of Israel, something else was going on in my head at the same time.

It had always fascinated me that a person could concentrate so diligently on his speech while thinking of something else entirely, but I didn't expect it to happen when I was preaching. Yet as I was establishing my unique credentials to make the point of what kind of a man God had chosen to bring the message of Christ to both Jew and Gentile, I noticed someone in the room who was clearly out of place.

I knew all the believers, of course—at least I recognized their faces. For one thing, they were Jews I had fellowshipped with in gatherings of followers of The Way after I had been converted. The other guests were strangers—I assumed friends or neighbors, perhaps even fellow attendees of the synagogues of these believers in Jesus. All the while I was speaking,

I carefully kept them in mind and worked to couch my phrases and arguments to best persuade them.

In the back by the wall, directly in the center of the room, sat a man perhaps five years my senior with large, pleasant, gray eyes looking me directly in the face, frequently smiling and nodding at my every point. I wracked my brain to recall how he had been introduced. Joseph, I thought Ananias had said. And I believed he said the man was from Cyprus. Joseph of Cyprus.

What I hadn't noticed until now, however, was that he was a Levite, for I could tell by his attire. What was a Cypriot Levite doing here? He couldn't have been a threat, as Ananias knew him by name.

Every time I looked at him, he raised a brow or appeared even more interested than he had the moment before. I found myself speaking as if to him alone.

My story was dramatic, and I had a flare for eliciting emotion in an audience, so I was careful not to exaggerate my tale. The details had to speak for themselves. I was not the hero of this saga. I reached the point where the young, passionate Stephen had had the gall to challenge the revered Sanhedrin council to their faces about their hypocrisy.

"Imagine their outrage!" I said. "And if *they* weren't insulted, I was insulted for them. How dare he? Who did he think he was, in our house of worship, not even a guest but himself charged with blasphemy, adding more to his offense?"

I took my listeners with me out of the great chamber as I led the venerated men of God against the impudent upstart, stirring them, appealing to their pride, holding their cloaks to make it easy for them to do the right thing.

"But the righteous death of that insurrectionist was not enough for me. If my superiors were impressed with that, I asked for the authority to keep the rest of those charlatans from spreading this heresy! I said, 'Issue me papers, give me men, grant me authority, and send me to Damascus where they're infiltrating the synagogues.'"

I told of the band of choice men awarded me by the high priest himself, "and the documents that allowed me access to every temple in this very city, where I planned to make a spectacle of rousting out every vestige of The Way and its pathetic rebels."

By the time I got to the light blinding me on the road and my horse throwing me to the rocky ground, everyone in the room was with me, especially the newcomers. The Levite's bright eyes shone with tears.

I told of the voice asking why I was persecuting Him, of my asking who He was, of His saying He was Jesus of Nazareth. "In that instant my world changed. I had believed that Jesus was an impostor who was now dead. There was no time to wonder, to question, to make sense of what was happening. Jesus was speaking to me. That light was the light of God, and it permeated my soul.

"I said, 'What shall I do, Lord?'"

And I stopped. Everyone sat waiting. The newcomers, interspersed with their friends, seemed as rapt as the rest. I let the tension hang in the air. Finally I said, "Do you know what Jesus said to me? Do you know?"

Some shook their heads. One said, "What?"

"Jesus said, 'Rise and stand, for I have appeared to you to make you a minister and a witness both of the things which you have seen and of the things which I will yet reveal to you.'

"Can you imagine? Men and women, I was blind! The Lord, the One I had been persecuting, Jesus, the Man who had been put to death on the cross and was now in heaven, told me to rise and stand! What would you do?"

"Rise and stand!" one said.

"Yes, you would!" I said. "And yes, I did! Now, listen to what He said next: 'I will deliver you from the Jewish people'—those are my own, you understand—'as well as from the Gentiles'—can you imagine? Hear this: 'To whom I now send you, to open their eyes, in order to turn them from darkness to light, and from the power of Satan to God, that they may receive forgiveness of sins. Now go into Damascus, and there you will be told all things which are appointed for you to do.'"

I paused again and looked expectantly at everyone. "So I did what any of you would have done. I obeyed." I told them of my three days of blindness, of my encounter with Ananias, of our mutual visions, his restoring my sight and filling me with the Holy Spirit.

"And then I was sent away for three years, where God prepared me to do just what He said he was going to send me to do. And here I am. And here you are. He turned me from darkness to light, and from the power of Satan to God that I might receive forgiveness of sins. That's what I offer you through Christ.

"Jesus died for your sins, was buried, and rose again the third day. Believe on the Lord Jesus Christ, and you will be saved."

My brothers and sisters of The Way wept and prayed. The Levite buried his face in his hands. Several of the new people glared at me. More of them looked terrified. One, sitting at my feet, prostrated himself on the floor and cried out, "I want to be saved!" As I knelt to pray with him another joined us. Several others stormed out.

About half the guests waited until I had finished praying and talking with the two, and then they shook my hand and thanked me before leaving. One said I should be very careful because some who left angry might cause trouble for me. I was not worried for myself, but I didn't want to bring danger upon Judas' home—especially after what my mere presence had brought upon the enclave at Yanbu. I had deliberately caused mayhem to believers before Jesus confronted me. I would spend the rest of my life repenting of that.

The exhilaration of my first experience preaching the gospel after three years in the wilderness was tempered by the fear that the persecution the Lord had predicted for me would be this curse—that I would be the reason many of my beloved friends would die. It was right that I should suffer for the violence I had committed in my former life. Yes, I knew I had been forgiven and that I stood before God innocent because of His grace and mercy and the miracle of the cross. That didn't mean I wouldn't bear the scars of regret and remorse. Families had been destroyed at my hands—even the family of the woman I loved.

But must I now face this prospect, that wherever I went and no matter how faithfully I served, regardless how willing I was to pour myself out in the service of Christ, I would bring upon the households of all I came into contact with the blight of peril, the threat of death? I had been the reason for the bloodbath at Yanbu. Would I now be the cause of the same in Damascus? God forbid! The last thing I wanted was to have to keep a tally, comparing the number lost to the number brought to faith.

Ananias told the new converts they were welcome to come back, and some of the others asked if they could return, too. When they were gone and only the followers of The Way remained, I noticed the Cypriot was still there. "Ananias," I said, "tell me more about your friend."

"Oh, I will," he said. "He's staying at my home tonight. As you are. And you'll be leaving for Jerusalem with him tomorrow."

Was there no end to the surprises? My new life had been one adventure after another, and I couldn't deny that appealed to me. I knew I was headed to Jerusalem, but tomorrow? And with this man? "I thought you said he had come from Cyprus," I said.

"I said he was from there. I sent for him from Jerusalem, where he has been ministering with the apostles."

"You sent for him?"

"Someone has to introduce you to them. They are certainly not about to lend you an ear on my say-so."

"They don't trust you?"

Ananias smiled. "They have been very good to me and to our fledgling churches and gatherings. But we are fairly new to all this, Paul. They heard the stories of what supposedly happened to you here three years ago—"

"Supposedly?"

"Paul, would *you* have believed that story if it hadn't happened to you? God Himself had to convince me. In fact when He told me to come and minister to you, I argued with Him! Can you imagine that? For the first time in my life, the God of Abraham, Isaac, and Jacob speaks to me personally, gives me an assignment, and I take it upon myself to explain to Him why He must have mistaken you for someone else!

"I told Him, 'Lord, I have heard from many how much harm this Saul has done to Your saints in Jerusalem. And here he has authority from the chief priests to capture all who call on Your name.' What kind of a man presumes the Creator needs to be informed of something? And you wonder whether the apostles trust me?"

"But they trust the Cypriot?"

"They have known him longer. He has proved himself." Ananias waved him over. "Joseph! Please!"

He was talking with the couple who had helped me escape Damascus and was apparently quite taken with them. "A basket!" he said, laughing loudly. "Come, you must introduce me."

As Judas busied himself with farewells to the rest of his guests, Ananias made the introductions, and Joseph seemed to enjoy my reunion with the husband and wife. "It sounds as if you owe these people your life," he said as they embraced me.

"I do indeed. Only the Lord knows what would have become of all of us had I been discovered dangling outside their window."

Joseph put a hand on each of their shoulders. "May He reward you richly for your courage and faithfulness."

They thanked him, and the wife said they needed to be going.

"We all should go," Ananias said. "Judas' home has not been his own since early this morning."

Moments later, with thanks all around and yet another eloquent expression of praise from Joseph—this time for Judas—I found myself in a covered two-wheeled, one-horse cart designed for two passengers. With my bag in my lap, I wedged myself between the other two for the ten-minute ride to Ananias' home with neither any idea what lay ahead nor an iota of concern about it. I had resigned myself to the fact that this was to be my lot in life. God would somehow get me where He wanted me, and I would do His bidding.

It wasn't going to be easy. I didn't expect it or need it to be. But there was a certain comfort in the idea that the details were not my concern. All I had to do was be prepared to plead the case for the gospel to anyone who would listen.

Joseph wrestled the skittish mixed breed through the narrow streets to a secluded alley and tied him near a small water trough and bale of hay. Ananias led us into his meager quarters and showed us where we would bed down, then poured us each a cup of wine at a small table with a stub of a candle set in the middle. "I recommend letting that wick determine the length of our discussion about your trip," he said. "It's been a long day for all of us."

15

JOSEPH

THE ROAD FROM DAMASCUS

THERE WAS SOMETHING ABOUT this man. His earnestness made my fatigue melt away. It didn't leave me for long, and I knew I would sleep soundly, in an actual bed for the first time in more than a month. I was indoors and safe in the home of Ananias, whom I knew and trusted. I had been weary with grief and from travel for a long time. Despite that I was healthy from all the walking and invigorated from finally having had the opportunity to preach, much uncertainly lay ahead and could have discouraged me—had it not been for Joseph.

He reached across the table and pulled me to within inches of his face, peering intently into my eyes. "I need to tell you, friend, you have a passion for your message."

"It shows?" I said, smiling.

"It does! I can tell you believe it with all your being."

"Well, my story is true, and who wouldn't believe it when Jesus Himself blocks your path and blinds you with His glory?"

"And this man," Joseph said, releasing me and gesturing toward Ananias, "he is such a loyal friend to you. When he sent for me, telling me of God's work in your life, I came at once. He told me how he had upheld you in prayer every day since you had escaped this city, though he never heard from you in all that time."

"Well, I couldn't—I wanted to send word, but—"

"Oh, I understand! He understands. I'm just saying he's a faithful friend. Now, about our journey. You noticed my horse is young."

"And energetic."

"Unfortunately, he has not learned to pace himself. It took me almost a week to get here, and it takes a mature horse but five days. Regardless, we will have plenty of time to talk. I thought you might like to take the western route around the Sea of Galilee so we could stay a night in Capernaum where the Lord spent so much time."

"I'd love that, Joseph! Did you know Him?"

"Sadly, I did not. I first heard of Him when I was in Jerusalem to observe the Feast of Weeks, but of course by then—"

"Pentecost."

"Yes. By then He was in heaven."

"And Peter and John got into so much trouble. Were you one of the thousands who became followers of The Way that day?"

"I was. I had thought myself devout. And I was! I was a Levite and had traveled all that way at my own expense because of my devotion to God. But like everyone else, I heard the commotion and found this uneducated Judean speaking with such fervor that I had to listen. I knew his language, but all those foreigners somehow miraculously understood him, too! I was astonished! And the more I listened, the more amazing I found it, beyond the miracle of the multitudes understanding in their own tongues. I was persuaded by the logic of the man's argument."

"Tell me what he said, so that I may preach like him."

"You must preach as the Lord directs you," Joseph said. "But I see that our candle is almost gone. Let me just say this, and I will tell you the rest on the road tomorrow: because Peter and the other apostles were speaking in languages so many could understand, and everyone could tell from their dress that they were Judeans, some accused them of being drunk. But Peter assured everyone that neither he nor his friends had been drinking. Then he quoted the prophet Joel to these Jews like myself and finished, saying, 'It shall come to pass that whoever calls on the name of the Lord shall be saved.'"

The flame had disappeared, and in the darkness I grasped Joseph's arm. "You must not stop yet."

"No, not yet," Ananias said. "Another moment, please. I'm not going with you tomorrow."

Joseph laughed. "Peter went on to quote David concerning the Lord, that David had foreseen Him before his face, at his right hand that he would not be shaken. His heart rejoiced, his tongue was glad, his flesh rested in hope."

"Praise God!" I said.

"Peter claimed that David was a prophet, knowing God would raise up the Christ to sit on his own throne, so he was speaking concerning the resurrection of the Christ. Then Peter said, 'This Jesus God has raised up, and we are all witnesses.' Well, my brothers, eyewitnesses are hard to refute! Peter said that God had made Jesus, 'whom you crucified, both Lord and Christ.'

"When I heard that, and I dare say most of those assembled appeared to feel the same, I was wounded deeply in my spirit. I called out to Peter and the rest, 'What shall I do?'

"Peter said, 'Repent, and be baptized in the name of Jesus Christ for the remission of sins, and you shall receive the gift of the Holy Spirit.' He said the promise extended to our children and to all who were afar off, as many as the Lord would call. It took until evening, but about three thousand of us were baptized that day."

I heard Joseph rise. "I must sleep," he said.

How I did not fully awaken I do not understand, but long before dawn I became aware of muffled activity and conversation and most pleasant smells emanating from the alley side of Ananias' home. But the man had provided such comfortable sleeping quarters that I remained immobile, trying to commune with God, allow my body to restore itself for the passage south, and organize my thoughts about how to find Taryn.

As eager as I was to get to Jerusalem and meet men who had known Jesus personally, using my satchel as a pillow with my journal and my treasured note inside, I also found myself yearning to be reunited with my love. I wanted to see her, to hold her, to look into her eyes. I did not want to forget the sound of her voice, her look, her gentle spirit.

And Corydon. What was life like for him? He had to be impressed, moving from a tent in the desert to the home of a Roman general. Would he be confused, or would he have enough memories of his father or grandfather or me to know the value of a man loving God above all else? What a tragedy if he became enamored with militarism or worse, pantheism.

My discomfiture was allayed somewhat by Joseph's consistently cheery disposition, which seemed to pick up where it had left off the night before. He exulted over Ananias' hospitality, his thoughtfulness at having arranged for two ladies of The Way to arrive early to prepare a bountiful breakfast, bake bread, and pack provisions that would feed us throughout our journey.

Joseph lauded our benefactors with all the descriptors he could think of, praising them until their faces were rosy. And before we boarded his cart with the basket of victuals stuck fast between us, he gathered the three in the alley and likely woke the neighbors, saying, "May you continue to live for God in generosity of spirit, setting your minds on His ways, not clinging to the things of this world, but taking up your cross and following Jesus. May God grant you a share in His eternal covenant, and may Christ Himself be proud of you when He returns in glory. Now may the Holy Spirit grant you strength in your faith and lead you in paths of righteousness for His name's sake."

When I offered to drive the horse, Joseph let me know that the very idea offended him. "You are my guest and my passenger. While he is a contentious youngster who tries my patience and my endurance, I will not have you struggling with him even for a few moments when your mind should be on the things of God."

"But so should yours, sir."

He let go of the reins with one hand to gesture, but while he was saying, "I'll not hear another word about it," the young stallion veered off route and had to be yanked back. That served only somehow to amuse Joseph and return him to the subject he had begun the night before.

"I had planned for a festival visit of only a fortnight, as I did every year on my sojourn to Jerusalem, but now I wanted to stay. I had a cousin and an aunt there who had also become believers, and with no family on Cyprus, I sent word back to sell my estate so I could look at settling in Israel, perhaps even in Jerusalem."

"You wanted to work with the apostles?"

"I was willing to do anything for the Lord. And providentially, by the time my land was sold and the money eventually found its way to me, thousands of others had made the same decision. Most had not come from as far away as I, of course, but we all spent our days sitting at the apostles' feet, studying doctrine and fellowshipping, breaking bread, and praying. Not once did anyone doubt the men's calling, because they performed many signs and wonders.

"We new believers shared everything in common, sold our possessions, and divided the money, giving to each other as anyone had need. We were all of one accord, praising God, and the Lord added to His church daily."

"I wish I could have been there."

"But you were there, were you not?" Joseph said.

"I wasn't far away," I said. "I received regular reports of you rabble-rousers."

"Yes, it wasn't long before the authorities took notice of Peter and John. One afternoon at about three o'clock they were entering the Temple for prayer through the Beautiful Gate when they were accosted by the lame man who lay there every day."

"I remember hearing that story. Peter told him he couldn't give him any money but what he had he would give. He told the man to rise up and walk in the name of Jesus Christ of Nazareth, correct?"

"That's the one," Joseph said. "But of course Peter could not just let the work of God speak for itself. I don't think your superiors would have had a case against him if he had just left it alone. But he demanded to know why everybody looked so surprised. He told them that it was through faith in the name of Jesus that this man was made strong. He insisted they repent and be converted so that their sins could be blotted out."

"That's what got back to us at the Sanhedrin and got him into such trouble."

"Yes, he and John were arrested and held till the next day, but many who had heard him believed and the number of believers grew to about five thousand. Were you there the next day when Peter and John were asked by what power or name had they done this?"

"I was there," I said, "when Peter said, 'Jesus Christ of Nazareth, whom you crucified and whom God raised from the dead, by Him this man stands here before you whole. This is the stone that was rejected by you builders, and it has become the chief cornerstone. Nor is there salvation in any other, for there is no other name under heaven given among men by which we must be saved.'"

I told Joseph I had been among the council when they threatened Peter and John and forbade them to speak anymore in Jesus' name. "But Peter and John said, 'Whether it is right in the sight of God to listen to you more than to God, you judge. For we cannot but speak the things which we have seen and heard.'

"We couldn't punish them, because we didn't know what you people would do."

Joseph said, "When Peter and John reported all that the chief priests and elders had said, we praised God."

"That's where they got the courage to defy the Sanhedrin?"

"All I remember, Paul, is that we had a prayer meeting that ended with a believer calling out to God to grant His servants boldness that they may speak His word. And when we had prayed, the place was shaken and we were all filled with the Holy Spirit, and we went from there preaching the word of God with boldness."

When the sun reached its zenith and the horse seemed as thirsty as we were, Joseph reined him in and forced him to walk the last six miles to a way station where we found shade. There he appeared to enjoy a bit of respite from the heat as he was watered, and we sat in a grassy area sharing a loaf of bread and a handful of figs. I dug through the basket to see what else lay in wait for us, thrilled to show Joseph a rich supply of dried fish that looked and smelled delicious. We decided to save it for special suppers as we neared Jerusalem.

Joseph insisted that for the next several hours I tell him all I could remember about my time in Arabia, before he finished his story of Peter and John's exploits. I told him everything. I even showed him Taryn's note to me.

He did not discount my pain or offer any easy solution. He merely comforted me and I became convinced he truly understood my agony. "I can only imagine how desperate you are to know where and how they are. And how it must wear on you to be unable to release her from her captivity."

"How will I ever find out where she is, Joseph?"

"Only God can tell you. What does He say?"

"He tells me His grace is sufficient."

"And so it must be."

Later I buried my head in my hands as the carriage jostled along in the gathering darkness. After a while Joseph stopped the horse and asked me to hold the reins while he relieved himself and got a closer look at a stone marking at the side of the road. When he returned he said, "We're a couple of hours from an inn, if you're up to it. We can get a good rest there and be off at dawn. I estimate we'll reach Capernaum early in the afternoon on the third day."

I told him I imagined the alternative to a couple of more hours of riding was sleeping under the stars, so I would endure if he would continue his story. I was fascinated by what had happened with the crowd I had found so threatening in the days after Jesus' crucifixion. Had someone told me that one day they would be my brothers and sisters in the faith, I would have thought them insane. I never imagined the cult would survive more than a year.

Gamaliel had tried to assure us that if this group was not of God it would die out soon after the death of its leader, as had all similar hero-led movements. But none of the other cults had seen thousands of new adherents join their ranks, especially in the face of such opposition.

The idea that Jesus had risen was a fresh approach, and then to counter demands to produce Him by saying He had floated back to heaven seemed laughable to me. But how to explain this burgeoning growth? Naturally now I knew it was the work of God Himself, but when it happened it was an annoyance that had quickly become a problem—one I thought we had largely solved by executing the popular Stephen.

Now Joseph told me that the more severe the Temple opposition grew, the more the multitude of those who believed became of one heart and one soul. "Every day it seemed that anyone among us who lacked benefitted by someone else who possessed lands or houses, bringing the proceeds of things sold and laying them at the apostles' feet. They in turn distributed to anyone who was in need. I considered it a great privilege to do the same."

"But it seems now you are very close to the apostles, someone they trust and confide in."

"I am humbled to say it is so."

"Because your land was worth so much?"

"Oh, I don't think so. Certainly many gave larger gifts than I."

"Then why you? Are there not others who are as willing to serve as you are?"

"Yes, I believe there are."

"But how many are as close to the Twelve?"

"Paul, I don't know, and I must say, deliberating on this makes me uncomfortable."

"Forgive me, Joseph, but that may be the heart of the matter. Your very humility makes the Twelve trust you."

"If I have anything to offer, being a Levite I do bring a certain knowledge of the Law—"

"But your reputation reaches as far as Damascus. You are the person who has even Peter's ear. He's Cephas, the Rock, the one everyone knows as the leader, the most courageous, the most outspoken. And you are his confidant."

"Well, I don't know . . ."

I laughed. "Ananias doesn't travel to Jerusalem! He hadn't met you! Yet he had heard enough to send for you, and you came. You are held in high esteem, even by the leader of the apostles of Jesus."

"I'm just grateful."

"Joseph, Ananias told someone my story and that I would now like to connect with the apostles. He was told forthrightly that they had heard a similar story and didn't believe a word of it. They believed me a wolf in sheep's clothing."

"That is what I thought, too, Paul. Reports from many outlying areas said our brothers and sisters were being treated as horribly as the followers of The Way had been—by you—in Jerusalem. Why should we not have suspected you?"

"No reason. But then I wonder, why *did* you accept Ananias' invitation to meet me?"

Joseph hesitated and looked away. "I knew none of the apostles would take the time. And I trusted Ananias."

"Why?"

"Because I had heard good things about him. And he said God had told him you were returning. A man of God dare not say something like that if it is not true.

"If you must know the truth, I had my doubts until I met him. When he told me of God's visit, he said it was so reminiscent of the vision he received at the time of your conversion, he knew it was of the Lord. His eyes shone and his face came alive in the very telling of it.

"If I have any spiritual understanding at all, I can tell when a man has had a real encounter with God. It wasn't possible that Ananias was mistaken.

"I couldn't wait to meet you, and I wasn't surprised when you walked through that door. When I heard your own story, I knew Ananias had chosen the right person to persuade Peter to meet with you. Peter does trust me, and if I tell him I believe you, he will give you an audience."

"He will believe me too?"

"I did not say that. But he will see you."

"He will convince the others?"

"You would do well not to assume too much, Paul. Peter may be the leader, but the apostles are not a military unit. Each has a mind of his own. Just because Peter meets with you doesn't mean anyone else will. James, the Lord's brother, probably will. He and Peter are often united."

I didn't tell him the Lord had already told me I would meet James. Naturally my wish was to meet them all.

Two days later, when we pulled into Capernaum, I was immediately intrigued to see that a garrison of Roman soldiers was stationed there. "Don't get any ideas," Joseph said.

"It's too late for that," I said. "I could ask about a campaign in Yanbu, say something about the heroic actions of General Balbus, see if someone might give me an idea where he's located."

"You're not thinking, Paul. No doubt that was a secret raid, and your knowing anything about it would only arouse suspicion. Let's ponder this before you do anything rash. Besides, you know who lives in this town, don't you?"

"Should I?"

"Peter's mother-in-law. Jesus once healed her."

16

RECOGNIZED

CAPERNAUM

I KNEW IT WAS foolhardy to sit out in the late afternoon sun, idly chewing bread and nibbling a fig next to the horse and cart. Joseph had arranged lodging for us in a tiny upstairs alcove at a modest inn, a mere pittance affording us two thin mats, use of the easement area out back, plus half a bale of hay and a few gallons of water for the horse. We were allotted no food or other provisions and agreed to leave the premises before sunrise.

Joseph advised me to make myself scarce till sundown while he set off to ask after people he knew from his association with Peter and James. I had no reason to be disagreeable and certainly not to disrespect my elder, but I had quickly tired of the dark, dank closeness of the diminutive upper chamber, and no other roomers were around at that time of day. So I fished my afternoon snack from the pack, stored the rest in the corner, and found my way back down and out, making the horse my only shade. I tucked my shoulder bag in the carriage, wanting it never far from me. The horse nickered and whipped his tail, probably curious at what I was up to, but eventually he ignored me.

My mind was on Taryn and Corydon and that garrison of soldiers whose colors I could still see near the city gate a quarter mile away. What would be the harm if I moseyed over there and struck up a friendly, curious conversation? I was a Roman citizen. A taxpayer. Of course, I hadn't realized any income for more than three years, so I hadn't contributed to the public till in a long time, but I still had a right to inquire about government services, didn't I? Who knew what I might uncover?

The longer I sat in the waning sun, the more bored I grew, and the more I knew I ought to be praying. What kept me from it, of course, was that I was not at all in the Spirit at that moment. It wasn't that I was obligated to obey Joseph, but I knew in my soul that he had spoken to me from a place of wisdom. And as much as I tried to rationalize and persuade myself otherwise, I was thinking only of myself.

As I had to learn all too often at times like that, the Lord chastened me by speaking to me when I was the least prepared for it.

I have stricken you dumb for a purpose.

You have stricken me dumb? I prayed, forgetting once more that God never repeats Himself. And then, thoughtlessly, as if there were some possibility He didn't mean what He said, I tested Him. I opened my mouth to ask why or for how long, and of course I could emit no sound.

At that moment I espied Joseph being led back toward the inn from the heart of Capernaum by three men who appeared put out with him. They gestured and remonstrated, but they were far enough away that as yet I could hear nothing.

Do not attempt to speak.

I was beginning to understand. Even if I wanted to help Joseph, I was not to get involved. Whatever power of logic or persuasion I might have, God had rendered it useless.

As Joseph and the others drew closer, I began to pick up their voices on the wind. It became clear he was trying to convince them he was innocent, a friend of Peter and his brother, and that he merely wanted to bring greetings from them to Peter's mother-in-law.

"And we're telling you, people saw you arrive in this town with a man who looks like Saul, the Sanhedrin's persecutor of people of The Way."

"No one has seen him for years!" Joseph said. "I don't know what you're talking about."

So the Lord had told him what to say as well! It would be suspicious if I pretended not to hear what was going on, so I finished my food and rubbed my hands together, standing as the men approached. The horse stutter-stepped and swung his head back and forth.

"This man right here!" one said. "Who is this?"

"Why don't you ask him?" Joseph said.

"Because I'm asking you! You tell us you have come from the apostles in Jerusalem, and I'm telling you we think you're up to no good."

"Well, this is my horse and my carriage," Joseph said. "If this were my traveling companion, he would have our provisions packed in it and we would be riding away right now, wouldn't we?"

"Who are you, sir?" the man demanded.

I stared at him.

"Are you deaf?"

I shook my head.

"Are you mute?" another said.

I nodded.

"Are you Saul of Jerusalem?"

I shook my head, perhaps putting too fine a point on the fact that God Himself had told me not to identify myself that way anymore, and walked toward the inn.

"Where are you going? Come back here!"

That caused the horse to stamp and whinny. I looked back to see Joseph give me a furtive glance as he grabbed the reins to steady the horse, and I also noticed no one had followed me. I hurried upstairs and grabbed our food pack, then rushed back down and waited in the shadow by the door.

The men shied away from the edgy horse and one said, "Control that animal!"

That was just what Joseph was waiting for. He leapt into the carriage and snapped a rein, making the steed bolt. The men fell back as the carriage swung around to where I waited. Joseph yanked the reins, causing the horse to rear—which kept the men at bay and gave me time to jump in, the pack in my lap.

The men lit out toward us, but rather than trying to get the horse to race away, Joseph gave the reins a mighty jerk that turned him to face them, clicked his tongue, and snapped the leather again. The young beast bounded straight at the men, forcing them to dive for cover, and we lurched off toward the city gate.

I turned to watch the men slowly rise and dust themselves off. They got what they wanted. They had kept Joseph and me from Peter's mother-in-law, wholly unconvinced we were brothers in Christ.

Joseph kept looking back until we were well down the road again and he was satisfied no one was in pursuit. "The Lord had to intervene there for no good reason," he said finally, shaking his head. "Have you found your voice?"

"I have," I croaked, testing it.

"That cost us, Paul. You know that, don't you?"

"Forgive me, Joseph."

"It wasn't much money, but the coins were not ours to waste. The horse needed rest, as we did. And while I am not your master, clearly I knew best, and you ignored my counsel."

"I'm sorry. Why did they not trust you, Joseph?"

"They suspected me from the moment I got near her home. Naturally they live in fear and must protect her. But I might have been able to talk my way in there had you not been in plain sight."

"You're right."

"Let's just hope word of this doesn't get to Peter before we do. I identified myself, but I had not told him I might try to visit her."

"I would so have enjoyed talking to her about her times with Jesus."

"You have no one but yourself to blame."

I nodded, but I also noticed a twinkle in Joseph's eyes. "You are not still angry with me?"

"I am still disappointed."

"You don't look it."

He looked at me and shook his head. "I am trying to look remorseful, Paul."

"So am I!"

"We behaved shamefully."

I nodded solemnly. "We did. And now we have to travel how far to find lodging?"

"Too far," Joseph said. "We'll be sleeping in the open tonight."

"We deserve it."

"*You* deserve it, Paul. You're the one who still looks like your old self after all these years. Nobody knows or cares what I look like."

We rode in silence a while before I said, "I'm glad those men didn't get hurt. We treated them like enemies, like threats, and they are our brothers."

"I know. I hope someday we will get to meet them again and laugh about this."

"You're a dreamer, Joseph."

Three days later we arrived in Jerusalem near midnight, weary and hungry. Due to the fiasco at Capernaum, we twice had to sleep under the stars, and our food had run out half a day earlier than we expected.

Joseph spent the last hour of the journey praising me for how I had held up on the trip, which I found strange, because the drive in the carriage was faster and easier than the painstaking caravan that had carried me from Arabia to Damascus.

He stopped at a trash heap outside the southeast corner of the city, tied the horse to a rock, and walked me to a smelly area where he pointed out damaged parts of the city wall. "People here got tired of bringing their refuse through the Dung Gate, so they broke through in a couple of places. Some have been repaired, but others have been reopened. If you are careful and stay in the shadows, you can slip through."

"How long has this been in such a state of disrepair?" I said.

"You would know better than I," Joseph said. "I have lived here only a few years and just recently became aware of it. Was it not this way when you lived here?"

"I didn't frequent this part of the city. I knew such squalor existed, but I didn't have to face it."

"Once you get in, find your way to the upper city and wait for me."

Joseph headed west to enter through the Essene Gate, and when we reunited an hour later, he had with him a quiet young man he introduced as his cousin, John Mark. "His mother, Mary, will put us up while we are here."

"How kind."

"I couldn't expect the apostles to let you stay with me just yet," Joseph said. "Mary may not be happy if she recognizes you, but we're family, so . . ."

John Mark sat between us as we rode to his home, and twice I thought I heard him refer to Joseph by another name, but I assumed it was merely a term of endearment. I was stunned when we arrived at the palatial home of Joseph's widowed aunt, a handsome woman not much older than he, who immediately assigned servants to wash our feet and feed us.

Mary, too, referred to Joseph by another name I did not catch, but it was also apparent to me that while she was cordial and polite, she was wary of me. As soon as she had opportunity, she spoke privately to him in low tones. When he returned he asked me for a sheet of parchment and a quill. He scratched out a note and asked John Mark to take it to the disciples. "Unhitch my horse and take him, but beware. He's tired and jumpy."

Joseph showed me where he and I would share a room. "She knows me, doesn't she?" I said.

He nodded. "She also knew the Lord. Would you like to see where He broke bread with the disciples the night He was betrayed?" He led me down the hall to a large room.

I stared, wide-eyed. "Here? She knew Him before you did?"

"She is not happy about your staying in the same house."

"I'm not sure how *I* feel about it, Joseph."

"You must tell her your story."

"In time. I want to tell the apostles first."

We heard fast young footsteps on the stairs. John Mark appeared breathless and shaking his head.

Joseph glanced at me as he whispered, "Excuse us" and led the boy away. He returned a few minutes later, alone. "I'm sorry, Paul. They won't see you."

"But surely if you—"

He held up a hand. "I will talk to Peter."

"Now?"

"Yes, but I cannot leave you here. You will come with me and wait outside. I will see if I can persuade him at least to meet with you since we have come all this way. He is a fair man. I believe I can talk him into hearing you out."

17

THE WATCHMAN

I SHOULD HAVE BEEN exhausted from the last leg of the trip, crawling through the crumbled wall of the city, finding the rendezvous point with Joseph, and meeting his cousin and aunt. But the hospitality in the spacious home had invigorated me, despite Mary's obvious guardedness. Fed, feet washed, and now learning I would sleep not far from where Jesus had dined with His disciples the night He had been betrayed—I could hardly fathom it.

Besides that, nothing could have kept me from the possibility of meeting even one of Jesus' disciples. I had been waiting for this since the day the Master Himself had confronted me on the road to Damascus. How many times had I rehearsed what I would say, what I would ask?

As I followed Joseph downstairs before we headed out, he said, to a secret location in the bowels of the upper city, I heard John Mark arguing with his mother in the parlor where we had been welcomed not a half hour before. He was begging to be allowed to accompany us, but she was having none of it.

"It's already third watch," she said, "and you're going to bed!"

The boy mentioned a name I didn't recognize who, he claimed, said he could go. Mary swung a door open, dark eyes flashing, and confronted Joseph. "Nephew, it is not your place to raise my child! I have enough trouble without you—"

Joseph raised both hands, smiling. "John Mark, save me from this woman! Tell her I said you could go only if it was all right with her!"

"That's what he said," the boy muttered.

"Saved from the gallows!" Joseph chortled, and Mary shook her fist at him.

John Mark trudged toward the stairs. "I never get to make my own decisions."

At the door Joseph turned back. "Aunt Mary, you're the best mother I know."

"No thanks to you."

"You *are*!"

"My sister wasn't a bad mother herself, may she rest in peace. But how many mothers do you know?"

Joseph shrugged.

"Just go."

"I don't know when we'll be back, but we'll have the gateman let us in so he won't have to wake you."

I caught her glance of disapproval. "I appreciate that," she said.

The horse appeared to be dozing. "I hate to wake him," Joseph said.

"I don't mind walking. How far is it?"

"Only a couple of miles. The activity will calm you anyway. You appear too eager."

"I can't deny that."

I even walked too quickly for Joseph's taste. "We're not racing," he said. "There's no profit in getting ahead of me when you don't know where you're going."

"But you're not so much older than I that you should have such a deliberate gait."

"Slow down and let me talk to you about John Mark."

"Do."

"He's a most unusual young man. He may seem typical in how he talks with his mother, but he is in many ways wise beyond his years. Would you believe he has been a counselor to Peter himself?"

"Truly?"

"The lad has never breathed a word of it, to his credit, but Peter told me that during some of his darkest hours, John Mark spoke such peace to his soul that Peter believes he may even have saved his life."

"How so?"

Joseph was a good but not quick storyteller, and I was intrigued by the difference in the man when he was being careful. He kept to the shadows and avoided watchmen with a natural ease that somehow did not make us look suspicious. We merely appeared to be changing sides of the street or turning when our normal course might otherwise have taken us a more noticeable way.

"This is a story for him to tell, but imagine yourself in the days immediately following the death of the Lord. You're grieving, having lost more than your best Friend, but also the Man you believed in with all your heart and soul. You left everything for this person because you were convinced He was the Messiah, the Son of God. You believed—and swore—you would have gone to your grave for Him, and in fact you hacked off a man's ear with his own sword in your zeal to see that no harm came to Him.

"And then, just hours after you had vowed you would never, ever deny Him, you do just that, and not once but three times, exactly as He predicted you would."

I shook my head and sighed. "I had heard that story and found it hard to believe, especially when Peter eventually became the most defiant one, virtually shaking his fist in the face of the high priest and telling him that he would obey God rather than men."

"He denied he even knew Jesus, the third time in the Lord's hearing where He could look into Peter's eyes."

"I would have been suicidal."

"Who wouldn't? But it was more than that, Paul. While many others, particularly before Jesus' resurrection, were sorely disappointed because they had believed Jesus was going to overthrow Roman oppression—and now their hopes were dashed—Peter believed he had lost forever any chance to right his terrible wrong. He had shown himself the worst of cowards, had discovered within himself something so odious he could hardly face it. There was no way to apologize, to repent, to seek forgiveness, to make amends."

"I cannot imagine."

"And John Mark somehow became a balm to his broken spirit."

"He's not an adult yet, Joseph! How young must he have been then?"

"Barely into his teen years, but he had already long loved the Lord and listened to Him. He was a believer. He helped serve the meal the night Judas betrayed Jesus. He followed the men to the Garden of Gethsemane. He saw everything that took place. I dare say that's why he felt he had earned the right to be with us tonight."

"He probably had."

"But my aunt rightly points out that he remains her responsibility," Joseph said.

"What must he have said to Peter?"

"That's between them," Joseph said, then put a finger to his lips. He pointed me to an alleyway, then signaled he would be going across the street to a low-lying building that sat half-underground and emitted dim light from windows at street level.

"This is where John Mark delivered your message earlier?"

He nodded.

"And where you stay?"

"We move around," he whispered, "but more stay here than anywhere else. There are usually about forty of us. You see our watchmen at the corners? They trade off those posts during the night. They will recognize me and allow me to pass. I will tell the closest one that you are my guest in case he notices you, but I will not tell him who you are."

"I understand."

"Do you?"

"Of course, Joseph."

"Do I need to remind you not to attempt what you did in Capernaum?"

"I deserved that."

"God may not strike you dumb again, but I will strike you dead."

"No you won't. You have grown too fond of me."

Joseph smiled and patted my arm. "Perhaps. But that is not true of any of the men across this street. If they even knew I brought you here before Peter had approved you, I would be under as much suspicion as you."

He stole away and paused to speak softly to the watchman, who turned and casually glanced my way. I stayed in the shadows as Joseph moved to the center of the building and disappeared down a short flight of stairs. A sliver of light broadened briefly onto the street as the door opened and closed, and a shiver of excitement rose from my feet to the back of my neck. Was it possible I was moments from meeting an actual friend of Jesus the Christ?

I knew I was of all men most privileged to have once encountered Jesus on the road. And then He had personally taught me His gospel and doctrine daily in the wilderness for three years, once transporting me into the third heaven where I heard holy utterances I dare not repeat. But before this night, the only people I had ever met who had seen Jesus with their own eyes had been the few in Yanbu who had encountered Him briefly.

Alastor had heard Him preach, seen Him heal the sick and give sight to the blind, and feed the multitudes with just a few loaves and some fish.

Taryn had marveled at His tenderness with her baby, whom He had cradled in His arms.

Even the gruff Zuriel had witnessed the Savior's crucifixion.

John Mark and his mother, Mary, had known Jesus, and I longed for the day when I might earn their trust so I could hear their stories.

But to be able to talk with those He had called and surrounded Himself with—the men He had loved and taught during the years He preached and performed wonders throughout this very land—what a privilege! What would they remember? How could they have forgotten a jot or tittle?

On the other hand, it had to have been harrowing for them every day to face danger and threats on their lives. Did that blight their memories, ruin whatever joy attended the adventure of pursuing an unknown future with Him?

My dream that Joseph would simply rush into the headquarters of the apostles and plead his case with Peter, then step out and wave me in, soon faded. As the minutes pooled and became an hour, the watchmen traded corners and the night air grew cool enough to make me fold my arms and hunch my shoulders and walk in place. My emotions shifted.

Hope became frustration and frustration despair. Part of me wanted to take matters into my own hands, to march across the street and announce myself and demand to see Peter. I would tell him that yes, I was who Joseph said I was. I used to be Saul of Tarsus, once served as an operative in the Sanhedrin, proudly led the charge against people just like him. But he could trust me now, and I could explain why.

It made sense that the apostles would suspect me, but why could their own man not get through to them?

I couldn't keep my mind from wandering. Here I was, a man Jesus Himself referred to as an apostle, the thirteenth living man to be called so, and I had become as impulsive as John Mark when his mother forbade him to run off with his cousin in the night. Had I been one of His disciples, would I have been an impetuous one the Lord would have had to harness, to correct in public? There had to have been some reason He had chosen me to be an apostle now. I so wanted to prove worthy.

But was I exhibiting worthiness now, losing my patience in a lonely alley in Jerusalem, creating lofty visions of myself as a close friend of the King of kings? Unable to control my restlessness, I edged into the street where the flickers of distant torches revealed any movement. The watchman immediately lifted his chin at me. When I only stared back, he surreptitiously gestured as if to wave me back into hiding.

What was wrong with me? In spite of myself, I felt my back stiffen, and I refused to comply! I could say this character trait made me the man I was, but it actually made me a monster, one who had led raids against people who were now my beloved brothers and sisters in Christ. This watchman was my fellow warrior in the cause of Christ, and I was making of him an adversary!

He faced me full-on and cocked his head, and I am sure he wondered why the guest of one of the most trusted men he knew would jeopardize the security of the people he was assigned to defend. What was I trying to accomplish?

Maddeningly, I had no idea myself. Some misplaced sense of authority or power? Christ Himself had been teaching me the holiness of humility. What I was doing, I did not understand. What I wanted to do, I did not do, but what I hated, that's what I did. In my flesh dwelt no good thing.

Lord, I prayed silently, desperately, *speak to me.*

Let this mind be in you which is also in Me, who, being in the form of God, did not consider it robbery to be equal with God, but made Myself of no reputation, taking the form of a bondservant, and coming in the likeness of men. And being found in appearance as a man, I humbled Myself and became obedient to the point of death, even the death on the cross. Therefore My Father highly exalted Me and gave Me the name above every name, that at My name every knee should bow, those in heaven, those on earth, and of those under the earth, and every tongue should confess that I am Lord, to the glory of God My Father.

Thank You, Lord, I said, nodding to the watchman and stepping back into the shadows. *Forgive me.*

Moments later the door across the street opened and closed and Joseph appeared, trailed by a shorter, thinner man who appeared younger than I. He wore his mantle hood up and hurried across the street with Joseph. I peered intently in the darkness, eager to know whom I was about to meet.

18

THE BROTHER

JERUSALEM

WITH ONE HAND ON my bag I reached to shake hands with the man Joseph brought into the alley. Joseph plainly tried to cover the awkwardness of the man's ignoring the gesture by gathering me in and saying, "Let's move to where we can talk."

He led me to the center of the alley where it was so dark I could see nothing. "Paul bar Y'honatan of Tarsus, this is James bar Joseph of Nazareth, a brother of Jesus."

I had to force myself to keep from gushing. "I—I—it's an honor."

James' voice was quiet and precise. "I did not intend rudeness, sir, but I reserve the right hand of fellowship for those I know without doubt are my brothers."

"I understand."

"Now then, the hour is late, so let me tell you that Barnabas has told me your story in some detail and—"

"I'm sorry. Forgive me, but who?"

"Barnabas here."

Joseph broke in. "It's a nickname Peter gave me long ago, Paul. No one calls me by anything else anymore. It means—"

"I know my Greek, Joseph, and it fits you. If you're not a 'son of encouragement,' no one is."

"Then please, stop calling me Joseph. I've been meaning to correct you since Damascus."

"It's how you were introduced to me!"

"Well, now you know. James, please continue."

"Paul, you must know that many among us—in fact almost all—find your story stretches the bounds of credulity. You would have us believe you were not seeking God, did not see the error of your ways, and felt no remorse over your atrocious acts against the believers—yet you were converted in an instant and three days later became an enthusiastic advocate of the gospel."

"It's true."

"So you say."

"James, I agree that it sounds preposterous."

"What does not sound so absurd is that not long after you proclaim this astounding message in the synagogues of Damascus, your life is threatened and you are forced to escape. If the former is somehow true, the latter is plausible. But how you claim you got to the enclave in Arabia, again—"

"I know."

"And then, may I say, the three years there of meetings with Jesus and God the Father in the desert, including a vision or perhaps even a visit to heaven—all while followers of The Way were being persecuted throughout the world in the same way you persecuted us before you disappeared . . . Well, you must admit, it sounds like a story invented to cover atrocities."

"I admit that."

"And now here you are, attempting to befriend those of us who knew my Brother intimately. Why should we not fear that your real motive is to infiltrate us?"

"I understand your fear."

"Yet you wish to speak to our leader. To what end?"

"To join you as your brother, to stand alongside you, to risk my life with you in order to propagate the gospel."

"If you are trustworthy, we will know immediately by the absence of the authorities. But if you are not, it will be too late. We will have put our brothers and sisters' lives at risk. How do we weigh such an expensive risk?"

"Seek the Lord."

"We have. He is silent on this."

"Ask me anything. I have learned the Lord's doctrine directly from Him, not from any man. If I were defrauding you, would I really know it? If I were a charlatan I would stumble somewhere, would I not?"

James fell silent, and as tempted as I was to fill the void, I held my tongue. I could hear Joseph's weary breathing and knew I needed to get him back to his aunt's and to bed. But how I wanted to somehow earn the right to speak with Peter that very night.

"Do you know," James said, "that my own brothers and sisters and I did not even believe Jesus was the Christ until near the end?"

I could not stifle a gasp. "And your mother?"

"She knew from before He was born. Gabriel himself told her. She tried to tell us, but we were full of ourselves, so of course we knew better. It wasn't that Jesus had done anything to indicate otherwise, but He made no claims until He left home when He was thirty. There had been occasional mysterious statements about doing His Father's business, like when He was lost for three days at age twelve and was finally found in the Temple confounding the elders. But it was only later, when I saw Him perform miracles, that I could no longer deny the truth."

"Test me, James. Ask me anything."

Again he fell silent. Finally he said, "All right. How were you, how is anyone, saved? What qualifies a person to inherit the kingdom of God?"

I felt as if God imbued me with His Spirit anew and as if I were standing before a crowd to preach, though I dared not raise my voice. I simply stated with confidence and authority, "Salvation came when the kindness and love of God toward man appeared. It's not by works of righteousness we have done but according to His mercy He saved us, through the washing of regeneration and renewing of the Holy Spirit, whom He poured out on us abundantly through Jesus Christ our Savior. Having been justified by His grace we have become heirs according to the hope of eternal life."

In the quietness I detected emotion in James' very breathing. His voice came thick. "Then what about works of righteousness?"

I said, "This is a faithful saying, and these things I affirm constantly: those who have believed should be careful always to do good works, because these are good and profitable. But by grace are we saved through faith. It is the gift of God, not of works, lest any man should boast."

James drew quavery breaths through his nose. Finally he managed, "I extend to you, my brother, not only the right hand of fellowship, but the embrace of a fellow sojourner in the gospel of truth."

The three of us awkwardly grabbed for each other in the dark and hugged tight. At last James said, "I would like to pray for you, Paul," and we knelt. "Father, as I have heard my brother Jude so affectingly put it, 'Now to Him who is able to keep us from stumbling, and to present us faultless before the presence of His glory with exceeding joy, to God our Savior, who alone is wise, be glory and majesty, dominion and power, both now and forever. Amen.'"

We remained kneeling there for many minutes until Joseph finally struggled to his feet. "I need to get some sleep," he said. "I'm sorry, Paul."

"There is no chance of my seeing Peter tonight?"

"No," James said. "He said he would hear my report in the morning, and if I was satisfied he would meet with you tomorrow night."

"Here?"

"No. In fact, you are not to come back here. The other ten have voted not to see you until after he and I have labored with you without incident. You must understand, most of them saw dear friends and loved ones suffer at your hands."

"I pray God will grant me the opportunity to prove my remorse and show that Christ has changed me."

"I believe He will," Joseph said. "Now we must go."

As we made our way back toward the street and I was thanking both men for their patience and trust, I referred to the elder as Joseph again. "No one even remembers his real name anymore, Paul," James said. "You need to resign yourself to it." I promised to try.

The next morning I gained a deep respect for Mary. Rather than simply make herself scarce or make it obvious again that she was upset that her nephew had forced her to play hostess to a man she did not like or trust, she pressed the issue. She said that as soon as we were able, she wanted to hear how our meeting went with the apostles, and because Barnabas had pressed John Mark into service as a courier—and because he knew the men and the situation—she felt he should be in on the discussion as well.

I welcomed the opportunity, and as she arranged for the four of us to talk in private in one of the far reaches of her airy home, I ran through in my mind the best way to open my argument and present my case. I needn't have bothered. This meeting was Mary's idea, and apparently she had thought a lot longer than I had about how it was to proceed.

While she was not unkind, the woman was direct and looked me in the eye as we sat at an ornate wood table. "Sir, as you are a guest, and because my cousin tells me you call yourself my brother in the Lord, I owe it to you to tell you why I have doubts about you."

"Please."

"Of course you know your reputation precedes you. The Lord Jesus was a dear friend of this family. He was treated shamefully by the Sanhedrin, turned over to the Romans, tried and convicted unjustly, and put to death in the most shameful way imaginable." Her voice caught and her eyes filled, but she did not falter. "His death broke our hearts. We missed His promise that He would rise again, but we did not miss His resurrection, because He appeared to many of us, myself included."

"Praise God," I said, knowing I appeared devious but unable to stifle my emotion.

"The persecution, *your* persecution, sir, of those of us who maintained our devotion to the Lord, was vicious and reprehensible. Many people I loved were imprisoned or forced to flee, and you stood by as the husband of one of my best friends was stoned to death."

"You were close to Taryn?"

Mary paled and glanced quickly at Barnabas. "How does he know her name?"

Barnabas raised a hand. "Finish your charges, Aunt Mary, and then give him the opportunity to—"

"I want to know how he knows her name!"

That I loved Taryn was on my lips, but I knew that would ignite a rage. "John Mark," I said softly, "would you do me a favor? I would like my bag from my room, if you would be so kind."

He hurried off as his mother continued. "She was not there the day her beloved was crushed by the rocks thrown by dozens of old cowards while you bravely guarded their coats, but I was. What kind of courage does it take for a mob of white-haired clerics to gang up on a beautiful young husband and the father of a baby—"

"Corydon," I breathed, immediately knowing I shouldn't have.

"He knows the child too!" she railed at Barnabas, arms flailing. "I suppose you know where they are now! And her father? Do you know him?"

"I do."

"Of course you do! The family fled the likes of you, but none of us knows where they went. Will we ever? Did you track them down and kill them as well?"

Barnabas reached across the table and spoke soothingly. "Mary, please. You have made your point and you must let Paul speak. He will explain how he knows Stephen's family. And Paul, set her mind at ease immediately about mother and child."

"I believe they are alive."

"And tell her the truth about Taryn's father."

"Alastor was killed by the Romans."

Mary set her jaw. "And you had nothing to do with that?"

"I was their target."

"You're telling me the Romans were after you."

"Ma'am, believe me, I understand your anger and I also understand your deep love for your friends. Grant me the courtesy of telling you what became of me after I perpetrated those crimes against Jesus and His followers, and I will accede to your wishes as to whether I am welcome in your house for another minute."

For a moment I wondered if she would allow me to proceed. John Mark had returned and slipped me my bag. I pulled from it the scrap of parchment that bore Taryn's note and set it aside while he poured his mother a cup of water. "I am prepared to listen," she said.

Mary sat with her hands folded so tightly her knuckles were white. I gathered from her expression that she would rather have thrown the water in my face and left the room. I told her forthrightly how justified I had felt in orchestrating Stephen's death and how proud I was to become the leading opponent of The Way in the days following Jesus' death. I even recounted my ridiculing what I considered the resurrection fable.

"So we were all lying," she said, "all of us who claimed to have seen Him."

"Let him continue," Barnabas said.

"That's what I believed, Mary. That you were deluded, a cult of conspirators." Then I told her of petitioning the high priest for authority and men to thwart the threat of the burgeoning sect expanding as far as Damascus.

When I got to the brilliant light that threw me from my horse and blinded me, it was clear Mary had moved from enduring my tale to truly listening. She seemed to be with me as I sat in deep remorse at Judas' home on the street called Straight, not eating or drinking for three days. The story of Ananias experiencing the same vision I had seemed to soften her.

She turned to her cousin. "This is the Ananias you know?"

Barnabas nodded.

I told her of the distressed horse, the gatherings of the people of The Way, of visiting the synagogues and amazing the scholars because I knew the Scriptures but argued for Jesus being the Messiah. She seemed to hang on my words when I told of the couple who helped Ananias lower me over the city wall, then the miraculous ride to Arabia on Theo.

I suggested I didn't have to tell all the details of my time in Yanbu, but when I described the old man and the young boy and she saw where the story was going, she said, "Yes! You do!"

So I left nothing out.

I told her even more than I had told Barnabas on the long trip to Jerusalem. Because Mary knew Taryn, I included our first embrace, our first kiss, and the anguish over keeping from her the truth about my involvement with the death of her husband.

In a normal circumstance I might have eliminated many of the horrific details of the slaughter of the innocents. But Mary was a woman who had suffered deep personal pain, who had lost her own husband when her son was young. She had been oppressed and persecuted because she had cast her lot with a Man who claimed to be the Son of God and then proved it by rising from the dead. And she had seen loved ones martyred for their faith.

Mary wept with me as I told of burying Alastor, and finally she dissolved into sobs when I showed her the note from Taryn I had found on the dead man's body. Barnabas and John Mark came around the table to comfort her, and I saved the rest of my story until she had control of her emotions again.

Mary was moved and as confused as I at God's wiping away all traces of Yanbu before I met the caravan. When my account brought her up to the previous night and James' prayer, her transformation was complete.

"I love James," she said. "Everybody does. Peter so depends on him. And don't worry. If James is with you, Peter will be too."

"And you?"

She clouded over again and gently ran her fingers over the parchment before her. "If Taryn is for you, I am too. And you must find them."

I shook my head. "I don't even know where to start."

"That won't stop you."

Barnabas rose. "The Lord has told Paul he will be here fifteen days."

"Oh, no," Mary said. "Is that all?"

I couldn't suppress a smile. "Earlier you didn't want me here at all."

"I didn't know the Lord and one of my best friends had forgiven you. You are welcome in my home anytime you are in Jerusalem."

At ten o'clock that evening, Barnabas and I took the cart about twenty minutes north of the apostles' main headquarters and tied the horse on a street in a quiet neighborhood that appeared to have shut down for the night. We walked two and a half blocks to a dark synagogue, and Barnabas led me around back where he knocked lightly on the door.

When it swung open, a low husky voice said, "Watch your step. I don't want to light the lamp till we're downstairs."

I didn't know how these people lived that way, skulking around in the dark most of the time. I gingerly felt my way down each step, wondering which was the last. When we finally reached the bottom, the air was cool and damp and our host lit a small lamp. There before me, in the flesh, was the man I had seen only from a distance a little more than three years before. The short, stocky fisherman was still muscled from when he'd spent all his daylight hours slinging nets into the Galilee.

He shook my hand without hesitation, apparently James' approval being all he needed. I was surprised by the edge of humor in his tone, a hint of sarcasm a constant just below the surface. He was uneducated but certainly not limited in intellect. "Your reputation is much bigger than you are, isn't it?" he said.

That made me laugh. "I suppose it is. Had me bigger and scarier in your mind, did you?"

"You scared me all right. You terrified a lot of people with the authority of the Sanhedrin behind you. But in person there's something almost charming about you."

"I've never faced that accusation before," I said, and he laughed.

"Well, I've heard your inspiring legend secondhand more than once, but that doesn't mean I don't want it straight from you. I've got all night, so let's have it."

"You really want to take the time?"

"We're going to be spending a lot of time together, Paul. You came here to preach, did you not?"

"I did."

"Then we're going to a place where you will do just that. But I want to know you first. Start from the beginning."

I looked at Barnabas, who merely raised a brow as if I should get used to doing as instructed. So I started my account in Tarsus and took more than an hour to tell it all. Peter proved the best audience I'd ever had, perhaps because I didn't have to convince him I was telling the truth. His face and eyes came alive as he responded to every twist and turn, every surprise and disappointment.

The man flinched and feinted, grunted and groaned, laughed and gasped, "Oh, no!" and "Really?" and "I can hardly believe it!" besides praising God. He even loved the story of my having won over Barnabas' Aunt Mary that morning.

"Isn't she the most amazing woman?" he said. "You never have to wonder what she's thinking! And that boy! He's going to make a great missionary one day."

"Or evangelist," Barnabas said.

"Now, Paul," Peter said, "you say the Lord has indicated you will be with us only a short time. He has not indicated why, but that's all right. Besides James and me and Barnabas here, my brothers are adamant about keeping their distance from you for now. Let's not worry about that either. There is a lot of work for you to do. Two weeks is plenty of time for you to prove yourself so that if the Lord should ever return you to us, the brethren will have forgotten their opposition."

"I'm ready to be put to work."

"I have in mind seeing how you would do, given your background and your fervor, holding forth for the kingdom among the Hellenists."

I glanced at Barnabas and stared at Peter in the low light. The Freedmen? The ones who conspired to have Stephen executed? "Do you know what you're asking?"

"I know exactly what I'm asking."

"You think the other apostles suspect me now, what would they think if I went straight to the same faction who delivered your first martyr to the Sanhedrin, complete with false witnesses?"

"They'll believe you're everything they fear you are—someone trying to infiltrate us."

"And what will that serve?"

"It will prove them right or wrong."

I sat back and studied the man. Had he misled me all this time? Had Peter encouraged me to a place where I could not but fail? "How long do you expect I would last, preaching Christ and Him crucified to the Hellenists?"

"That depends on you, Paul."

"I don't understand."

"Explain to me your calling."

"I have."

"Make me understand it in the simplest terms. What propels you? What sends you out? You preached in Damascus a few times three years ago, then once more a week or so ago. Now you come here, ready to fulfill what you believe is God's call on your life. You had better be able to articulate it if you are to accomplish it in a city where you are widely known as an enemy of the argument you now so enthusiastically espouse."

I found myself unable to hold his gaze, so I studied my hands and considered my words. "I am a prisoner of Christ Jesus," I said. "The dispensation of the grace of God was given to me by revelation. He made known to me the mystery of Christ, which in previous ages was not made known to the sons of men as it has now been revealed by the Spirit to His apostles and prophets.

"I became a minister of His promise in Christ through the gospel, according to the gift of the grace of God given to me by His power. I consider myself less than the least of all the saints, yet this grace was given that I should preach the unsearchable riches of Christ to make all see the fellowship of the mystery, which from the beginning of the ages has been hidden in God who created all things through Jesus Christ. Now the manifold wisdom of God may be made known by the church to the principalities and powers in heavenly places, according to the eternal purpose He accomplished in Christ Jesus our Lord, in whom we have boldness and access with confidence through faith in Him."

"Boldness and access with confidence!" Peter thundered, slamming a fist on the table, making me jump. He grabbed me by the shoulders and pulled me close. "You are not going forth in the power of your own flesh, but in the power of the resurrected Christ! You have nothing to fear but death, which we know is only life eternal!"

"Oh, I long to know Him and the power of His resurrection and the fellowship of His sufferings."

"That's all He asks. Let us do His bidding until He sends us elsewhere. You have long since surrendered your standing before the council, the Sanhedrin, the high priest. You never had any official standing in the government except, as you say, as a citizen. Unless you're mistaken and the horse you called Theo never made it back here, you have a closed account with your former superiors. So while they might be curious about you and take notice that you're back in the city, they have no legal interest in you. You are free to go about your business, and your business is the Lord's work. If you are making yourself accountable to me—"

"And I am."

"Then I have work for you. Tomorrow you venture into the Hellenist Quarter. Preach on the street corner, preach in the market, the square, the amphitheater, the bathhouses. They will argue, they will rage, they will accuse, they will try to shout you down, but stand your ground and preach till they chase you away."

"Am I to go alone?"

"What if you were?"

"I'm willing."

I was offended when Peter laughed. "The Master Himself never sent us out alone," he said. "We always went at least in pairs. Tomorrow the three of us will go. Then it will be you and the Son of Encouragement here. He can make you feel as if your worst address was a gift from heaven."

"Which it had better be," Barnabas said.

19

FLIGHT

JERUSALEM

REFRESHED EXHAUSTION. I KNEW no other way to express it.

Peter's strategy of speaking unbidden in public areas among the Hellenists proved prescient, as their leaders quickly invited Barnabas and me to formal debates, where I became the chief speaker.

My days and nights were full, and at first I felt God must have put in abeyance the persecution I was to endure as I fulfilled my calling to preach the gospel. Since the horror at Yanbu, I had suffered no personal persecution beyond the terrible loss of the family I believed was about to become mine. I could not deny that after my evening prayers I often wept bitterly, unable to do anything about my beloved Taryn and her son, Corydon. This went far beyond missing her touch, her kiss, her love, the sound of her voice, and the future I had believed was ours. I was nearly mad not knowing where she was.

I comforted myself with only the hope that General Balbus, motivated by his lust for her, would not mistreat her or the boy, that he would provide for them and not cast them aside. But what basis for marriage—God forbid—was his mere attraction to Taryn's beauty? And what was to become of her if she could not convince the general she cared for him at all? Would he soon tire of her and move on to his next conquest? Or was she already just one of many? Did he already have a wife and family, and were Taryn and Corydon mere trifles who would prove inconvenient and not worth hiding? Then what?

I prayed God would spare them, see they were, at worst, abandoned somewhere I could find and rescue them. I could look past any indignity to reclaim her.

It was the not knowing that wore on me.

Barnabas' Aunt Mary proved a balm to my spirit, for she had been such a good friend to Taryn that she enjoyed talking about her. And she was older than I so I respected her as a wise counselor.

Every morning for the rest of days I stayed in her home, Mary asked insightful questions of Barnabas and me about our evenings of ministry, and she urged John Mark to ask questions too. She would not allow him to come along, as she agreed with us these were dangerous meetings and that the Greek-speaking Jews may pretend to enjoy the debates with me, but they could not be trusted. "While they smile and compliment you on your knowledge of their language and culture, behind your back they are plotting your demise."

"She's right," Barnabas said. "You have to know they recognize you."

"So much for your nickname," I said.

"Oh, there are many things for which I can easily compliment and encourage you, Paul. And Peter agrees with me. You preach with passion and power, and you stay focused on your message. But he also agrees your time here is providentially limited. You have no friends among these people."

Every day I stopped in the tiny temple where I had first met Peter, making sure it was between services so I could be alone. There, before venturing back into the Hellenist district, I sought the Lord—sometimes with Barnabas, but often just by myself. God always met me. Whether He spoke or not, I sensed His presence and felt settled in my spirit.

Coming out of there one evening on my way to meet up with Barnabas, eight days into my Jerusalem visit, I was intercepted and greeted warmly by James, whom I hadn't seen since that first night.

"I have a suggestion for you," he said. "Are you still convinced the Lord has you here for only a fortnight?"

"Yes, just a week to go."

"You know the Sanhedrin is aware you're in the city."

"It doesn't surprise me."

"Well, it wouldn't surprise me if they've infiltrated these meetings. Why not show you do not fear them? While you never formally resigned your position there, the worst response you can expect is an expression of disappointment for rudeness."

"And I am sorry about that."

"Then say so. Make the first move. Go to Nathanael. Go to Gamaliel."

"Do you think they'd see me?"

"Of course! Out of curiosity if nothing else."

"I treated Gamaliel shamefully. I revered him as my mentor for so many years, and then I ignored his counsel—cavalierly dismissed it, really."

"Do you not think he would want to hear that?"

"And what would I say to Nathanael?"

"You can think of nothing? You were close for many years."

Suddenly the idea of a visit to the Temple Mount began to appeal to me. "I would not care to visit the high priest."

"I would not recommend that either."

That night Barnabas and I debated the Hellenists, and I sensed the tenor changing. Their questions grew sharper, more accusatory. I attempted to keep the focus on the prophecies that pointed to Jesus as the Messiah. This did not mollify them.

The next morning I went straight to the Jerusalem Temple unannounced and asked to see the vice chief justice. A young aide, apparently my replacement, asked the nature of my business.

"My name is Paul, but Rabbi Nathanael knew me as Saul when I worked for him."

The young man blanched. "Y-you, you're Saul?"

I had learned from the Lord the lack of a need to repeat oneself. I merely smiled and he hurried off. He was soon back, beckoning me to follow. On our way to the vice chief justice's familiar chambers, we passed a slow-gaited, white-haired cleric. "Excuse me, Saul, is that you?"

I stopped. "Sir?"

"My name is Nicodemus. I—"

"I remember you, Rabbi."

He pulled me aside and whispered, "Would you have a moment while you're here?"

"Certainly."

"I'll be studying in the catacombs when you're free."

"I'll find you."

Nathanael stood in his doorway squinting and bearing a wry grin. He pointed me to a stool, then excused his aide, who looked quite disappointed. "I wondered whether I would ever see you again, Saul," Nathanael said, settling behind his desk. "I didn't imagine I would. I hear you've joined the other side."

"You're a scholar, Rabbi. If you still study I could show you how Jesus is the Messiah we've awaited for so long."

He held up both palms. "I'm familiar with what The Way believes. You taught me years ago, remember?"

"That was before I knew it was true."

"And now you *know* it's true."

"Beyond doubt."

"How nice for you. All I want to know, Saul, is who delivered that stallion back here from Damascus."

I smiled at him as kindly as I could muster. "My old friend, if you don't care to consider the evidence that Jesus is the Messiah, you'd never believe me about the horse."

"Try me."

"Let me just say he came from a lot farther than Damascus."

Nathanael shrugged. "Your men did say he was still there when they left, and they wouldn't have given a drachma for his chances. Or yours for that matter. I heard you'd gone blind."

"The horse returned from Yanbu by himself."

Nathanael went rigid. As crisp and lucid as he had been, he abruptly sounded as if he needed to clear his throat. "By himself, you say?"

I nodded.

"Yanbu in Arabia?"

"Yes, you know it?"

"I've heard of it."

"Where?"

"I don't recall."

And suddenly I knew why the Lord, through His brother James, had led me here. "Sure you do. That's where you thought the Romans had finally caught up to me." No wonder he thought he'd never see me again.

He affected a look of incomprehension and shook his head.

I stood. "Well, I just came to urge you to study the messianic prophecies."

Nathanael seemed to have somehow gathered himself and remained seated. "Few are as learned in the prophecies as I."

"Oh, I know. The Lord healed my blindness—but no man is so blind as he who will not see."

I left before he had a chance to respond and hurried to see Nicodemus in the subterranean hollows where the council members prayed or studied in private. The old man peered about to be sure no one else was within our hearing, then pulled me inside. "Gamaliel will join us in a few minutes," he said.

"Excellent."

"You know I have been *persona non grata* within the council since my sympathies toward the Lord were made manifest after His death."

"I apologize for my role in their attitude toward you, Rabbi."

"You knew no better, but I pray what I have been hearing about you is true."

"If it is that I now preach Christ, it is true."

"Praise God! But it is more than just a rumor here. You are not safe. You cannot leave today the way you came."

"What do you suggest, sir? I worked here a long time. The secret exits are known to those who would mean me harm."

"Gamaliel and I and a few of the others have learned to be creative."

"Gamaliel was always a voice of reason, but he is fully a Christ follower now?"

"He can speak for himself."

I felt my old rabbi's hands on my shoulders and turned to greet him. "Master, I owe you so many apologies, I don't know where to begin."

"You were following your conscience, my son. Let us leave it all in the past. Now we must get you out of here."

Nicodemus pulled from behind a cabinet a cloth bag containing a thick, dark, hooded robe. "With this you won't need a secret passageway. Leave it with one of the brethren and they'll get it back to us eventually."

I pulled it on over my clothes and even over my bag. It was nearly a foot too long so I gathered it at the waist and tucked the material under a braided sash. "How is it you two have survived?"

"To my shame," Nicodemus said, "my wealth has made me visible enough that if anything happened to me, the public would know. And Gamaliel has been able to maintain his aura of wise neutrality, so these scholars—educated beyond their intelligence—still have not gathered that he has taken a position opposed to theirs."

"Brilliant."

I told them of my joust with Nathanael and asked if the Roman raid on Yanbu was common knowledge among the council. "I'm afraid so," Nicodemus said. "But the rumor about you was mystifying. Everyone knew you had disappeared, but some thought you had been reassigned. Others heard that you had converted. But when news of the attack emerged, some caught wind that you had been the target, while most thought it was just another foray against a faction of The Way."

"I don't know where I'll go from here," I said, "but I'll be gone from Jerusalem in a week. Do you know Barnabas among the brethren?"

"Of course," Gamaliel said.

"Everyone knows him," Nicodemus said.

"If either of you ever happen to become aware of the location of General Decimus Calidius Balbus, who led the assault on Yanbu, could you get it to Barnabas for me?"

"Certainly," Nicodemus said.

"Now go," Gamaliel said, and the two walked me toward a flight of stone stairs. "Just cover your head and look to neither side until you are far from the Mount. And beware, because much of the council remains in league with the Freedmen."

"Peter has assigned me to the Hellenists."

"He has assigned you to certain death, Saul."

"It's Paul now, Rabbi."

We three embraced, and Nicodemus said, "Go in peace with the risen Christ."

Somehow I knew I would never be mature enough to perfectly rest in the Lord and trust that He knew best. That seems a logical place to reach if one simply acknowledges that the One who created heaven and earth and mankind is Lord of all. But though He had clearly told me the number of my days in Jerusalem, as the time drew to a close, I actually began to wonder if God had got it wrong.

Perhaps it was the quality of Barnabas' gift of encouragement that made me prize too highly the progress we seemed to be making with the Hellenists. These were bright, incisive thinkers. Snakes, no doubt, but interesting, exciting men with whom to debate and argue. It seemed they actually listened and heard my arguments. And because God had chosen me for the very reasons that I was educated and erudite, a Roman citizen, a Pharisee and Greek, my old nature reared its ugly head as it was so often wont to do. I began to see myself as important to the potential spiritual development and maturation of these people. The Hellenists had possibilities. God needed me to win them to His cause!

How good it was to feel necessary. The very danger He predicted for me I found invigorating. I was traveling easily in and out of Jerusalem,

speaking boldly, arguing vociferously, preaching Christ, following my calling, and—while I didn't feel particularly persecuted, as I expected I might
and was certainly willing to be—I could only praise God that He had
prepared me the for the task to which He had called me.

After the fourteenth night of my visit, Barnabas had been particularly
encouraging and, I felt, rightly so. The leaders of the Hellenists had been
so taken with the stimulating nature of the deliberations that evening that
they suggested a more ambitious venue for the next meeting. If Barnabas
and I could come deeper into the Hellenist sector, they would arrange
to host the affair at the largest indoor arena available—allowing them to
invite all the interested parties in the area. What an opportunity for the
gospel! What an opportunity for me.

Even Mary and John Mark agreed and prayed fervently for us late the
next afternoon before we left. On our way to the temple to pray, we met
Peter and James outside a private home where they were to have a meeting
of their own, and they seemed more subdued about our prospects than I
had hoped. But still they prayed for us and said they looked forward to a
full report.

About an hour before our meeting—to which Barnabas had given
detailed directions—he steered his horse and cart up the narrow street
to the little temple where it had become my practice to pray before our
nightly debates.

As Barnabas began to rein in the horse, the cart lurched with the
steed's every step, and we both leaned out to see what was causing it. The
animal was heavily favoring his right foreleg. "There's a livery not three
blocks away," Barnabas said. "Help me unhitch him and I'll walk him up
there while you go in and pray."

"You're sure you don't mind?" I said.

"Not at all. He's probably just picked up a stone. I can see to it, and we want you fully prepared."

Even helping him with pulling the reins off the horse and leaving the straps in the cart allowed me to start organizing my thoughts. The Hellenists would field their best minds against me to argue the doctrines of Christ, but I believed I had the advantage, not just of truth, but because Jesus Himself had taught me.

With the wagon angled into a curb and Barnabas slowly walking the gimpy horse up the street, I made my way into the small temple and set my bag on the bench, settling into an attitude of prayer. How I loved these times alone with God.

As I prayed I began framing my argument into my testimony concerning Jesus, believing I should be straightforward about the man I once was. I would say that in my former life I was just as they were. Even though they had craftily not let on that they knew who I was, I would make plain that it had been my job to go into every synagogue and either imprison or beat those who believed on Jesus. I would reveal that when the blood of the martyr Stephen was shed, I stood by consenting to his death, even guarding the clothes of those who were killing him.

Yes, this would be a dramatic announcement by someone who had once been dead in his trespasses and sins, now redeemed through the blood of Christ shed on the cross. Had there been any doubt about my identity, this would end it.

But for once, when God spoke to me, it was not a silent impression upon my soul and heart. Rather, this night it was as if I had fallen into a trance and saw Him standing before me, saying, "Make haste and get out of Jerusalem quickly, for they will not receive your testimony concerning Me."

It dawned on me that none of my message would have been a surprise to them. I said, *Lord, they all know what I did in the synagogues and with Stephen.*

And He said, "Depart now, for I am sending you far from here to the Gentiles."

If I had learned nothing else as a bondservant of Christ, besides the maddening intrusion of my old nature at the worst possible times, I knew that when He spoke, I was to respond. He had said to "make haste." He had said, "Get out quickly." He had said, "Depart now."

And so I did.

I grabbed my bag, marched directly out, and traded it for the pile of leather straps in the seat of the cart. I shook them into a semblance of order, draped them over my arm, lifted the wagon tongue, and swung the carriage out into the street, wheeling it toward the livery. Barnabas was already coming the other way with his healthy horse.

Without a word, as if the Lord had spoken to him too, he worked with me to reattach the animal. "Take me to Peter and James," I said, and we set off at a gallop.

Our brothers were waiting outside as we pulled up, and yet another man emerged from the house, shook my hand without introducing himself, and said, "God bless you, Paul. Are you ready to go?"

I nodded blankly as he climbed into the seat between Barnabas and me, and Peter and James each put a foot inside the back wheels and hung onto the roof as Barnabas started off again. The horse labored with the weight of five men.

The man between us pulled from deep in a pocket of his mantle a leather pouch with a drawstring, teased it open, and began counting out coins. "Do you have a place to carry these, Paul?" he called out over the din of the rattling carriage.

I opened my bag.

"This will pay your fare to Antipatris, one night's lodging there, a ride to Caesarea, a few nights' lodging there in case there's not a ship to Tarsus for a few days. Then—"

"Tarsus? That's my hometown!"

"We know. Your fare is here, too, plus enough to cover a few days of uncertainty. Then you will have to depend on the believers there, or family, or find work. Any questions?"

Any questions?

This was happening too fast. I didn't even know this man, and God had clearly used him to save me from the Hellenists. And I was going— home. To my family for the first time in nearly four years.

Had there been no change in my circumstances since the last time I'd seen Father and Mother, my sister Shoshanna, and her husband and their four little ones, they would be angry with me just for the lack of contact. But if they knew one speck of what had become of me, I expected they had wholly disowned me.

"May I know your name, sir?"

"It's not important. I am one of the brethren here. Any questions about Tarsus?"

"What am I to do there?"

"That is a question for Peter."

I craned my neck and looked out at the fisherman, dangling off the back of the rig, the hem of his tunic in his hand to keep it from getting caught in the wheel. "We'll talk when we stop!" he called out.

That came twenty minutes later when Barnabas had driven us far outside Jerusalem to the start of the descent that led to the port city. Everyone clambered out or off and we stood at the side of the trade route. Peter took charge and told us to watch for some transport that could get me to Antipatris, the city on the border between Samaria and Judea. Most providential to me, it was also the site of a Roman military operation. But then Caesarea was the headquarters of Roman rule and home to the Roman Tenth Legion.

There had to be a way I could find information about Taryn from one of those two places.

Peter said, "We are going to bless you and pray for you and wish you Godspeed. Then I have some news for you. Finally, after I have found you a ride and have negotiated a price, the rest of us will return to Jerusalem and commend you to the remainder of the brethren, in the event our paths cross again someday."

"News?"

"All things in order," he said.

He and James and Barnabas and the unnamed brother encircled and laid hands on me and Peter raised his face toward heaven. "Father, bless our friend and your servant with safety, with health, with courage, and with his every need in Christ Jesus. Give him Your words to say to people You want to hear them, and may his path be straight and smooth. Amen."

The others added their amens, and I said, "Thank you all. Now I need to know what I am to do in Tarsus."

Peter said, "Paul, when the Lord sent you to Jerusalem, I wasn't sure I even wanted to meet with you. I didn't know if I could trust you or expose my friends to the dangers you posed. When you proved yourself worthy, you put yourself under my authority. I did not ask for that, but I accepted it as from the Lord. But now that you are leaving, you are also leaving my authority. We believe God would have us send you away with the provisions we have offered, but beyond that, you are again under His direction."

"But you laughed at me, ridiculed me when I suggested I go alone.

And now you're sending me by myself—"

"Hear me, Paul. *I'm* not sending you anywhere. I do not feel I am shirking my responsibility when I say this is God's doing. He called you. He taught you. He trained you. He told you to come here for fifteen days, and you did. All I am doing is turning you back over to Him. What are you to do in Tarsus? Whatever He tells you to do."

I hung my head and nodded. I confess I wanted it to be easier, or at least clearer. But I could not argue with Peter's logic. And the Lord had been sufficient up to now. I knew He would lead me. "You said you had news."

"Yes, Paul. Nicodemus has been murdered."

Barnabas steadied me as my knees nearly gave out. "How? Where? By whom?"

"Between the Temple and his home. It was made to appear to be a band of robbers. He was a wealthy man, as you know, but it was also known he never carried great amounts of cash. Frankly, we have feared this for a long time. The council has hated him since some learned he'd had a clandestine meeting with Jesus without Sanhedrin approval."

"Everywhere I go I bring such things about," I whispered.

"If showing yourself at the Temple Mount instigated this," James said, "I share as much of the blame as you. I urged you to go."

"Neither of you is the cause," Peter said. "It was inevitable. Nicodemus was a courageous man to have returned to the Sanhedrin after the crucifixion."

"You were next, Paul," Barnabas said.

"Why do we pose such a threat?"

It was a question without an answer.

From the horizon above us a slow-moving cart shambled into view.

Peter flagged down the driver, who proved to be transporting military messages and equipment to both locations I needed to reach. He negotiated a price for which he would take me to the Plain of Sharon, where Antipatris lay, and also on to Caesarea the next day. Moments later, after a tearful farewell, I climbed next to the driver and found myself surprisingly weary. Grief has a way of causing that.

"We won't pull in till around dawn," the man said, "but I'm grateful for the company because night is not the safest time to travel. But I'm not a talker, in case you're wondering."

"Are you a listener?"

"Not a willing one."

"But you've been paid, so for almost forty miles you don't have much choice, do you?"

"No, I don't suppose I do."

"Let me tell you about a carpenter from Nazareth who was crucified and came back from the dead."

"Back from the dead? This supposed to be a true story?

"Actually it is."

"You know this man?"

"Yes, I do. I talked to Him today."

"And you believe he was really dead and now he's alive?"

"Absolutely."

"Well, I'm not saying I'll believe it, but I'll listen."

I set my bag behind me. "I was working for the vice chief justice of the Sanhedrin in Jerusalem a few years ago when we began hearing about a man, a carpenter from Nazareth, who was becoming popular among the people. It wasn't just because of what He was saying, although it was interesting and often paradoxical—we'd dealt with that kind of thing before—but this one was performing signs and wonders, even miracles."

"And he wasn't a holy man?"

"That was the thing. Sometimes He claimed to be. But people kept saying, 'Isn't this the carpenter's son from Nazareth? Don't we know Him? Who does He think He is?'"

20

THE SLAVE

ANTIPATRIS

THE LORD HAD HARD lessons to teach me, and not all came in threats on my life, being chased out of cities, or even feeling I had been the cause of the deaths of others, including the people at Yanbu and then Nicodemus. I yearned to be victorious for Christ, a conqueror—more than a conqueror. Not just because I had always been a competitor; I believe my heart was pure in this. As a bondservant of Jesus I longed for Him to instill within me the conviction that it was not I who lived, but Christ, so that anytime I proclaimed His truth, His gospel, His message, His story, no one could dispute or deny or reject it.

Yet that is just what this courier driver did! I told the story of Jesus and my own testimony to show how the risen Christ could redeem the darkest of hearts, could bring life from death. It wasn't as if the man did not find me credible. He didn't even seem to suspect an ulterior motive.

He acknowledged I was not trying to sell him anything. It was simply that at the end of it all, when I explained to him the way of salvation—that if he believed on the Lord Jesus Christ he would be saved from his sins and become a new creation—he was not interested!

How could this be? I begged, I pleaded, I argued, I cajoled, I wept, I explained again! Finally I realized I had gone too far, had inserted myself too wholly in the equation, told him he should forget about me, about my personality, my character, my insistence. But he said that wasn't it at all.

He was even smiling in the light of dawn when he said, "I believe you have found something, someone, who completes your life, friend. It works for you. I'm happy for you. Good for you, and I say it again, good for you."

"You don't want to be saved?"

"No, thank you. But I am grateful to you for telling me about this. All about it. About this man. Very interesting. Very inspirational. Good for you."

"But it's for you too! It's for everyone."

"So you've said. But no, it's not. It's not for me."

At last he convinced me. To go any further would offend him. For the last hour of the ride I tried to think of anything more I could say. Finally I thanked him for listening and asked if I could pose just one more question. He sighed and nodded.

"What would it take to persuade you that what I spoke to you of *is* for you?"

He shrugged. "I suppose if I were to have the experience you did, I would have little choice, wouldn't I? Just like you?"

"But sir, no one had told me about Jesus the way I have told you about Him. It's not a matter of—"

He held up a hand. "All due respect, my friend, but you have talked about this all night, and you just wanted to ask one more question. I have grown weary of it and am through talking about it, if you don't mind. Now I'll thank you just to go with me to where we lodge, and if you can't agree to abandon this subject for the next leg of the trip, I'll be happy to refund that portion of your fare and ask you to make other arrangements."

"Forgive me. I'm sorry."

Weary as I was, I found sleep elusive. I'm not one who surrenders easily, but I sensed the Lord teaching me that not all my efforts, regardless how well meaning, would prove successful. It was exasperating, sour medicine, but I determined not to let it impede my efforts. My assignment was clear. Success was not the goal; obedience was.

As I lay staring at the ceiling, I also began crafting a plan for the next day. In the event, unlikely though it might be, that I might be known by sight to any of the Roman military personnel, I decided to make my first order of business changing my appearance. With so many men stationed in two locations so close together, there had to be a tonsorial service some-where—if not here, certainly at Caesarea.

Late in the morning the driver informed me that his courier work for the relay station required about two hours before slaves would load cargo onto his wagon and he would be ready to leave for the port at Caesarea. That gave me time to explore and ask questions as a curious Roman citizen on his way back to his homeland. That's when I discovered that yes, all manner of services were provided for the troops in Caesarea—including barbers—and also that many generals were headquartered there.

Was it possible I would get my first clue to where my almost-family might be, before setting sail to reunite with my parents, sister, brother-in-law, nephew, and nieces after so many years? I longed to see them but had no idea whether they had an inkling of what had become of me.

Certainly I would have heard by now if anything had happened to either of my parents. Shoshanna surely would have let me know before I fled to Arabia—unless she heard I had become a follower of Jesus. Had that reached as far as Tarsus, Taryn and Corydon might be the closest thing to a family I had left in the world.

Waiting has never been my strength, and I resorted to what I knew would be my practice during the long voyage home: I prayed. I prayed for my driver. I prayed for my family—both my families. I prayed for the brethren in Jerusalem, for Barnabas' aunt and cousin, for Nicodemus' family, and for Gamaliel.

What I really wanted was to be preaching. If not all would come to a saving knowledge of the Savior, I would preach to as many as would listen so that any who heard me might come. I prayed for smooth sailing so I could get to Tarsus soon enough to learn what God had for me there. Peter had taught me that when nothing had been arranged, I could preach on street corners or in any public place. People would gather just to see who the crazy man was who had started shouting.

Pray for your enemies.

Thank You, Lord.

I prayed for Nathanael, for the Sanhedrin, even for the high priest.

Pray for your enemies.

I prayed for them again and added the Hellenists and the Roman troops who attacked Yanbu, even for General Balbus.

Pray for your enemy.

Whom am I neglecting, Lord?

Pray for your enemy.

I pondered. Aah, yes. *Thank You, Jesus.* I prayed for Nadav.

Pray for your enemy again.

I prayed for Nadav again.

And again.

I did.

And again.

I am Your servant, Lord. Your will is my command. How many times?

As oft as I bring him to mind.

As You will, Master. Strangely, this did not become a chore, not monotonous. Praying for Nadav seemed in some way a privilege. And the Lord continued bringing him to mind until the courier found me.

"When the slaves finish loading the wagon, we'll get under way," he said. Six thin but heavily muscled, barefoot men wearing only loincloths, their skin reddish-brown from the sun, quickly filed past me in a tight line. They hoisted heavy wood boxes on their shoulders and kept their eyes straight ahead, peering out from deep eye sockets above protruding cheekbones. They situated the cargo in the wagon just so and jogged back for more, sweat dripping.

I carefully set my bag behind the driver's bench and was reaching for the strut to pull myself up into the passenger seat when I noticed him, second from the last returning to the wagon with another heavy box. He had to have lost twenty pounds since I had seen him, but it was definitely he.

"Nadav!" I hissed, and he turned with a start, the box slipping from his bony shoulder and leaving a gash. The man behind him deftly slipped around him.

Nadav's eyes filled, and he stared at me as if I were a ghost. "Balbus used me," he moaned. "Forgive me!"

"Used you how?"

"Sold my children as slaves. Took Anna."

"Where's—"

An overseer rushed up and savagely whipped Nadav, leaving welts on his neck and forehead. "Get that box aboard and get back there for more!"

As Nadav loaded the box, I said, "I'm a Roman citizen and I have need of him for a moment!"

"Make it fast. He's on this detail!"

I motioned Nadav to follow me inside.

"Kill me, Paul! All those people! All that blood on my hands! Put me out of my misery!"

"Stop! Pray God will forgive you!"

"He's abandoned me, as He should! How can He ever forgive me? How can you?"

"Nadav! Help me find the others! Where are your children?"

"They sell for more than adults. Balbus made Anna a concubine and sold the children to a trader in the south. I couldn't find them if I were freed today!"

"Where is she?"

"With him in Caesarea, where Taryn and Corydon are."

"Taryn—"

"He divorced his wife and married her, but he also has a harem of concubines. It's awful for all of them."

"How do you know this?"

"Government slaves are transferred back and forth. People talk."

The door burst open. "Hurry and get him back out here!"

"Go!" I whispered. "I'm praying for you, and I'll do what I can. I'll try to get to Anna and tell her I saw you."

"Tell her I'm well, Paul. Don't tell her I won't last long here, that they're starving us. And if you can ever find it in your heart—"

"Nadav, we're still brothers in Christ."

Outside he was whipped again on his way to the cargo stack. He lifted a box to his good shoulder as the overseer followed close and seemed to examine the bleeding wound on the other. Any hope that this might afford Nadav some reprieve was crushed when the man stopped and appeared to calculate the distance, then unleashed the whip so the tip cracked directly into the open flesh.

Nadav dropped to his knees with a shriek as the man blankly turned away, as if he had swatted a fly.

The cargo pile had shrunk to a single row of boxes, and the courier's wagon was already laden to where the horses would labor all the way to the coast. The driver was up in his seat and signaled me aboard with a nod, but I was so repulsed I could barely move. The inhumanity I had witnessed was, in truth, nothing compared to the atrocities I'd seen in Yanbu. But it all flowed from the same steaming pot of putrid poison that made up the Roman Empire.

At its beginning the realm may have seemed a grand design for the common good, and though I had never believed in a plurality of gods, for all I knew the original philosophers and thinkers were well intentioned. But with their conquests had come a reach and a power that resulted in a toxic elitism, a bloated entitlement scheme that seemed to necessitate supporting itself, despite its no longer working for the people.

"I'm cracking these reins when the last box is loaded, friend," the courier called out, "whether you're aboard or not."

I nodded, still finding it hard to move. Nadav retrieved the box that had tumbled when he fell and shuffled to the end of the line, sliding it onto the wagon and going back for another, appearing desperate not to endure one more lash. I fought every urge within me to attack the overseer myself, reminding myself of everything I would lose in the process— my freedom, my calling, any chance to see Taryn, let alone rescue her or Corydon. And it would surely mean the end of Nadav.

As the slaves heaved the last of the boxes onto their shoulders and the courier tightened his hands on the leads to the horses, I mounted the wagon. All the while, my mind was on the Empire and what it had meant to me as a child in Tarsus as compared to when I was a student in Jerusalem and then an employee of the Sanhedrin.

I slouched on the bench, but I turned to face Nadav as the wagon slowly began to move and the slaves were herded away. I tried to communicate with my eyes that he should stay strong and courageous and know that God had not abandoned him, that He would forgive him, and that he should never stop praying for his family.

In his eyes I saw only hopelessness.

As a child I had heard pride in my father's voice when he informed me we were Roman citizens besides being Jews, and not just Jews but Pharisees. Oh, it was good also to be Greek and of Tarsus. It's no wonder I became so full of myself. But when I became a rabbinical student I learned what a complication it was to live under the rule of a foreign power.

Then strangely, those of us associated with the Sanhedrin despised and resented the Romans and yet used them for our own purposes when the need arose. Indeed, we used them to do the dirty work when the Miracle Worker from Galilee began stirring crowds. And when we wanted to eliminate Stephen. And we tried to use them against Peter and John.

When I became a believer, I became an enemy of both my own people and the Romans, but the massacre in Yanbu and what Nadav had just told me made me face the truth: regardless how expansive, impressive, powerful, intellectual, or mythological the Empire appeared, it could not, must not be allowed to continue.

I did not know what would lead to its demise or how long it would take to finish it, but end it must. I prayed it would be a spiritual end, for then perhaps I could have a hand in it. God had not called me to be a military leader. I would not likely ever carry a weapon or defeat an army. Neither would I fight this battle in the great halls of justice or academia, though I would have loved to debate the great minds of the Empire. If only God would allow the future of Rome to hinge on the efficacy of its spiritual foundations, I might be granted the opportunity to play some role in its downfall.

As the great cart loaded with boxes full of military equipment precariously shifted side to side, I held tight, closed my eyes, and prayed silently for the Empire's end.

When I opened my eyes the early afternoon sun made me squint. "General Balbus," I intoned casually.

The driver grunted.

"You've heard of him?"

"Who hasn't?" he said.

"I hadn't until recently."

"Decimus Calidius Balbus," he said. "Ahala."

"Pardon me?"

"His nickname. It means 'armpit.' And it fits."

"How's that?"

"I have to explain it? You seem like such a smart man. I haven't met him, but I gather he's not pleasant. Decorated. Feared. But a hothead, some say."

"Decorated for what?"

"Volunteers for the unsavory assignments. Leads his troops long distances over rough terrain to carry out unpleasant tasks. He doesn't demand a popular battle in a major city that results in a parade with music and banners and dancing maidens. He'd just as soon drive his men for days to pillage an entire town, then return with the severed heads of his foes to present to his superiors."

"Charming."

"Ahala."

"Long live Rome," I said.

The man shrugged. "I just deliver the packages."

"You've never seen this General Decimus—?"

"Decimus Calidius Balbus. And don't care if I ever do."

"I'd like to get a look at him," I said.

"Truly?"

"I would."

"What would it be worth to you?"

"You could make this happen?"

"A couple of the boxes behind you are for Balbus. They are delivered by an actarius, but you give me a couple of drachmas, I give one to him, and he'll be happy to tell you where General Armpit lives. Whether or not the general is there, I keep the money."

"I'll take the risk."

"Give me the coins and I'll show you the man to talk to at the unloading station two hours after we arrive."

Twenty miles and fours hours later we arrived in Caesarea, the salt breezes off the Mediterranean reminding me of more than twenty years before when my father and I sailed from there to Tarsus to bring back Mother and Shoshanna so I could attend rabbinical school under Gamaliel.

But now, unable to erase the images of the emaciated Nadav from my mind, I was consumed with finding Taryn. Like Nadav and Anna, she and Corydon were paying the price for his awful betrayal. How could he ever forgive himself? Had he really thought the general would honor him for being a traitor?

I don't know if I would want to survive, had my actions gotten my wife used by a tyrant and our children sold into slavery. How could he ever face her or expect her to forgive him? I no longer knew how to pray for Nadav, that he live or die. I prayed he felt God's peace, but knowing the depth of my own guilt and shame, I found it hard to imagine.

The courier pointed out the man he was confident would trade places with me and tell me where to deliver my packages later.

I walked to the harbor of the city of more than one hundred thousand people, learned that the next ship to Tarsus left late the next morning, and booked my passage. I decided to get my hair cut in town rather than at the military outpost, for if I was recognized by anyone, it would most likely be by someone in authority. Half an hour later my purse was a few shekels lighter and my head and face were bare.

The voyage to Tarsus would be more than three hundred miles, giving me time to grow back my beard and what little hair I had, or not even my own family would recognize me. Already enough about my character and personality would shock them. What would Rabbi Daniel and the people of the synagogue who had known me since childhood think of me now?

21

FREEDOM

CAESAREA

THE WALK TO WHERE the Roman Tenth Legion was stationed brought the familiar quiver that always preceded the unknown. I prayed God would allow me not only to see Taryn but also get a chance to talk to her. Ideally, I wanted to rescue her, spirit her away to Tarsus, and marry her. I knew in my heart God could do anything.

What would it take to extricate a woman, who amounted to a spoil of war, from a general in the army of the Empire that rules a quarter of the people on earth? My beloved and her son and I would become fugitives, marked for death. It was a risk I was willing to take.

Yet God gave me no peace about such a plan, and common sense ruled it out. Only some miraculous turn of events resulting in the conviction—or death—of the general could create a positive outcome.

Still I pleaded with the Lord to speak to me about this, rather than just leave me with a troubled spirit that told me there was no future in such a delusion. I wasn't certain I wanted an answer. Whenever God impressed something on my heart and soul, because He cannot lie, it was always, naturally, the truth—and rarely easy. This time was no exception.

I have called you to a lonely task. And when I provide you a companion after three years, it will be Barnabas.

As always, I did not have to ask God to repeat Himself or clarify. While I had wished for news that Taryn might be thrust back into my future, plainly that would have to wait, if it was ever to be. I cannot deny disappointment, and yet I clung to hope as well. It is not all bad news when the Lord gives you a glimpse of your future, even when it doesn't match what you might have designed for yourself, if it includes a gift like Barnabas.

The man deserved his nickname, for he was more than just someone with a cheery outlook. He was a fount of encouragement—genuinely seeing and helping produce the best in everyone. I was a better person when I was with him, and because I was with him.

But what was I to do in Tarsus for three years? When the Lord sent me quickly from Jerusalem, He had said, "I am sending you far from here to the Gentiles." Did that mean immediately to Gentiles in Tarsus? I had learned that His messages did not always mean what I thought they meant.

When He had sent me from Yanbu, I thought I was to preach to the Gentiles in Damascus. But no. Then when He sent me to Jerusalem for fifteen days, I thought I was to preach to the Gentiles there. But no. Now I would have to see what God had for me in Tarsus. My first audience would be my own family and childhood friends, because it would be the height of effrontery for me to return home and not see them immediately, though they were anything but Gentiles.

But I was prepared for anything. I would speak and preach and debate with anyone God put in my path. While He had called me to be an apostle to the Gentiles, He also said I would preach to kings and the children of Israel. My mission was to obey. I would not stop praying that my work would one day include Taryn and Corydon, but neither would I stop preaching while waiting for that to come to pass.

When I approached the man I was supposed to see and informed him it was I who had sent the money and was to replace him as deliveryperson to General Balbus, he said, "Oh, I don't think that is correct, sir."

Imagining no good reason for this, I immediately said, "Do not even attempt to steal my money without satisfying your end of the bargain."

"I would never do such a thing, stranger, but prove yourself to me by telling me to whom you gave the money, and how much you paid him."

What if the driver had taken the two drachmas and paid the man only half a drachma? That was between them; I could only tell the truth. "I paid the delivery driver two drachmas. He was to give you one."

He looked thoroughly perplexed. "That is correct, sir. But he told me to look for a bearded man with a rim of thinning reddish hair."

I smiled. "I've been to the barber in the meantime." When still he frowned and hesitated, I added, "How else would I know the details?"

"I would be in serious trouble if these deliveries were lost or stolen."

"Have no fear. My life would be worth nothing if I dared steal from the Roman army. Any idea what I am delivering?"

He set two boxes before me and looked none too comfortable with the arrangement. "I never ask and no one ever offers to tell me. It could be weapons, uniforms, equipment, anything. Of one thing I am certain: the contents are none of your concern."

He told me how to get to the general's residence and said it was about a ten-minute walk. "Avoid the government center by taking the slightly longer route to the west."

I stiffened, hoping he hadn't noticed. How could he possibly know I didn't want to be seen by the authorities? No one had seen me for years, and they weren't likely to recognize me bald and clean-shaven, but still I was determined to circumvent them. "Why is that?" I said as causally as I could manage.

"Prefect Marullus is in his headquarters this week, so his entire staff is here as well. Many of them know me, and if they see someone else making my deliveries, they're bound to ask questions. What would you say?"

"Ah, good counsel. Thank you."

I slung my bag around to the back, but when I set one box atop the other and bent to lift them, I nearly collapsed under the weight. I could not make two trips and was not willing to hire a conveyance. I would have to make this work.

Arms and legs straining, I set off, knowing it would take much longer than ten minutes but also praying the trip would be worth the effort. With the first step the top box shifted, and I instinctively shuffled to keep it balanced.

"You going to be all right?"

I slowly turned to see him eyeing me with a deeply concerned look.

"You have your money," I said. "Don't worry about me."

Nearly twenty-five minutes later I drew within sight of the general's home, my tunic and mantle drenched and my arms scraped raw. I set down the boxes and studied the spacious dwelling at the corner, which boasted open porticoes and a wide expanse of land, set off from a row of three-story apartments. Six heavily armed legionnaires patrolled the front, their backs to the entrance. I imagined they were there to keep two people in as much as to keep intruders out. Who would try to invade the home of a Roman general?

I assumed the general kept his concubines in the apartments. Looking for signs of Taryn or Corydon, I saw near the house only a colorful pole that could have been a toy. My heart leapt when the boy scampered around the side wearing what appeared to be a cape made from the red cloth of a Roman uniform. He jumped and skipped and grabbed the pole, thrusting it like a spear, but still he bore the visage of the lonely. I ached for him.

I hefted the boxes again and moved toward the house, whereupon the two middle guards closed ranks and one lifted his chin, squinting at me. "Delivery for General Balbus," I said. He gave the boxes a cursory glance and nodded toward the door, and as I headed past him Corydon stopped and looked at me. Leaning idly on his toy weapon and staring, as children do, he seemed to study me as I set the containers near the door and knocked. Could I trust him not to holler my name and come running?

But it was clear Corydon did not recognize me. Nor, at least at first, did the beautifully dressed and artfully adorned woman gazing at me from a patio directly overlooking the door from ten feet above. Taryn would know enough not to react aloud if she did realize it was me. I checked to be sure the guards were facing away from her, then turned back to look directly at her. The dryness of the desert had been refined from her. Her billowy dress was an elegant white, she wore no veil, and her olive skin and dark hair shone from creams and oils. She wore gold bracelets, rings, a necklace, a brooch, and another tasteful bauble in her long, flowing tresses.

Dazzling as she appeared, Taryn, too, emanated a depth of solitude and despair clouded by what perhaps began as curiosity at a new delivery-man. But that seemed to have become an affront over my lingering gaze.

I now pleaded with my eyes for her to see me, to know me. Abruptly a hand flew to her mouth and she turned away, then back, her eyes filling.

"Excuse me!" she called out, and I busied myself situating the boxes as all six guards spun to look up at her. "Have him bring the boxes around back. The general will want them there."

"We can bring them," one said.

"No, thank you, I prefer you remain at your posts."

"Go on, then, man, and move along!"

Desperate not to attract more attention, I tried to look experienced but nearly tripped lifting the boxes. As I leaned the load against my chest and straightened, I noticed a miniature statue set into a small shelf over the door, as if standing sentry. Curious.

In the back I discovered four more guards. Ten to watch the house of one general? Where must he be, and how important was it that his "family" be confined to his home?

Taryn opened the door, pulled me in past the eyes and ears of the guards, and we communicated more in the few moments we dared spend alone than we had in any previous half hour together. We kissed deeply, she insisting that she had been forced to marry against her will and would never consider herself wed to a pagan in the eyes of God. "Decimus doesn't even believe in the Roman gods, let alone the one true God. He claims he fancies the Greeks' idea of some unknown god, but he lives like the devil."

I asked if she would call in Corydon, but she feared he would say something when the general got home from a meeting with the prefect. "You must be gone before he gets back, Paul. He thinks you're dead. He mistook Brunon for you, paraded him around in a royal robe made from one of his men's capes, and then cut off his head before he crucified him."

"I wondered what that was all about," I said.

"Please!" Taryn said. "I'd risk my life to spend the rest of it with you, but I won't risk Corydon's or yours. You must go!"

I told her I was on my way to Tarsus but would try everything I knew to get messages to her, and I gave her the address of the synagogue.

I also told her of her father's last words, finding her note, burying him, of Damascus and Barnabas and Jerusalem and Nadav, and I asked her about Anna. She confirmed what Nadav had told me and said Anna would be relieved to hear he's alive, "but she still won't expect to ever see him again—or her children."

"She's probably right."

"Just as I'll probably never see you again, Paul."

"We must not give up hope. I think of you always and pray for you and Corydon."

"I love you, Paul."

"I love you."

Hearing something out front, she put a finger to her lips. "That's him! Go!" When I hesitated she rushed to the foot of the stairs. "Paul, please!"

Leaving her was agonizing, but when I heard the front door I rushed out the back as she trotted upstairs.

"Hey, yah, you're dead!" Corydon shouted, thrusting the pole at me. I nearly fainted.

"You got me," I said, disguising my voice and turning away so he wouldn't recognize me.

And as I returned to the front of the house, my heart was full of gratitude and grief. Thankful for getting to see Taryn, I feared she was right—it was likely the last time. But when I breathed my thanks to the Lord, He filled me with a fresh touch of Himself. I was unexpectedly emboldened, my shoulders reared back, and my chest expanded.

A couple of the soldiers turned and watched as I went directly to the front door. "Forgot something," I said, and I knocked loudly.

The general opened the door. "What do you want?"

"God sent me," I said, staring up into the face of a man at least ten years my senior, forty pounds heavier, all muscle, and six inches taller.

"He did, did he?" Balbus said, looking miserable. "How'd you get past my detail? Commander!"

"I'm not talking about one of the phony gods the Romans want you to believe in. You know better than that. I'm talking about the One you think is unknown, the One you don't even know how to depict on your door here."

A guard appeared behind me and addressed Balbus over my shoulder. "Have you already forgotten we've been decommissioned?"

"Disregard, Commander."

"I no longer report to you, sir."

"All right! Round up your men and—"

"That's what I was trying to do."

"Just carry on!"

What was this? The guards were leaving? Those from the back had joined the ones in front, and they were climbing into a wagon that had just pulled up.

"Changing of the guard?" I said.

"It certainly doesn't concern you. Now I don't have the time—"

"You consider yourself a religious man, General, I see that. I proclaim that this One you purport to worship without knowing is the God who made the world and everything in it."

"I am not inclined to talk about this. I've just returned from a meeting where—"

"You would do well to take the time, sir, as the unknown God I am referring to is not happy that but two months ago you attacked and slaughtered people who bear His name."

The general narrowed his eyes and cocked his head. "Are you from the prefect's staff? I told him I would surrender my equipment and leave this—"

"I told you. God sent me."

"Prove it."

"The Arabian Desert."

"Whom have you been talking to?"

"God."

"If one of my men—"

"Your orders were to spare no one."

"How well I know. But you know nothing of my orders. I make one mistake in dozens of campaigns, after having established my own strategies—"

"You have well said your 'own purposes,' for three of the seven you think you spared live under your own roofs now. You delivered the wrong head to your prefect, and look what it has cost you."

"It has cost me everything. Just because the one who eluded me turned up in Jerusalem."

"If you knew who it is who speaks to you, you would have invited him in to sit with you."

The general waxed pale and stepped aside so I could enter and we sat across from each other. His voice came labored and hoarse. "Who did you say you were?"

"I speak for the unknown God. He is Lord of heaven and earth and does not dwell in temples made with hands. Nor is He worshiped with men's hands, as though He needed anything, since He gives life, breath, and all things to all."

Balbus appeared to try to gather himself. "I was a senior officer of the greatest Empire on earth. I—"

"General, God has created from one blood every nation to dwell on the face of the earth. He has determined their preappointed times to live and die, as well as where they will live, so that they should seek Him in the hope that they might find Him. He is not far from each one of us, for in Him we live and move and have our being.

"Since we are His children, we ought not think that His divine nature is like gold or silver or stone, something shaped by art or man's devising. God commands men everywhere to repent, because He has appointed a day on which He will judge the world in righteousness by the Man He has ordained. He has given assurance of this to all by raising Him from the dead."

Taryn appeared at the top of the stairs.

Balbus said, "God ordained a man by raising him from the dead?"

"He has. Would you like to know who He is?"

He nodded.

I began telling him my story, and his eyes darted past me to where his guards had stood out front. Clearly it had dawned on him that I was the man he was supposed to have crucified in Yanbu sixty days before—either that or an impostor, a ghost, or an avenger. Plainly I was unarmed and no match for him. Yet without question he was scared.

I told him of my journey to Damascus and all that had happened. "General, He wanted me to open other peoples' eyes, so they could turn from darkness to light and from the power of Satan to God, that they might receive forgiveness of sins and be sanctified by faith in Christ."

Balbus' hands shook, though he tried to hide it. "I want you out of my house."

"God does not want me out of your presence until I have told you everything He wants me to say. I am not at liberty to be disobedient to my heavenly calling but must declare the truth to you as I did first to those in Damascus and then in Jerusalem, and soon to the Gentiles, that they should repent and turn to God. For this reason people have tried to seize me and kill me—including you yourself. But with help from God, to this day I stand. And woe to you should you try again."

"How did you elude me?"

"By being obedient to God and saying no other things than those that the prophets and Moses said, that Christ would suffer, that He would be the first to rise from the dead and would proclaim light to the Jewish people and to the Gentiles. God will defend whom He will defend, and no one—including you—shall be able to stand against them."

The general stood. "You are mad. How do you know I can't have you slain where you sit with but a command to my troops?"

"I don't know. But I am not mad. Rather I speak truth and reason."

Balbus grabbed the neckline of my tunic and lifted me to stand before him. Drawing me close to his face he said evenly, "I could have had the men surrounding my house in here with the snap of a finger. If you are who you claim to be, that makes eight who survived. By my hand alone, four of you could be dead in minutes, and I would do it without remorse."

I had not taken my eyes from his and felt not a grain of trepidation. "I command you in the name of Jesus Christ to unhand me or suffer the consequences."

His blink told me it had likely been decades since anyone had spoken to him with such audacity. He released his grip but appeared to be fighting to maintain his look of intimidation.

"Decimus, is your personal seal close by?"

"Why do you—?"

"I am here under authority of the God of Abraham, Isaac, and Jacob,

Creator of the universe and the unknown God. Do not make me ask again."

"Yes, but—"

"Get it, a flint, a candle, and an inkwell, and do not delay."

"But I—"

"You delay at your own peril, sir."

As he strode away I swung my bag around to the side and pulled from it a sheet of parchment and a quill and set these on a table. When Decimus returned, he said, "I don't know what you think is going to happen here, but—"

"Sit down," I said, as I sat.

He sat with his arms crossed as if he were through obeying.

"Taryn," I called out, "would you come down, please?"

"Oh, Paul," she said, a whine in her voice.

"Do not fear, love," I said. "The Lord reigns."

As she descended, looking terrified, Balbus slowly craned his neck. "What is this?" he growled.

"Is Anna next door?" I said.

"I believe so," Taryn said.

"Bring her and Corydon here, please."

"Paul . . ."

I looked directly at her, willing her to trust me. "All is well. I would not endanger any of you."

Balbus scowled at me. "If you think for a moment—"

"No doubt you were a student of history, were you not, Decimus?"

"I still am."

"Then you know how Herod the Great died. Fever, unbearable itching, intestinal pain, foot tumors, abdominal inflammation, gangrene where you least want it, asthma, convulsions, and foul breath."

"So?"

"God wants you to know that if you do not do exactly as He instructs, through me you will suffer more. The death of Herod the Great will be forgotten in light of the demise of Decimus Calidius Balbus the Worse."

Anna arrived, pale and thin and appearing even more frightened than Taryn. "Paul?" she said, peeking timidly at Balbus, who glared at her. "You saw Nadav?"

"And so shall you."

Corydon stopped and stared, then ran and jumped into my lap, shouting, "Master Paul!" I held him close and asked him to be quiet while I finished talking with the general.

"Now, Decimus, let us be civil in front of the child."

"Just tell me what you want," he snarled.

I slid the parchment and the inkwell in front of him and handed him the quill, while I used the flint to light the candle. "Simply write what I dictate. Sign, press your seal in the wax, and then we will be on our way to the government offices to execute your wishes."

"What if what you dictate does not represent my wishes?"

"That is your decision, sir. The option is the demise of Decim—"

"Get on with it."

I directed him to date the document, then identify himself by his full name, and write:

I hereby grant Taryn bat Alastor of Jerusalem a divorce and her unconditional freedom, effective immediately, and unimpeded passage to her hometown at my expense.

I hereby grant Corydon bar Stephen of Jerusalem his unconditional freedom, effective immediately, and unimpeded passage to his hometown at my expense.

I hereby grant Nadav bar Jeremiah and his wife, Anna of Emmaus, their unconditional freedom, effective immediately, and unimpeded passage to their hometown at my expense.

I hereby grant the three children of Nadav bar Jeremiah and his wife, Anna of Emmaus, their unconditional freedom, effective immediately, and unimpeded passage to their hometown with an adult patron to accompany them and ensure reuniting with their parents, at my expense.

Further I pledge full recompense to the buyer of the same children.

Further I pledge no recriminations to any above-named individuals.

Signed and sealed . . .

Balbus slouched as I fanned the document till the wax hardened. Taryn, Corydon, and Anna took several minutes to gather their meager belongings.

"Keep the jewelry and the clothes," Decimus muttered as he stood slowly and meekly joined us at the door.

"I want none of it," Taryn said, avoiding his eyes.

"Just something to remember me by?" he said.

"I'll try to forget every moment."

"Have you no pity?" he said. "I've lost everything. My title, my rank, my commission, my home, my salary, my future. Now you."

"You never had me."

"You were my wife."

"I had no choice."

"Was there nothing you liked about me, at least respected about me?"

"No."

"I don't believe you."

"Then I was a good actress. I hated everything."

"You didn't come to care for me?"

"I came to loathe you more every day. You can't massacre a woman's father and all her friends, kidnap her, force her to marry you, and expect anything else, you fool."

Taryn led the way out, Corydon in hand, Anna close behind.

"Oh," I said, "two boxes were delivered in back for you."

I waited nearby and stayed out of sight as the women presented the document at government headquarters. I no longer feared being recognized, as the Lord had made it clear He was going before me on this trip. But I didn't want to cause undue turmoil.

I saw furrowed brows and heard much murmuring as the superiors and the clerks talked among themselves, agreeing the document was in the deposed general's own hand and looked in order. They studied the women and the boy, and I knew events were set in motion when they began checking schedules and counting money, scratching out vouchers, and telling Taryn and Anna where to find inns, transports, and the like.

They were also instructed where to lodge that night, what transport they would take back through Antipatris to pick up Nadav, and how they would get to Jerusalem. When asked if they had arrangements there, Taryn mentioned her friend Mary, who we both knew would be overjoyed to help her and Anna.

Yet another official told Anna when she might expect the return of her children, which caused her to dissolve into tears.

The inn where they were to stay that night was not far from where I was staying, so we agreed to eat there together. Just as the women were receiving the last of the details, a legionnaire ran into the room and spoke urgently to a commanding officer. I followed him back down to the street and pulled him aside. "Pardon me, but I have accompanied General Balbus' former wife here. Did I just hear—"

"He's dead, sir. The prefect sent me to retrieve the last of his government-issued equipment and to order him out of his home immediately, and I discovered Balbus had taken delivery of some weapons, one of them a spatha—the new long sword. He had fallen on it and run himself through."

"An accident?"

"Unmistakably not. He had to wedge the hilt under the stairs and set the tip under his belly. It was ghastly, a gruesome scene. Reminded me of the worst battlefields I've witnessed."

I nodded. "Like one I saw not long ago, which included women and children."

The officer shook his head and spat. "Who would do that?"

"Only one who deserved the same fate," I said.

That night as the four of us sat outside eating a light dinner, Corydon nodded off. He had been puzzled but excited about the news of a trip back to Jerusalem, a city he barely remembered. Anna was still bewildered about all that had happened. I tried to explain how God had intervened, but I was still reeling myself.

She said, "I know that, Paul. I know He is able and I have seen Him do it before. But I can't believe Nadav and I didn't forever break ourselves from Him with our sin. And from you! We were selfish! We were horrid. And look what we brought upon our brothers and sisters in Yanbu! We will never be able to forgive ourselves.

"We don't deserve to live, let alone to be free, to have each other, to get our children back. How could you help me? How could you do anything but leave me to get what I deserved?"

"Truthfully, Anna, when I saw the general's house guarded like a fortress, the most I hoped for was a glimpse of Taryn and perhaps to sneak a message to her and to you. And yes, in my flesh I confess I'm not capable of that kind of grace. Can I deny I wished the worst for Nadav and you? I cannot. God Himself had to remind me that I was no better. It was I who drove you and those like you to the desert. I was one who brought pain and persecution upon the people of The Way, the children of God. If I am to be forgiven, I must forgive."

"I don't deserve it."

"None of us do."

Taryn had wept through the entire meal, and when Corydon was awake he had pestered her, asking her why. She would not answer. I knew it had all been just too much for her, had happened too fast. Finally she said, "Anna, would you sit here with Corydon so I can talk to Paul? We leave before he does in the morning."

This brought a new flood of tears from Anna. "That you would trust me with your child after what I have done . . ."

Taryn took both her hands in hers. "Please. We won't be long."

22

THE ACHE

CAESAREA

JUST TWO DAYS BEFORE, I had no idea where General Balbus had taken Taryn and I despaired of ever seeing her again. I pleaded that God would grant me the fortitude to carry out my calling in spite of such pain.

I admit that, despite the myriad ways He had proven Himself to me since my conversion, my faith was weak. I missed her, longed for her, needed her, worried about her, prayed for her.

To now be able to take the hand of this free woman with whom I was deeply in love, to stroll the dark, deserted streets to the harbor and feel the warm ocean breeze on my face, was a privilege that overwhelmed me with gratefulness.

Yet even as we walked, a battle raged within me. I knew beyond doubt that if I simply asked her, Taryn would join me in the adventure of a lifetime, and we would follow the Lord wherever He led—taking His gospel to the ends of the earth, facing every trial together.

Everything in me longed for God to bestow upon me this priceless gift, yet I dared not ask, knew better than even to broach it with Him. Deep in my heart, I could not hide from the painful truth that mine was a human, fleshly, selfish wish. God had called me to die to myself. He had called me to slavery. Willing as Taryn might be to come alongside so I wouldn't have to confront such adversity alone, I could not, would not ask her. In fact, even if she herself suggested it, I would not allow it.

In all this I was touched by God's compassion for me. The prospect of this great solo venture for the rest of my life was a fearful thing that I could at least comprehend approaching with Taryn at my side. Yet I trusted Him, believed in His sovereignty, His goodness.

Difficult as it was, I knew sacrificing our love was the right thing. I rested in the knowledge that He knew best. I did not understand His purpose in having weaved me into her family only to ultimately keep us apart—especially after using me to help free her from captivity.

But His leading was clear.

The time is short, for this world is passing away. Serve Me without care, without encumbrance. I have ordained that you will suffer persecution beyond what you can imagine now. He who is unmarried is free to care for how he may please Me. But he who is married must care about how he may please his wife. The unmarried woman cares about the things of the Lord, that she may be holy both in body and in spirit. But she who is married cares about how she may please her husband.

I say for your own profit, serve Me without distraction. My grace is sufficient.

Taryn and I walked in silence until we saw the silhouette of the great ship that would carry me toward my hometown in the morning. The hour was growing late, and torches encircled it as dozens of hands loaded cargo and trimmed the riggings.

I carefully scanned the area to be sure no one could see us, then found a low piling about forty feet off the starboard bow, brushed it off, and we sat. As Taryn settled between my knees with her back to me, I encircled her waist, my hands clasped, and she leaned back, her head on my chest. We sat without speaking for several minutes as waves lapped at the side of the ship and gulls mourned. We were far enough from the working men that though we could hear them talking and laughing, we couldn't decipher their words.

"I'm incredibly sad," Taryn said at last.

"Yes, love. I am, too."

"You agree, then?" she said.

"Of course."

She looked up at me and I kissed her. I brushed tears from her cheeks as she turned again to stare at the ship. "This is all there is for us," she said.

"I know."

"When I wrote my last message to you, I believed you would ask me to marry you one day."

"Had I gotten it a day earlier I probably would have. What would you have said?"

"You know, Paul."

"I still have your message. It's with me all the time, even now." I pulled it from my bag and tilted it toward a faint torchlight to make out the writing.

"When did you know?" she said.

"Know?"

"That he had damaged me, made me unfit for you?"

My breath came shallow and I fought to find words. "Taryn," I managed finally, "you must hear me. When your father told me you and Corydon had been the only ones spared, I knew what that implied. That you were alive was all that mattered to me. I—"

"But it meant—"

"That you were alive was *all* that mattered to me. That was the Taryn I knew. You did what you had to do, not to spare your own life but for the sake of your son! And by doing that you protected the people I love most in this world."

"But the general—"

"Taryn, don't breathe another word about that ogre. I wanted to kill him, but God has taken care of that, and none of it changed how I feel about you."

"But you couldn't—"

"None of it changed how I feel about you."

"How could you marry a woman who was treated like a—"

"Taryn, I would have married you regardless that he forced himself upon you."

"But he changed how I feel about myself, Paul. I can kiss you and let you hold me because I never felt wed in the eyes of God, but I could never . . ."

"That would not have stood in my way, Taryn."

She sat quiet for a long time. "That's kind of you, but I would have felt pitied."

"I feel bad that you were shamefully treated, but God has judged him. I certainly would not have judged you."

"You would still have married me?"

"Absolutely."

"Even if we could not have been . . ."

"Intimate?" I said.

"That's what I'm saying."

"Because he made a victim of you? I cannot accept that. If you refused to marry me for that reason, that would be your decision, but certainly not mine. Never mine."

She faced me again. "Then Paul, what are we agreed upon? Are we not sad because we know tonight is the end for us?"

"Yes."

"Yet you would have married me, in spite of it all?"

"Yes."

"Then, what?"

"I cannot."

"You see?" she said. "I'm not worthy."

"I don't believe that."

"Especially not worthy of a man of God, a man called as you have been. He has someone else for you, Paul, don't you understand? Someone the Lord has prepared for you, someone pure."

I shook my head. "I'll not even look upon another woman. My calling leaves no room for a wife. It will be hard enough for me, let alone for a family. I would be asking too much of you to travel with me and face the hardships I must endure."

"You need to know that if I felt worthy, I would be willing without question. I love you with all that is in me."

"That is all I can ask, save one thing."

"Name it, Paul. If it is within my power, I promise—"

"Acknowledge that nothing forced upon you in any way changed your value. I'll be unable to live with myself if I leave knowing you feel diminished at all by what the general did to you. You remain the same pure woman I fell in love with."

Taryn turned back to face the ship and the water, the warm salt breeze, and the sounds of the harbor. I believe I at least convinced her of my feelings. And I believe we shared an ache so deep it needed no more words.

We stood and she embraced me long and tenderly. "What did you mean about the general," she said, "when you said God had judged him?"

"It isn't pleasant."

"Tell me."

"Not long after we left him, he fell on his own sword."

She drew in a breath and looked deep into my eyes, then thrust out her chin and looked away. "I shouldn't be surprised. There's no way he could have lived with the humiliation of losing his position. God forgive me, I should mourn that he didn't repent of his sins. But I find myself grateful for justice."

"No one would fault you. I feel the same."

"And you have no pangs of conscience?"

"Had I not given him the gospel, I might," I said. "But you heard me tell him plainly."

"I also heard him try to turn you out of his house."

We walked slowly toward the inn, each with an arm around the other's waist, promising to stay in contact by letters, no matter where we found ourselves over the years. "I will never stop loving you," I said. "And if God should ever grant me the freedom—"

"You could do me no greater honor, Paul. And know you take with you all my love forever. I pray God's richest blessing on your every step."

A block from where we left Anna and Corydon, Taryn and I kissed for the last time, and I feared I would never see her again.

We found Anna on a stone bench with Corydon asleep in her lap. I offered to hold him so Taryn could give her the news about General Balbus.

"What about him?" Anna said, handing me the boy. He lay his head on my shoulder, and I kissed his cheek. How I would miss him!

Taryn pulled Anna away and spoke quickly. The woman soon exulted, then remembered to quiet herself. "Some of the others and I were plotting to kill the pig ourselves," she whispered.

After final embraces all around, I placed my hand on Anna's forehead. "Father, I ask that my sister be filled with the knowledge of Your will in all wisdom and spiritual understanding, that she may walk worthy of You, fully pleasing, being fruitful in every good work and increasing in her knowledge of You."

I touched Taryn and Corydon's foreheads and prayed, "Father, strengthen these, my beloved, with all might, according to Your glorious power, for all patience and longsuffering with joy, giving thanks to You who have qualified them to partake of the inheritance of the saints. In the name of the Father, the Son, and the Holy Spirit. Amen."

Anna turned away as Taryn, Corydon draped over her shoulder, nodded a silent farewell—tears streaming.

The walk to where I would spend the rest of my sleepless night near the harbor was longest and loneliest of my life.

23

BECALMED

FOR SOMEONE WITH MY disposition, fatigue does not contribute to a productive day. My normal course consisted of vigorous daily activity resulting in sound sleep and an early awakening. With the day I had endured, full of the whole gamut of emotions, from fear to elation to sadness and longing, compounded by great physical exertion and then the inability to sleep, I boarded the ship bound for my homeland with a weariness that draped over me like a thick, woolen cloak. I felt as if my legs were wood, my arms rock.

I bore no earthly belongings but my leather bag containing my parchments and writing implements. A wool cloak would have been a welcome addition. In my sluggish morning prayer time, as I sat topside nodding and forcing a smile for those cordial fellow passengers who deigned to greet me, I apologized to the Lord for bringing less than my best self to His work for the day. I feared that if He brought opportunities to share

His gospel with anyone, I might not be vigilant enough even to recognize the prospect.

Fortify yourself with rest, for in due time I will trouble the waters to make pliant the ears of the voyagers.

I went below decks to the tiny area I had been allotted, secured my bag, slipped off my sandals, and set about stretching out on the hammock of rope affixed to the beams. It was good I was the only one with a nap in mind at that hour, as it had been years since I had attempted this and looked anything but a seaman.

The contraption swung toward me when I put my foot in, then pitched me to the floor when I attempted to roll onto it. Eventually I had to hold tight to the ropes on either side, steady myself with one foot and leap off the other, hoping to land square on my back on a moving target. I accomplished this, only to cause the bed to bang the side of the ship then sway perpendicular to the floor, forcing me to hang on lest I be hurled out anew.

When I was sore and exhausted from the effort, the wild rocking finally slowed and the movement of the ship lulled me nearly to sleep. I became only vaguely aware of conversations and footsteps topside as the great vessel was readied to leave the dock. With shouted commands and running about, the crew loosed the lines, and amid cheers and groaning and squeaking, the craft shoved off.

I was the only passenger below, and I slept all day, for it was twilight when I finally extricated myself from the rope bed—no more gracefully than how I had mounted it—and made my way above. Passengers drew shawls about their shoulders as they crowded the sides to watch the moon rise and await a dinner of fresh fish. Crew members scampered about the rigging and trimmed sails as the ship cut smoothly through the Mediterranean.

I asked how fast we were going and told a crewman to consider me a non-seaman. "If we were on land," he said, "I'd estimate us at about seven miles an hour, sir. She's a big craft."

I felt rested and had grown hungry. I found a secluded seat and prayed for Taryn while also asking God to prepare me for whatever lay ahead—in the water and in my homeland.

An hour later, our section of the ship sat about forty passengers who passed bowls of steaming whitefish and vegetables with bread. I was told that about 160 other passengers were eating elsewhere. I may have been the only one who noticed whitecaps forming in the moonlight. I drew my mantle closer around my neck and wasn't surprised when a deckhand called for attention and announced the crew would be picking up the serving bowls early, as the captain and navigator anticipated strong winds.

We passengers were instructed to make our way below decks until dawn or an all-clear announcement, and we were advised to stay away from beams and protrusions should the ship begin to shift or roll. "We don't foresee anything severe, but we want you to avoid being tossed about. Should our angle spill any lamp oil, it's safest to douse all the lamps to avoid fires."

I sat in the middle of my hammock, finding that much easier to manage, and felt reasonably secure with my arms spread, holding fast to the outer ropes. As I was positioned in the front corner of the quarters, I would not have to move to shout for everyone's attention.

It wasn't long before the excitement began.

I had noticed many aboard wore Jewish garb, as well as Greeks I surmised were sober people of some faith. They were organizing their belongings and preparing their sleeping arrangements when the ship began to rock and sway, gradually at first and then with more force.

Many immediately commenced to pray, which told me that when God brought on the crisis He had foretold, they would be ripe for listening.

Suddenly the bow of the ship came out of the water and must have risen nearly ten feet, as I was pressed back and heard shrieks as lamps went out and oil spilled throughout. Several shouted to douse the lamps, which many rushed to do, just as the keel slammed back to the surface and a number of people fell, screaming.

Within moments all the lamps had been snuffed and numerous people sniffled in fear.

"Be not afraid!" I cried out. "God is with us!"

"Be quiet!" someone said.

"Shut up!"

"What?" came a plaintive call from a woman. "Let him speak! I'm frightened."

"Yes, speak!"

"God is with us!" I said. "Men and women, sons and daughters of the family of Abraham, and all those among you who fear God, to you the word of salvation has been sent!"

"What do you mean?"

"I bear a message from God on high if you care to hear it!"

"Yes, yes! Speak! Please!"

"Very well! The God of Abraham, Isaac, and Jacob sent His Son Jesus to Jerusalem as the promised Messiah. But those who dwell there and their rulers, because they did not know Him or understand the voices of the prophets that are read every Sabbath, fulfilled those prophets by condemning Him. And though they found no cause for death in Him, they asked Pontius Pilate to crucify Him anyway.

"When they had fulfilled all that was written concerning Him, they took Him down from the tree and laid Him in a tomb. But God raised

Him from the dead. The risen Christ was seen for many days by those who came up with Him from Galilee to Jerusalem, who are His witnesses to the people. I myself saw Him later on the road to Damascus and declare to you glad tidings—the same promise that was made to the fathers of old.

"God has fulfilled this promise of the Messiah for us their children, in that He has raised up Jesus. As it is written in the second psalm: 'You are My Son, today I have begotten You.'

"I am making it known to you, brothers and sisters, that through this man Jesus comes the forgiveness of sins. By Him everyone who believes is justified."

"I believe!" someone shouted.

"So do I!"

"I as well!"

The sea continued to roil and the ship to toss.

"Pray Jesus will save us all!"

I prayed, "Father, calm the sea in the name of Jesus!" and it was as if the ship stopped dead in the water.

"God is real!" someone called out.

"Praise God!"

"I believe in Jesus!"

Many cheered, then all fell silent. From above we heard cautious footsteps, then running. The hatch opened. "Light the lamps!"

Tiny flames appeared all over and people called out to know who the preacher had been. I stood and raised a hand. "I will pray with any who wish, and I will tell you how the Lord Jesus Himself met me on the road to Damascus. Peace be unto you!"

As people rushed topside, most stopped to shake my hand and tell me they would find me later to talk. Within minutes I followed the last of them up and found the ship absolutely still in the water. Regardless what the crew did with the sails, the Mediterranean was not moving, and not a puff of wind could be felt. It was nearly as disconcerting as the storm had been.

"Are there oars?" someone called out. "Are we stuck here?"

"It's not that kind of a vessel!" a crew member said. "We're what is called 'becalmed,' but it won't last long. It never does."

But it did. It was midnight before a minor swell turned the ship slightly, then a gentle breeze caused a dull thud in the lower sail and broke the craft's inertia. Cheers arose from the passengers and many began making their way back down to the sleeping quarters.

Wide awake now, I remained topside enjoying the warm stillness of the night and the slow, quiet movement of the ship. And people began seeking me out, asking about Jesus. Some had heard about Him. To others He was just a name. Many were curious about my having come from such a religious background, opposing Him and the people who believed in and revered Him, even to the point of violently attacking them—then becoming a most enthusiastic proponent of His gospel.

That night a Jewish couple from Joppa became believers in Jesus the Messiah and said they were eager to get back to their family and congregation to tell them the good news. I warned them they might not find everyone so welcoming.

A young man, a Greek who said he had always been a devout follower of God but who had never heard of Jesus, also became a believer. He asked if he could find other followers of The Way in Pisidian Antioch.

"Some are being sent from Jerusalem to preach and teach in that area. If you ask the right questions and listen for the right answers, you believers will find each other and churches will grow there." I also told him to write to me in Tarsus if he found no fellow believers and I would encourage him and tell him if I knew of anyone coming to his region.

The next morning several others asked me to talk more about the Messiah, but I learned that God had other plans for me on this voyage. He had apparently not designed it merely to train me in ministering to strangers. He also gave me a taste of opposition.

I was holding forth about the truths of God to a group of about a dozen when I was interrupted by a boatswain who told me the captain wished to speak with me in his quarters. I told him I would come as soon as I had finished teaching the group.

"You don't understand, sir. The captain of this ship is like the governor of a province. He holds your life in his hands."

I smiled. "So if I don't come immediately he can throw me overboard. Is that what you're telling me?"

Several chuckled. The boatswain did not. "That is exactly what I'm telling you, and I've seen him do it. You are entirely under his authority as long as we're at sea. He can marry you and bury you, and if you haven't noticed, not one sliver of land is visible from here."

"I believe you had better go," one of the men in the group said.

I followed the boatswain amidships and he pointed me to the captain's quarters. "Have I gotten myself in trouble?" I said with a light tone.

The captain neither smiled nor looked up from his charts. He merely pointed to a chair. "This is my meeting," he said, "so allow me to ask the questions."

"I apologize."

He referred to a long sheet of parchment and traced a finger down a list, stopping midway. "'Paul bar Y'honatan, no city listed, full fare paid, disembarking Tarsus.'" Finally he looked up at me. "Occupation?"

"Tentmaker."

"Then why don't you make tents and keep me from hearing complaints about you?"

"Complaints?"

"Some worry that you are a sorcerer."

I covered my mouth to hide a grin.

"This does not amuse me, Paul. I employed all my skill to fight through a squall last night, when suddenly the wind and the waves unaccountably stilled. More than one person says you commanded them to do so."

"I assure you I possess no such power. I prayed and God answered."

"I do not believe in the gods."

"Neither do I. I believe in the one true God, Maker of heaven and earth. The wind and the waves obey Him."

"Well, Paul, I'm grateful for whatever part you played in stopping the storm. Another swell like the first could have done serious damage to this ship. But some Jewish passengers are even more exercised that you seem to ascribe to a certain man the qualities of the messiah. As I said, I am not a religious person, but I know when you are disrespecting someone's beliefs. The Jews believe in a prophesied messiah, and they didn't book passage on my ship to have some tentmaking drifter claim that man has already arrived and that you've met him."

"Sir, with all due respect, I am not only a Jew myself but a Pharisee of the highest order."

"For whatever that is worth."

"I studied under Gamaliel."

"I'm sure that means something import—"

"And the Messiah *has* come and I *have* met Him."

The captain stood. "If you want to reach Tarsus, you will keep that to yourself. Do we understand each other?"

"Are you a god or are you a man?"

"You well know the answer. I told you I do not claim even to be religious."

"Then I give you fair warning: I choose to obey God rather than man. If God tells me to speak about the Messiah, I will."

"And I will cast you into the sea if you challenge my authority."

"I answer to a higher authority, sir."

"Aboard this ship you do not." As in Balbus' home, I felt not the least hint of fear, yet the Lord did not permit me utterance. "You are dismissed, and I warn you, not another word about the messiah until we dock at Tarsus next week."

I had promised the people I would be back to teach them, so I rushed from the captain's quarters. For the first time on the voyage every sail billowed to its maximum and the ship seemed to slice through the water. The crew seemed excited about the efficiency of the craft, the wind, the weather, and the progress.

My little gathering seemed to have grown, several having joined while I was away. I sat and said, "I was quoting from the prophet Isaiah. But some aboard are offended at my claim that Jesus could be the Messiah, and the captain has ordered me to stop talking about this."

"How dare he? Talk about whatever you wish! If someone doesn't want to hear it, he doesn't have to listen!"

"Fair enough. If you care to listen, stay."

A handsome, gray-haired couple quickly rose and left, I continued, and within a few moments the captain and several of his crew came and dragged me to the side of the ship. I desperately pressed my leather bag to my chest.

"What is happening?" a woman cried out. "What are you doing to this man?"

Several others joined the fray, and a crowd of well over a hundred quickly gathered. The captain called for order. "This man is guilty of contempt of the captain, punishable by death!"

"What has he done?"

"Let him apologize and stop what he's doing!"

Two crew members lifted me off my feet and carried me to the edge of the craft, awaiting the captain's orders. Passengers came running from all parts of the ship.

"No, no!" several shouted. "Let him speak! What's he done?"

"He's taught blasphemy!" a man yelled. "He calls himself a Jew, yet he claims he's met and talked to the Messiah!"

"So he's a crazy man! Don't kill him for it! Let him live! Let him live!" Several took up the chant.

"There's nothing crazy about him," the captain said. "I warned him! Told him not to talk about this till we get to Tarsus! I don't care what he thinks, what he believes, I'm responsible for this ship, and every passenger does what I say or pays the consequences! I'm a fair man. I'll ask him one more time, give him one more chance. Paul, will you stop talking about this Jesus as the messiah, yes or no? If you stop, you live! If you don't, into the sea with you."

"I will not!" I shouted, and screams and shrieks arose from the crowd.

He gave a wave, and over the side I went.

Tunic and mantle flapping in the warm breeze, I wrenched the strap from around my neck and thrust my bag over my head, wanting it to be first to resurface. Not a person aboard ship would have given a shekel for my chances with no land visible, but I knew God would not end my mission before it had barely begun. I needed to keep my parchments as dry as possible.

Fortunately my knees were slightly bent when my sandals finally smacked the surface, for the force raced all the way to my shoulders and head. With my hands aloft cradling the bag, all I could do was hold my breath and wait till my momentum stopped and I began to rise. I kicked as hard as I could against my waterlogged tunic and mantle, and when the bag and then my head popped out of the cold sea, the sun warmed my scalp and face, and the cheers of my fellow passengers warmed my heart.

I found the captain's dark, glowering eyes among the many faces on the deck. He appeared stumped by what had to be a funny-looking little sojourner some thought was a sorcerer, bobbing and grinning with his bag aloft.

As one, the crowd turned to look at the masts, where the sails had suddenly lost their tension. Every expanse of fabric hung limp in the face of not even the hint of a zephyr. The sea lay still, its surface smooth as a marble floor.

Almost imperceptibly, but unmistakably, the ship began to glide. I was as fascinated by this as anyone, for nothing seemed to propel it. I set my bag on my shoulder to rest my arms and merely caressed the water with my feet to stay afloat. The captain barked for the helmsman to take the wheel and set the craft back on course, but regardless how the man spun the great rim, the massive vessel appeared to have a mind of its own.

As I remained suspended, left to die in the cold Mediterranean, his seemingly rudderless ship, sans wind or current, inexplicably circled me for hours.

The chant started low, then gained volume until all the passengers— no doubt eager to get on with the voyage—joined in clear and strong: "Pick him up! Pick him up! Pick him up!"

Finally the crew gathered solemnly around the captain, causing the chant to cease and allowing me to hear the first mate say, "Give the order, Captain."

He nodded and turned toward his quarters, muttering, "Pick him up."

The passengers erupted.

The crew tossed ropes to me.

As soon as I was back aboard, the sails fluffed to life and never flagged again.

My parchments were dry.

I preached Christ and Him crucified, and many more became believers.

The captain never showed his face again.

24

SHUNNED

As you can imagine, few passengers doubted the Lord's hand was upon me. Daily many milled about, pleading with me to speak with them, pray for them, teach them from the Scriptures, and tell them about Jesus.

I remembered the gray-haired couple who had joined the little group when I had been in the captain's quarters and had slipped away when I resumed speaking of the messianic prophecies. They were at the edge of every crowd now, looking both troubled and curious. Finally I sought them out and asked to speak with them privately.

The man, perhaps a dozen years older than I, introduced himself as Kaduri, a supplier of cilicium to tentmakers in Tarsus, and his wife, Nait.

"Perhaps you did business with my father, Y'honatan," I said.

"That was your father? Of course I did, God rest his soul. Anyone who supplied tentmakers worked with the best in the trade. Now, I knew your father only in business, but surely he was not—"

"Pardon me, sir," I said, holding up a hand, overcome. "Did you say, 'God rest his soul'?"

"Oh! Forgive me! I assumed you knew! I'm so sorry, Paul!"

"When?"

He looked to his wife. "When was it we went to the funeral, Nait? Not a year ago. The daughter and grandchildren were there with your mother. She is not well either, did you know?"

"Yes. Is she failing?"

"She does not remember things. She kept asking where Y'honatan was."

"Oh, no."

"I'm sorry. Your father was so highly thought of. Many from his congregation and the community were there, and of course countless who had known him in business. You knew he had retired and been ill."

I nodded.

"The son-in-law has taken the business," Nait said. "Whom do you deal with now, Kaduri?"

"Ravid. Very knowledgeable. Paul, I am very sorry. I would not have said anything."

"No, it's my fault. I lost touch, and my sister and I, we . . ."

"I understand. But if it's not too painful, I was going to say, as devout Jews ourselves, we knew your father and mother as most observant. We did not attend the same synagogue, but I believe it would be fair to say they would not share your views."

"That is correct."

"Is that the reason for the estrangement then?"

I had asked for this conversation, hoping to draw them out, to see if they had been the ones offended by my speaking of Jesus as the Messiah. Now I was certain they had been, but I hadn't expected to be interrogated myself.

"No, I have been unreachable for some time. But I wanted to let you know that I do not bear any animosity for your reporting my offense to the captain." Both appeared as if they wished they could deny responsibility. "Truly, it's all right. Before I became a believer in Jesus as the Christ, I would have done the same. It is a mark of your devotion to God, misguided as I believe it is—and mine was. But I have seen by your faces since then that you have started to wonder."

"We're far beyond wondering," Nait said. "Isn't that true, Kaduri?"

"Yes," he said. "When this ship went from near-breakup to becalmed because you prayed, I won't deny we thought you were praying to some god we didn't believe in. But when it became clear the Lord Himself wouldn't leave you in the sea, and now we've been sailing straight for port since you've come back aboard, well . . ."

"You're ready to listen."

"More than ready," Nait said.

By the time we reached Tarsus, Kaduri and Nait had become followers of Jesus, praying with me daily and inviting more and more passengers to meetings and seeing several added to the kingdom of Christ. They wanted me to come to their synagogue as soon as they could arrange it. I told them I would be happy to but warned them they were likely to be received the way they received me initially. "Don't expect that our church will begin in your temple."

"Then it will begin in our home!"

They offered me a ride from the Tarsus harbor to my old homestead, which I accepted, but I alighted half a mile short of where I had grown up. All things considered, I couldn't simply appear unannounced on the doorstep of my childhood home. Despite all, my sister would feel obligated to offer me hospitality, at least temporarily. So I first stopped at a bathhouse and washed not only myself, but also my clothes. Then I paid a young man to deliver a message to Shoshanna, letting her know I would arrive in an hour and that I looked forward to seeing Mother, my sister herself, her husband, and their children.

I waited for any response before leaving for the place of my birth, but the young man returned to say my sister had merely read the message, thanked him, and turned away.

"No response? No sign of emotion whatsoever?"

"No anger, if that's what you mean, sir. But she may have wept. I couldn't be certain."

I thought the walk would calm me and help shape my thoughts, but the closer I came the less settled I felt. I would decide on how I wanted to begin and in the next minute scuttle the plan and start somewhere else entirely. I prayed God would grant me wisdom when I needed it, but I didn't want to arrive unprepared either.

When the familiar landscapes of my childhood came into view, the only thing I was sure of was that I would be kind to Shoshanna, regardless how she took the news of my conversion. Even before I had disappeared she had been right to resent my shameful neglect of my ailing parents. I would have to gauge the depth of her pain.

I found her outside, dressed as if expecting a guest.

"We're each going to say how much the other looks like our parents," she said. "So I'll begin. You do remind me of Father."

"That's exactly what I was thinking, Shoshanna. You do look like Mother. And no matter what is between us, you are going to let me embrace you."

To my great relief she came to me and we held each other tight, weeping on each other's shoulders. "Mother and the children are inside. Don't be alarmed by her."

Mother and my nephew and three nieces sat on a reclining couch in order of their ages, like museum pieces to be studied. The children looked shy and uncomfortable, as if they had no idea what was expected of them. Mother wore the blank stare of a child.

I bent and pressed my cheek to hers. "I've missed you," I said.

"I've missed you too, Y'honatan," she said.

"I'm your son, Saul, Mother."

"No, Saul died. We had his funeral."

"That was Father," Shoshanna said. "This is Saul."

Mother smiled at me. "Saul is dead."

I squeezed her shoulder, a sob rising in my throat. "I love you, Mother."

"I love you, too, Y'honatan."

I could barely tell the girls apart. Shy and pleasant, they reminded me of Shoshanna when she was very young. They seemed eager to get through the greeting and relieved to be excused.

I had not seen Uzziel since he was about five, and I was struck by how tall and lanky he seemed now at age nine. He face showed definition and his hair was long and curly. He was not at all shy but looked me in the eye and answered questions in complete, thoughtful sentences.

"You'd be proud of him, Saul," my sister said. "Rabbi Daniel says he has many of your qualities."

"Oh? A reader? Memorizer?"

"That and a thinker, aren't you, son?"

"I like to believe I am," Uzziel said. "The other boys read and memorize, too, but they don't ask questions. I have many questions. The rabbi encourages that. Sometimes he and I are the only ones who talk about what the prophets were really trying to say."

"Interesting, aren't they," I said, "the Scriptures?"

"Often I think I'm the only one my age who thinks so, Uncle."

"Let me tell you, they become more fascinating the older you get, especially when you come to know the God behind them all."

"Well," Shoshanna said, more as a statement than a question, "wouldn't we all like to think God is knowable."

"Oh, but He is," I said.

"Uzziel, it's time for your uncle and me to talk. You may go outside."

"It's all right, Mother," he said. "I don't mind staying here with Grandmother."

"Go outside and play with your sisters," Shoshanna said.

He frowned but rose and shook my hand. "I hope I'll get to talk with you more, Uncle Saul."

Shoshanna said, "Perhaps he can ride with you when you visit Rabbi Daniel later." When the boy was gone she added, "Ravid built him a cart his little donkey colt can pull. He uses it when he goes to the temple for lessons. I assume you'll want to see the rabbi."

"Very much. Will I fit in the cart? Can the colt can handle us both?"

"Of course. And you'll spend tonight with us?"

"I don't want to be a nuisance."

Shoshanna crossed her arms and sighed. "I wish a nuisance was all you were. I've heard you're no longer going by Saul of Tarsus, once a title of such honor. What is it you want to be called these days?"

It felt strange, saying and hearing such things in front of my mother, realizing she didn't even know who I was. "I would be honored if you would just call me your brother."

"Oh, I know *that* is not true, and you do as well. But I mean it, I will call you whatever you wish to be called."

"Call me Paul."

"And where are you hailing from? We hear things of you from Damascus and rumors from other cities. No longer Jerusalem?"

"I will be here for the time being. I will be Paul of Tarsus."

She seemed to study me. "When you were Saul, you were my champion. You had to know that."

"I did, Shoshanna. And I was proud to be your brother. I still am."

"Are you? Why?"

"Because I know the woman you are, the wife and mother, the daughter. I admire you, respect you, like you, love you."

"Is that true?"

I studied my hands.

"You do well not to answer, Paul. For so many years you were the brother any sister would want—the finest, the smartest, the most devout. You went all the way to Jerusalem—at thirteen!—to study under Gamaliel himself. You became his best pupil, worked for the Sanhedrin, assisted the vice chief justice, advised the council. My revered brother: working at the Temple.

"It didn't surprise *me*. I knew before anyone that you were doing what you were made to do. I could not have been more proud. Or at least I thought I couldn't be—until you led the way against the blasphemers. Again, the perfect person for the task.

"Even the high priest recognized your value, sending you to put a stop to the menace. Oh, I was so proud, Paul. Unfortunately, so were you. Father and Mother had fallen ill, which you well knew, for it was the reason we moved back here. But you had become too busy for us, too prominent, too important."

"To my shame and regret, Shoshanna. You're right and I am sorry. Forgive me."

"I am not finished. The fact is, I thought my letter might get your attention, and—knowing you—when you didn't respond, I believed it had. I expected you would ponder and come to your senses. But what did you do? The next thing I hear, you're no longer rousting out charlatans in the name of the God of Israel, you've become a fraud yourself. And not just a common one, oh no, that would not be enough for Saul of Tarsus, not he of the engraved parchment letter that wound up on local synagogue's wall. You've got a story that sweeps the world, and it's a monster.

"Tell me this, Paul: If you think so much of me, why have I had to hear your tale from everyone but you? Why couldn't I hear it firsthand?"

I looked up at her as the question hung in the air. "You're serious? You want me to tell you my story?"

"Apparently you've told everyone else."

So I did. And as was my practice with anyone who offered an ear, I did not leave out anything. Beyond every detail of my encounter with Jesus on the road to Damascus and how I had come to see that all the prophecies I had memorized as a child had pointed to Him, I gave a full account of the ride to Yanbu, my times with God in the wilderness, falling in love with Taryn, the Roman massacre, standing up to the deposed general, even being thrown into the Mediterranean and the Lord causing the ship to circle me until the captain was forced to have me rescued.

Throughout my lengthy recitation, Shoshanna's reactions reminded me of Barnabas'. She raised her eyebrows, shook her head, leaned forward, recoiled. In the end she told me that, if nothing else, she believed that I believed.

"It's hard not to when God Himself speaks to you," I said. "I've given up my entire previous life for a new one. I have committed the rest of my days to be a slave for the cause of Christ. The question is, what do *you* make of it? Do you see that Jesus fulfills all the prophecies of the Scriptures, that He brings salvation to everyone, including you?"

Shoshanna appeared to think deeply, to consider my question. Silently I prayed. Then she threw her head back and laughed heartily—which caused Mother to smile broadly. "I think you're as crazy as she is!"

"Shoshanna! You think I'm delusional, that I invented all this? Do you really?"

"I do! I want nothing to do with Jesus or with you, and I don't want you trying to instill any of this nonsense in my children. As for Ravid, the truth is he's always been a bit jealous of you. He needn't worry about that anymore. When I tell him that what he's heard about you is true, he'll know no longer compare himself to my successful brother."

I could barely find the breath to form words. "Will you allow me to speak to him?"

"He's an adult, but he will agree with me."

"And you're sure you want me to stay here tonight?"

"Actually no, if you want the truth. Tell Uzziel not to bring you back when he returns from the synagogue, that you have made your own arrangements. You are no longer welcome in this house."

"Shoshanna, you can't be serious. Mother, the children, you, Ravid—"

"You might see him somewhere. He can speak for himself. But if Mother were able to speak for herself, she would say what the head of this household would have said, had you come here while he was still alive: it is a serious thing to turn your back on your upbringing, Paul."

"I have done no such thing."

"You have dishonored your traditions, your race, your religion, your people, your history, your forefathers, your god, and the Holy Scriptures. You have rendered yourself unqualified to call yourself a member of this family, and you are banished from this home."

"Shoshanna—"

"Please leave."

I stood, my mind in a stupor. A stoning could not have been worse. I embraced my mother and kissed her on the cheek. "I love you, Mother."

"I love you too, Y'honatan."

"I love you, Shoshanna."

She opened the door and called for Uzziel. "Bring your cart!"

I reached for her but she turned away. "Sister, don't do this."

She stepped outside and the girls came running. I squatted, hoping they might come to me, but they hung back and Shoshanna would not have allowed me to embrace them anyway. I fought my tears for the sake of the children, knowing I could not explain.

When the cart rattled up, the colt looked too small to pull Uzziel, let alone a grown man. I hesitated, but the boy looked so proud, patting the seat next to him, so I climbed aboard, making the entire rig lean. His mother told him to deliver me straight to the rabbi and that I would not be riding back with him later.

"But I thought—"

"Just do as you're told, Uzziel."

I waved at the girls and they chorused their good-byes, but Shoshanna would not look at me. How many hours had we played together in this very place? The memories flooded me, and as Uzziel urged the colt forward and the little animal stutter-stepped to try to get the surprising load moving, I called out, "Farewell for now, dear sister! I love you with all my heart and always will!"

She pretended to busy herself with the girls as the tiny wheels of Uzziel's cart finally began to slowly rotate and the donkey lowered its head, straining, straining to tow its prodigious cargo.

Rabbi Daniel must have seen us coming, for he emerged from the synagogue and met us on the road. I leapt from the cart to embrace him, but his look stopped me and he pulled me away from Uzziel, whispering urgently.

"I need know only one thing. Is it true? Have you become a follower of The Way?"

"Rabbi, you are one of my oldest and dearest—"

"The question requires a yes or a no."

"I must be able to explain myself, Rabbi Daniel. In fact, I would love to address the congregation using the Scriptures and—"

"No! Now I demand an answer! Yes or no? Are you still a Pharisee or have you—"

"Yes!"

"What? You are?"

"Yes! I am a Pharisee and will always be a Pharisee, but I have come to believe that Jesus is the long-awaited Messiah, and—"

"No!" He held up both hands and shook his palms in my face. "No! You tarnish the very name of the Pharisees with such blasphemy and I'll not hear another word of it. I prayed it was not true, but you confess it with your own mouth."

"And I will preach it from the rooftops, if not in your temple then in others in this town! I am not going anywhere, Rabbi Daniel. I will preach Christ and that there is no other name under heaven by which one must be saved."

Daniel was running from me now, back to what he thought was the safety of the temple. At the last moment he turned. "Uzziel, come! Class begins soon!"

And to my astonishment, the boy stood in the cart and yelled back, "Do not worry about me, Rabbi! I will be there. Just let me say good-bye to my uncle!"

I was shaken and there was no way to hide it, even from a nine-year-old, especially one as bright and discerning as Uzziel. But I might as well have been talking to an adult. "Would you like to sit down, Uncle Paul?"

Even in my agitated state it was not lost on me that the boy called me Paul. I cocked my head and stared into his eyes as I climbed back into the little seat. "I have to confess something to you," he said. "I disobeyed my mother."

"What are you saying?"

"I didn't go outside when she told me to. I stayed by the door and listened."

"You heard our conversation?"

He nodded. "I've heard Mother and Father talking about you for a long time. When she told us you were coming, I wanted to ask you something, but now I know the answer."

"Tell me, Uzziel, because if you heard us, you know that you and I aren't likely to get many more opportunities to talk."

"Well, it's just that everything you have said about Jesus and the prophecies makes sense to me, and I know I cannot say this to anyone else. I don't want to be thrown out of my house or my family or my temple. But I believe Jesus is the Messiah."

I tried to respond, but I could not.

"I want to hear more, to learn more. And I understood, at least I think I did, when you told the rabbi that you can be a Pharisee and still be a follower of Jesus."

Rabbi Daniel appeared at the door of the synagogue. "Uzziel! We are about to begin! Stop listening to him!"

Again the boy stood in the cart. "I'm coming, Rabbi! And I am not listening to him! He is listening to me!"

It took everything in my power not to explode with both laughter and tears. "You'd better go, Nephew," I said. "You are wise and you are brave. I will be praying for you. The Lord has told me I will be in Tarsus for three years, and I already have friends here who will help me start telling others the gospel of Jesus. Maybe someday you will be one of those. That would be a great gift of God to me."

I thought it best that the rabbi not see me embrace my nephew for fear of the message that might get back to his mother. So I merely reached for Uzziel's small, dark hand and we shared a firm grip. I prayed, "May the God of our Lord Jesus Christ, the Father of glory, give to you the spirit of wisdom and revelation in the knowledge of Him, and that the eyes of your understanding be enlightened so that you may know the hope of His calling, the riches of the glory of His inheritance, the exceeding greatness of His power toward us who believe, according to His mighty power.

"And I pray He would grant you, according to the riches of His glory, to be strengthened with might through His Spirit in your inner man, that Christ may dwell in your heart through faith, so that you, being rooted and grounded in love, may be able to understand the width and length and depth and height of the love of Christ that passes knowledge, and that you may be filled with all the fullness of God. Amen."

Uzziel grabbed hold of my hand with both of his and drew it to his face, pressing a kiss on my knuckles. I stepped out and he drove the colt on, whirling to wave and smile before I turned away, my heart full.

I settled my bag of parchments over my shoulder and started walking toward town, in search of the residence of my new friends, Kaduri and Nait. Whether they could secure me an audience at their temple so I could plead my case for Jesus as the Messiah, I did not know. But I was confident they would provide a meeting place to which we could invite the curious, and I was certain they would work alongside me to begin spreading the gospel in this great city of my youth.

For this evening at least I knew they would offer me a place to lodge until I could find somewhere to ply my trade and pay my own way. Besides a bed, all I needed tonight was a table and a lamp where I could pen a letter to my beloved, telling her of young Uzziel, who—in the face of disowning, banishment, and shunning—stood on the shore of my future, shining a bright beacon of hope.

POSTSCRIPT

TO SEE WHAT BECAME
OF THE NEPHEW OF PAUL,
READ ACTS 23.

ACKNOWLEDGMENTS

Dr. James S. MacDonald (JamesMacDonald.com), founding and senior pastor of the Harvest Bible Chapel, is a Bible teacher *nonpareil.* Access to his inexhaustible mind and research was a treasure, as is his friendship.

Thanks to Dr. Laurie Norris, formerly of James's staff and now a member of the faculty of the Moody Bible Institute of Chicago, who so ably and quickly tracked down every detail I needed.

Dr. Charlie Dyer was another always at the ready with a thorough response to any question about the Holy Land.

I'm grateful to the following for their helpful input on the New Testament at various stages: Dr. Wallace A. Alcorn, Joe Buonassissi, Dr. Michael Easley, Dr. Gene Getz, and Dr. Grant Osborne.

Christopher (Kit) Denison served as nautical consultant.

Chuck and Krissie Cilano helped with the Italian for the prequel, *I, Saul.*

Thanks to my agent, the delightfully irrepressible David Vigliano of New York.

Thanks to Worthy Publishing CEO Byron Williamson for greenlighting the project.

Jeana Ledbetter, editorial vice president at Worthy, has been steadfast in her support and encouragement throughout.

Copyeditor Holly Halverson added her deft review to the make the final product the best it could be.

More than three hundred people came alongside from the first announcement of this project and agreed to pray for and encourage me. I cannot think of *I, Saul* or *Empire's End* without a deep sense of connection to that team, too numerous to list here but wholly appreciated nonetheless.

Thanks to my executive assistant, Debbie Kaupp, and her husband, Lynn, our properties manager, whose innumerable acts of service and kindness seem to double my productivity every day.

I could not be a writer, and certainly not a novelist, without my wife, Dianna. It would take another book as long as this one to list all she does for me and means to me.

Jerry B. Jenkins's books have sold more than 70 million copies, including the phenomenal mega best-selling Left Behind series. Twenty-one of his titles have reached the *New York Times* bestseller list, including seven that debuted at number one, and also the *USA Today, Publishers Weekly,* and *Wall Street Journal* bestseller lists. Jenkins has been featured on the cover of *Newsweek* magazine. He and his wife, Dianna, live in Colorado. Jerry coaches writers at JerryJenkins.com.

WORTHY®
PUBLISHING

IF YOU ENJOYED THIS BOOK, WILL YOU CONSIDER SHARING THE MESSAGE WITH OTHERS?

- Mention the book in a Facebook post, Twitter update, Pinterest pin, blog post, or upload a picture through Instagram.

- Recommend this book to those in your small group, book club, workplace, and classes.

- Head over to facebook.com/jerry.b.jenkins, "LIKE" the page, and post a comment as to what you enjoyed the most.

- Tweet "I recommend reading #EmpiresEnd by @JerryBJenkins // @worthypub""

- Pick up a copy for someone you know who would be challenged and encouraged by this message.

- Write a book review online.

You can subscribe to Worthy Publishing's newsletter at worthypublishing.com.

**WORTHY PUBLISHING
FACEBOOK PAGE**

**WORTHY PUBLISHING
WEBSITE**